PLANTATION
THE SPANISH OAKS SAGA

PLANTATION
THE SPANISH OAKS SAGA

RICHARD KANE

richard.kane72@yahoo.com

iUniverse, Inc.
New York   Bloomington

Plantation
The Spanish Oaks Saga

Certain characters in this work are historical figures, and certain events portrayed did take place. However, this is a work of fiction. All of the other characters, names, and events as well as all places, incidents, organizations, and dialogue in this novel are either the products of the author's imagination or are used fictitiously.

iUniverse books may be ordered through booksellers or by contacting:

iUniverse
1663 Liberty Drive
Bloomington, IN 47403
www.iuniverse.com
1-800-Authors (1-800-288-4677)

Because of the dynamic nature of the Internet, any Web addresses or links contained in this book may have changed since publication and may no longer be valid. The views expressed in this work are solely those of the author and do not necessarily reflect the views of the publisher, and the publisher hereby disclaims any responsibility for them.

ISBN: 978-1-4502-5681-0 (sc)
ISBN: 978-1-4502-5682-7 (dj)
ISBN: 978-1-4502-5683-4 (ebk)

Library of Congress Control Number: 2010913914

Printed in the United States of America

iUniverse rev. date: 09/09/2010

PREFACE

≈

"If it bleeds it leads." This is the common and everyday vernacular and verbiage of the print and broadcast medium used today in order to get people to purchase, watch, and listen to them. It is usually successful for their target population and corporate gain. Bad news, human suffering, tragedies, and misery attract an extended audience worldwide. Well then, so be it. Now, take that amalgam of evil, sinful, and unrighteousness of human bondage and enslavement, inject a wholesome, invigorating, and uplifting theme, and we have something special for everyone everywhere.

We have all heard the phrase: "When life gives you lemons, make lemonade." That is what the main character and his family have done. They go against the standard paradigm of the times and society in which they live. They defy the powers that be and do what is right, just, and hold true to their principles. The turbulent times in the 'pre-Civil War South', have been thrust upon them, yet the family holds true to their convictions. It would be too easy to sell everything off, leave with their fortune, and never look back.

This is a 'feel good' story set amongst the winds of adversity and tides of afflictions during these historical times. The main character uses his knowledge, training, and wisdom from a lifetime of experience to make life better for everyone that he can, irrespective of the outcome.

The family is not immune to the enigmas and uncertainties that life holds. The 'Good Book' says: "It rains on the just and unjust."

The book is fiction and the language that the Kahanes use is modern, but I have tried to make it historically accurate. The USS Constellation did work in the African Slave Patrol during the 1850s and captured several slave ships. Although slave importation was illegal and the traders were legally pirates, they didn't give up. The accordion was introduced to North America around 1840 and Zydeco music was played about that time growing from a 150 year history. Even the introduction of "Here Comes the Bride" is plausible. It was written in 1848 as part of an opera and it is possible that it was performed in New York shortly thereafter.

I had a lot of fun writing this book. Adult humor that I've heard over the years has been modified for the times. There is violence, adult language, brief nudity (use your imagination), and adult situations. I just hope that I do not offend anyone. So be pre-warned. I even found myself tearing up at some emotional passages and I wrote it.

Two sequels are planned and I am entertaining the idea of doing a prequel. That would tie in a lot of scenarios throughout the books. I have even bantered around the idea of carrying the main character's offspring clear up into modern times. That would be contingent upon there being enough years left in my life.

I closely paralleled the main character's family after my own family with our names slightly changed. I wrote this as if I were alive and living in that time era with my family. I wrote the way I would handle things as if I were right there at that time in history. The main character's last name, Kahane is pronounced Kuh Hane. Close to my last name but not exactly.

So, please, enjoy the book. As I continue to write these first undertakings in my life of this nature.

Richard W. Kane

PLANTATION:

THE SPANISH OAKS SAGA

I

⁓

On April 14, 1855, the USS Constellation is on African Slave Trade Patrol off the Ivory Coast. On board with the marine detachment assigned to this duty, is First Sergeant Dirk Kahane, affectionately known as 'Top", on his last tour of sea duty after a 30 year career with the marines. He is really looking forward to his retirement. Chasing down illegal slave dealers isn't how he wants to spend the rest of his life, but he knows the slave trade had to be stopped. Someone has to enforce the laws and treaties between England and America.

As he stands on deck with Lieutenant Roarke, who is in charge of the detachment but still a newbie on his first sea tour, he pulls out his telescope and looks out to sea.

"It's a slaver, Sir. She's a riding real low in the water. It must a have full load of slaves in the holds."

From high above in the crow's nest, the lookout yells, "Body afloat, two degrees off the starboard bow."

Lieutenant Roarke calls up to the captain on the bridge asking the ship to change course in order to retrieve the body, then yells "Grab a cargo net."

As the ship glides up to the body, the net is thrown over and the body hauled aboard. It is an African male obviously captured for the slave trade and seems to be in his late twenties or early thirties. His back is covered with wounds from lashings and there are open abrasions on his wrists and ankles from shackles.

"This one must have given the slaver crew a rough time, " says the First Sergeant.

"How do mean, Top?" Lieutenant Roarke says.

"These slaves are worth a lot of money to the right person, especially a young healthy male."

The Captain calls the ship's chaplain, crew, and Marine detachment to gather around.

"Chaplain", says Lieutenant Roarke, "we need to pray for this man's soul and give him a proper burial".

After the body is placed in a canvas hammock, weighted down and sewn shut, it is ready for burial at sea. The body is laid on a plank. Everyone removes their head coverings and then bows their heads. The chaplain prays for the man, the plank is lifted, and the body slides into the ocean. Some say "amen" and some make the cross sign across their chests. Along with the ship's Captain, First Sergeant Kahane and Lieutenant Roarke raise their telescopes towards the slave ship again. The delay cost them precious time in overtaking the slave ship.

"Captain", says the First Sergeant, "Even though we could head straight toward them, I recommend that we alter course 90 degrees to port to throw them off. We have their heading and it is only a couple of hours till dark. The slaver is 'low and slow' in the water, Sir. We have the speed and sleekness to overtake them just before dawn."

"With the ship in a 'blackout mode' we'll over take them in the dark." Lieutenant Roarke replies.

"Make it so First Sergeant", the Captain agrees.

"Aye Aye Sir."

The ship then turns 90 degrees to port.. The slavers are observing their every move. As the ship changes course a cheer can be heard through the entire slave ship. The slave ship captain yells out,

"We beat those bastards. Break out the rum, rum for everyone."

After darkness falls, the U.S.S. Constellation changes its course to intercept the slave ship. The ship is completely in 'blackout mode' with the exception of one shielded candle for the helmsman's compass. The lights of the slave ship are sighted at about midnight and the helmsman puts out his candle. With each passing moment, the lights on the slave ship get bigger and brighter.

"First Sergeant", says Lieutenant Roarke, "Have the men form on deck."

"Aye Aye Sir," replies the First Sergeant

The only sounds that can be heard are the sounds of the ship creaking and splashing as it effortlessly glides through the water on its intercept course. With the Marine Detachment and sailors assembled on deck, the Lieutenant addresses them:

"Our mission is simple. Capture the slavers and free the captives. The ship and crew will go to Philadelphia for trial and the Africans will be given to the proper authorities. Marines, sailors, we are about to overtake the slave ship just before dawn."

"Marines," says the First Sergeant, "Ten rounds of shot and powder with fixed bayonets. Sailors, you will be armed with boarding axes and swords."

"First Sergeant", says the Lieutenant, "pick out your four best sharpshooters, they will be up topside in the rigging for targets of opportunity and fire suppression should the need arise."

"Aye aye Sir", replies First Sergeant Kahane.. "I need one volunteer to swing over on a rope to knock out the helmsman with a belaying pin."

Three hands are raised up.

"You," says the First Sergeant "Standby. I want to talk to my sharpshooters. You four, protect and defend as you see fit. Lives will depend on your judgment and well-aimed shots. Okay, get topside."

The four scramble up the rigging to their positions. The First Sergeant thinks to himself: odd, no lookouts on the slaver, no alarm, and no activity whatsoever.

The U.S.S. CONSTELLATION slides up alongside the slave ship. The one Marine swings over on the rope and hits the helmsman in the head with a resounding "pop" and knocks him out. Grappling hooks are thrown over to the slaver as the ships are wrestled closer together. The boarding planks are put in place as the Marines and sailors then board the slave ship. The Marines have their muskets with fixed bayonets, and the sailors have swords and boarding axes at the ready.

"Very odd," the First Sergeant whispers to those around him. "No sign of the slave ship crew anywhere."

Still wary, the First Sergeant says in a low voice, "Prepare for an ambush, pass it along."

First Sergeant Kahane has his sword and Navy Colt thirty-six-caliber revolver ready for anything that comes his way. He signals for one group to go one-way and another with him.

"Four of you sailors go into the ship's quarters and reconnoiter. Anyone found asleep, wake their asses up and bring them topside."

"Yes First Sergeant" one sailor replies. As the boarding party cautiously continues on, a couple of empty rum bottles roll down the deck and one comes to rest at the First Sergeant's boot. The boarding party is still moving about the deck with great fear and trepidation. More empty rum bottles are strewn about the deck. Some of the slave ship's crew is either passed out from being drunk on rum or in various stages of intoxication. As the dawn approaches it is noticed that there are rum bottles scattered all over the deck.

"This will be my easiest mission yet," the First Sergeant says to himself. The First Sergeant yells "Put the crew in irons and tell the Lieutenant that all appears to be secure."

The sailors bring up the crew from inside the quarters and put them in irons. Too slowly they start to sober up. The sun is getting a little higher now. The first thing the slave ship crew notices is the armed guard around them. The captain of the slave ship realizes how hasty he was to celebrate, and tries to hide his shame with a show of anger, scowling and cursing.

Lieutenant Roarke says to the First Sergeant, "Top, see to the captives and bring them out on deck."

"Aye aye, Sir," replies the First Sergeant. As the cargo holds are opened, an awful gut wrenching and nauseating stench emanates from down below. The odor of human waste, body odor, and festering wounds is more than some can handle. The odors are so strong, two of the sailors start to throw up before they even get to the opening. The smell and sight of the incarcerated humanity is almost too much to bear.

"Somebody get me a lantern," yells the First Sergeant

With lantern in hand they venture into the ship's hold. Once inside the hold, the lantern gets very dim due to the lack of air. The rescuers try to contain themselves, but the lack of ventilation, stagnant air, and the nauseous emanations making their way through the opening of the hold is too much to contain. Some of the boarding party start to get sick to their stomachs. Still trying to contain themselves, the boarding party cannot believe the mass of humanity packed, cramped, and chained together. The Africans are all crying, whimpering, and moaning. They have not a clue as to what is going on. They all show fear and horror on their faces. Wherever the chains and irons touch skin, there are various stages of infection.

The First Sergeant yells to Lieutenant Roarke, "Lieutenant, we are going to need hammers, chisels, and wrenches to free these people."

No response is heard. One of the privates hollers down, "First Sergeant, the Lieutenant is over the side puking his toenails up. I'll get the tools. Soon the sounds of hammering can be heard throughout the ship. The captives are being freed and helped out of the deep dark hold of captivity and horror. They are weak from weeks of captivity and all need help to stand and walk. They all have to shield their eyes from the sun as it is now mid-morning. There are several empty shackles which only mean one thing; several had died and were thrown overboard. Several of the slave ship's crew slowly get to their feet, still hung over and are surprised to see that they are shackled and chained. As the captives come out on deck they are given water and food. The former captives talk amongst themselves still not realizing the gravity of their situation. Close to two hundred former African captives are on deck breathing in the fresh air and wondering what his new situation is going to bring. First Sergeant Kahane goes to one of the female former captives and gives her a smile and a loving pat on the shoulder. She starts crying and falls to her knees kissing the First Sergeant's boots while talking in her native tongue. He immediately picks her up and smiles again, looks deep into her eyes and says,

"You are free, all of you are free," well knowing that she cannot understand a word he is saying. The First Sergeant observes that one of the freed captives, a young African maiden, perhaps barely a teenager is noticeably more battered than the rest. As the First Sergeant looks at her more closely he can see that she was beaten about the face, eyes were blackened and partially swollen shut. He also notices fresh blood running down in between her legs.

The First Sergeant said to her, knowing she wouldn't understand a word he said, "My God child, you've been beaten and raped." As he helps her along the deck she looks at one of the slave ship crew and screams out hysterically and hides behind the First Sergeant still shaking in horror and crying in uncontrolled agony. First Sergeant Kahane stands the shackled slaver up on his feet. He notices that he has fresh blood all over his clothes and in particular in the groin area. The First Sergeant realizes that this is the son of a bitch that raped the poor young girl. He looks the slaver straight in the eyes with contempt, animosity, and anger written all over his face. The slaver crewmember was ugly as sin itself, ill kept, no personal hygiene whatsoever. He has a hairy mole on the end of his nose, several missing teeth, and breath that would make a skunk puke its tail up.

"Corporal," says the First Sergeant,

"Yes Sir First Sgt," replies the corporal. "Take my pistol and sword and give me your rifle. Take this young girl to the corpsman and have her wounds tended and then show her to the Lieutenant."

"Aye Aye First Sergeant."

The First Sergeant then takes the rapist to the stern of the ship and leans him up against the ship's railing and says, "If I had a dog as ugly as you, I'd shave his ass and make him walk backwards."

The slaver looks back at him and says, "Why the hell do you care about these fuckin' darkies? They are only good for one thing."

The First Sergeant looks at him with hate and disgust in his eyes and says, "Vengeance is mine sayeth the Lord God Almighty. I pray you be with me now O Lord." The First Sergeant takes the rifle and gives the man an upper butt stroke under his jaw smashing it and killing the slaver instantly. He then takes the rifle to the slumping body, puts the barrel behind his legs and flips him backwards into the ocean. The sound of the body splashing into the water is the last thing that can be heard as the weight of his shackles takes him to the bottom.

Lieutenant Roarke says, "Top, lock up the prisoners in the ship's hold. Let them have a taste of their own actions and take care of the Africans."

"Aye aye, Sir," replies the First Sergeant

The Captain of the U.S.S. Constellation sets a course for the Philadelphia Naval Ship Yard, with partial crews aboard each vessel. The newly freed Africans are still shock in from their ordeal but are slowly getting accustomed to their newfound freedom and the trust of the new white men.

On the voyage back to the Philadelphia Naval Yard, the Lieutenant and the First Sergeant have a chance to talk. The Lieutenant asks the First Sergeant about his career and life.

"Well Sir," he says, "I was born in Chester, Pennsylvania, just outside of Philadelphia. As soon as I turned seventeen, I joined the Marines. That was in July of 1825. Recruit training was a son of a bitch, please excuse the language." The First Sergeant continues, "I should have jumped over the wall and never looked back. I'm glad I stuck it out though; it did me a world of good. Now, thirty years later, I am going to retire and be with my family. I've been married for fifteen or sixteen years, I can't remember exactly, although my wife has several ways of reminding me."

The Lieutenant chuckles and Kahane continues: "When I enlisted there weren't very many Marines, about eight hundred if I recall and that included the officers. The new Officer's sword was introduced for the dress uniforms a year later.

In my early years, I fought a lot of Pirates in the Aegean Sea off the coast of Greece and off North Africa, but I sure didn't care much for that swordplay. I realized that if I were to survive, I needed to be better at sword fighting than anyone else. We had a few pirate prisoners that were willing to teach us some of their sword fighting techniques. I learned how to fight with a sword better than anyone else and I always taught those in my unit that were willing to put in the extra time how to sword fight to improve their chances of survival.

It even came in handy fighting the Seminole Indians in the Florida Swamps about 1836 with Col. Commandant Archibald Henderson. The fighting continued for me on into 1838. The Seminoles can have the swamps as far as I am concerned. The last I heard, they never signed a peace treaty and are technically still at war with the U.S. Government. Lieutenant, am I boring you?"

"Not at all, I am enjoying this bit of living history, please go on" replies the Lieutenant

First Sergeant Kahane continues, "I did other slavery suppression duty along with the British Navy in the early 1840's and I fought in the war with Mexico. In one battle just outside of Mexico City, we lost one hell of a lot of Officers and NCOs. Later on I found out it was called the Battle of Chapultepec. I continued on fighting up and down in California. even traveled with Captain John C. Fremont fighting more Indians near Klamath Lake in the Oregon territory.

Next I sailed to China to protect American interests after a rebellion broke out. As recently as just a few years ago and again, just last year, I sailed into Japan with Commodore Perry's trade delegation. I was part of the Honor Guard and we really impressed the Emperor of Japan and his entourage. I was in charge of the 'Close Order Drill. The Calling Cadence had them all bowing at us. The Japanese people are a very polite and gentle and we must have stayed for a couple of months. I had some very strange food while I was there. Did you realize that fish heads have a lot of meat inside? There were eggs with un-hatched ducks inside, and animal testicles too. My most memorable experiences were with the palace guards. I made it a point to become friends with a couple of the palace guards. Samurais are what they were called, which I found out means 'to serve'. I learned a lot of some special fighting techniques, the likes of which I have never seen. The Samurai were particularly adept at a special fighting with their feet, open hands, and a style of sword fighting that sent shivers up my spine. One of them could cut a candlewick off a lit candle and have the wick still lit on his sword. They slap kick a person three ways from Sunday before he hit the ground.

This one Samurai I must have really impressed. I learned how to say, 'thank you, good morning, how are you, and goodbye' all in Japanese. We became good friends in my short stay there, Tanaka was his name, he taught me a lot of his special fighting 'hand to hand' and some fancy sword fighting techniques. I wish I had one of those swords. In fact," says First Sergeant Kahane, "I became such a good student and became real good and adept at what he was teaching. He had some of his Samurai guards observe me. That is, I was real good for the short time we were there, not to be compared to their lifetime of training. I brought Tanaka to the ship a couple of times for chow. Tanaka ate as well with a fork as well as I ate with those little sticks. That was entertaining for all. When it came time for the delegation to leave Japan, I gave him a jug of one of Kentucky's finest Shine. You should have seen him smile and his eyes light up. I said goodbye to him in Japanese and made motions that we had to leave. We bowed to each other and then shook hands. I turned and never looked back.

I made several stops to some of the South Sea island nations when American business interests were being threatened. I also managed to learn some of their special fighting skills. Some of those experiences I passed on to those within our unit."

The First Sergeant continues. "I had a stint training raw recruits at the Brooklyn Navy Yard. That was something else. Those raw recruits didn't know their left from their right. This last assignment, saving this bunch of Africans, I feel is why I was put on this Earth. After several duty assignments and skirmishes from South America to the Pacific Northwest, I find myself here and in my present rank."

The First Sergeant says. "Lieutenant, I hoped I haven't made your ears bleed too much."

The Lieutenant says, "Top, I have enjoyed every minute of your living personal history." "I just wish I could have been a part of it."

The seas turn a little rough for the ship. All that can be heard is the 'hogging and sagging' of the ship's construction as it plows its way through the heavy seas.

"I am looking forward to becoming a full time husband and father to my two children. " My wife Janine, my daughter Babette, we call her Babs, and my son Edgar. They all have blonde hair and blue eyes. Babs is 14 and Edgar is 13. Janine is a bookkeeper for a local accounting firm, kind of unusual to have her working, but she likes it and I don't mind. We sure can use the money. I haven't figured out what I m going to do after retirement. Thirty years is a long time!"

The First Sergeant then asks the Lieutenant, "What about you Sir?"

"Well," says the Lieutenant, "My life is going to be boring after listening to yours." The First Sergeant smiles. "I was born and raised in Boston. My folks own a hotel there. My father wants me to get some life experiences under my belt before he hands over the reins of the hotel to me. So, after college, I joined the Marines. I don't plan on making a career out it. I have no wife, just a special lady friend back in Boston."

The slave ship crew is brought out on deck a few at a time for fresh air and water. The emanating stench from down below is still unbearably nauseating, but slave ship crew remains there for the duration of the trip with the exception of their short daily trips out on deck.

After five weeks of travel, the lookout spots land. In another few days, the ship enters the river for the trip up to port. The Marines make ready the prisoners for transfer. The signal flags are run up and the signalman communicates with the Navy yard as to the situation on board. The Marine Band is on station to play for them as the ship comes into the harbor and ties up at the dock. The prisoners are marched off to the brig for holding until trial. The Africans are released to the proper authorities for their processing. The ship's crew and the Marine Detachment leave for some well deserved leave time.

II

─≋─

Taking the stagecoach, First Sergeant Kahane arrives home in Chester surprising his family. Janine is overcome with tears of joy. Babs and Edgar run screaming, "Daddy you're home, we love you," as they all embrace. Everyone cries, even the soon to be civilian First Sergeant

That night at the dinner table Dirk says, "I'll be retiring next week. I just haven't figured out what I am going to do for employment. But for now, I just want to enjoy all of you and catch up on what has been going on last six months. Here, let me help clear off the table."

"You know, I don't think I'll ever get used to you helping around the house," says Janine "but I like it."

"Well, you know we weren't wealthy people growing up, and my mamma insisted all us boys help out. Guess she was kind of unusual herself."

After a week with the family, they all head to the Philadelphia Naval Yard for First Sergeant Dirk Kahane's retirement ceremony. A formal dinner is enjoyed by all. The Marines are in their Dress Blues. The Marine Band plays dinner music in the background. After the dinner is over, the Commanding Officer of the Philadelphia Naval Yard takes the stage along with Lieutenant Roarke who is carrying a rectangular wooden box about two inches thick. Wine glasses are being tapped. The dinner party quiets down immediately.

The Commanding Officer then says in a loud and commanding voice, "First Sergeant Dirk Kahane, front and center."

The First Sergeant stands up smartly to his feet, makes a right facing move and marches up to the Commanding Officer, stopping with his right should facing him and executes a right face turn and says, "First Sergeant Kahane reporting as ordered Sir," and gives a snappy hand salute. The Commanding Officer returns the salute and the First Sergeant returns his hand to his side.

"At ease First Sergeant and please stand between the Lieutenant and me." He does so. The Commanding Officer addresses the First Sergeant and the dinner guests.

"First Sergeant Dirk Kahane, United Stated Marine Corps, you have served and made personal sacrifices for your country for thirty years. You have never wavered in your duties and for that your nation is grateful and your fellow Marines take great pride in you and applaud you."

Janine has tears rolling down her cheeks, trying not to cry out loud. The Commanding Officer calls on Lieutenant Roarke.

"Thank you Sir," replies the Lieutenant "First Sergeant Kahane, A Top Sergeant is hard to find. You are the benchmark from which all others are to be measured."

From the crowd can be heard several 'here here's and the sounds of several glasses being tinkled. That is all it takes for Janine. She can be heard blubbering uncontrollably.

Lieutenant Roarke then says, "Top, as a token of our personal appreciation we have this parting gift for your retirement." The Lieutenant hands him the box. Dirk looks on it with great appreciation.

"Well, hurry and open it!"

Dirk opens the wooden box. His jaw drops open in surprise. Dirk lifts the box to the crowd and shows them the most beautiful Bowie Knife. It has pearl inlay on the handle with a shiny brass finish with his name etched at the base of the blade near the hilt.

"I don't know what to say. This is beautiful and I'll be carrying this with me wherever I go. Thank you very much, I love this knife already and I already have a name for it." Dirk says in a loud voice, "I christen thee, 'Sweet Thing'."

The crowd stands and cheers. "One more thing First Sergeant" says the Commanding Officer. "We have one more gift for you. Here is your own Marine Corps flag."

"Thank you again Sirs. I'll fly this on my front porch," says Dirk.

"First Sergeant," says the Commanding Officer.

"Yes Sir", replies Dirk.

"You are dismissed and enjoy a well deserved civilian life."

"Thank you again sir." Dirk salutes and shakes his hand and salutes the Lieutenant, and shakes his hand. The crowd stands and cheers resound through the banquet hall. Janine is still crying and clutches Dirk's arm. The Marines all file by and shake his hand with Janine still by Dirk's side.

"Thank you all very much. I need one more thing before we leave." Dirk says. "I'll be wanting several sew-on patches with the anchor and the U.S.M. over it, an equal amount of the small sew-on First Sergeant rank."

"No problem Top, you'll have them in the morning," says Lieutenant Roarke.

"We are getting a room and will head home in the morning."

"I'll see you in the morning." Lieutenant Roarke responds. They mingle some more and then depart.

———

At home the next day, Dirk says to Janine, "Honey, I am now Mr. Kahane, but my retirement checks won't be enough to keep us afloat. I need to find some sort of income for us. I'll go into town and see what is available in the morning."

In the morning Dirk fashions an extra leather piece inside the sheath of "Sweet Thing' so that the handle doesn't need to be tied. He fashions a couple of leather straps so he can put 'Sweet Thing' over his shoulder and makes a strap to tie around his waist so that the knife rides with its handle in the small of his back. Dirk then puts on a shirt over Sweet Thing so it won't be too noticeable. Off Dirk goes into town that morning. The new Dirk Kahane goes from business to business to see what is and is not available. Retail sales don't appeal to him. Hotel employment is not in his repertoire. Manual labor, no way! After thirty years of a regimented lifestyle, Dirk finds his first day as a civilian hard to adjust to. Going home that evening, he finds himself feeling low and dejected.

At dinner that evening, Janine can see his frustration. "Don't worry dear, something will turn up" she reassures him.

———

Up and at it the next morning, Dirk tries the shipping terminals and freight companies. Nothing happening there. Dirk tries the railroad. The only thing available there would keep him away from home for long periods of time. "Not that again for me," Dirk thinks to himself. He heads home again. Janine greets him at the door with a loving kiss and hug. "Tomorrow is Saturday," says Janine. "Just relax for the next two days."

"Yes Maam", Dirk replies with a smile. Monday morning Dirk straps on Sweet Thing and heads to Philadelphia to waterfront. He sees ships coming in from the Southern ports with the shipments of cotton, sugar cane, and coffee. He sees them being unloaded and carted off to the various destinations. Off across the harbor Dirk sees Navy ships tied up and one headed out to sea. Dirks eyes start to tear up at the sight of the one ship headed out to sea with the detachment of Marines aboard. Dirk has to find something fast before they have to tap into their savings. Dirk is in a real dilemma as to what the future would hold for him and his family if he doesn't find some sort of gainful employment. Working on the waterfront doesn't appeal to him at all, not to mention the minimal pay.

That evening sitting around the dinner table with the family, Dirk doesn't have a lot to say. Feeling sad and downtrodden at the job prospects, Janine knew what was going on inside her proud and powerful husband. Hitting the streets daily was starting to put a 'chink' in his armor. Janine puts her hand on his and looks deep into his sky blue eyes and says, "Honey, don't worry, something is going to come, I know it and I feel it deep within my soul." Babs and Edgar come over and give their daddy a big hug. Dirk looks back at everyone with a tear in his and says, "I love you all very much and thank you for being my loving family." Dirk gives each one of them a hug and a kiss.

The next day Dirk and 'Sweet Thing' are back at it again. He goes to the dockworkers and carters, construction companies, and even manufacturing factories. Still nothing appeals to him. Dirk thinks to himself that he is going to have to swallow his pride and accept the lesser of several evils in the employment situation. He goes home a little early that afternoon.

III

J anine meets him at the door. "Hi dear, there is a dispatch from some attorney firm in Charleston, South Carolina on the table for you. Quick, open it up."

Dirk opens the dispatch and meticulously digests every word as Janine waits anxiously to find out the contents of the dispatch. Dirk looks up and says, "Well my dear, I do believe that the employment issue is no longer a problem."

A puzzled look overcomes Janine's face.

Dirk says, "What do you know about growing cotton in the South? Apparently, my uncle died and I am the only living heir he has. He died about a month ago and his overseer, a Nash Snidley, is running things till we figure out what we want to do." Sitting down at the table, Dirk is in a dilemma. Not knowing the first thing about a plantation, he says, "Well, what do you think?"

Janine replies, "I am ready for a change. There are some bad influences here that I don't want the kids to be around. I believe that that change would be a positive life-altering event that would do us all good in the long run. God willing, we'll do well, I'm sure, but not without hardships, trials, and tribulations."

"Hardships are nothing but stepping stones in the learning process," Dirk adds. "Well my dear, I hope I don't let us down. The first thing tomorrow, I'll send a wire to the attorneys in Charleston that we will be arriving 'post-haste'. Tell Babs and Edgar we're moving."

In the morning, Dirk takes Edgar with him for company. As they are walking they stop to say hello to one of the neighborhood residents that he notices in his yard. It is one of the young sons of his neighbor.

Dirk says, "Well, if it isn't Ernest Jones. How are you doing?"

"Mr. Kahane, welcome back to Chester and how are you doing?" says Ernest. "It is really good to see you again Sir. Hello Edgar."

"What have you been up to since I saw you last?"

"Well Sir," Says Ernest, I am going to start my third year at West Point soon."

"West Point!" exclaims Dirk.

"Yes Sir, I have an uncle on my mother's side that has some sort of influence in Washington D.C. with one of the politicians."

"Whatever it takes to get you there." Dirk says. "What are you studying?"

Ernest then replies, "My major interest is Engineering, Artillery, and a lot of military tactics and warfare thrown in."

"You keep up the good work Ernest, the country will always need good officers, even if it is the Army." Dirk and Ernest smile and laugh.

"Mr. Kahane, and what are you and your family doing these days?"

"Ernest, I just retired from the Marines after thirty years and I just inherited a plantation outside of Charleston, South Carolina. I am on my way now to send a wire that we will be arriving in two to three weeks. Ernest, I must be going now. It was really a pleasure talking with you and I am proud of what have done and what you will become. If you are ever down our way, please do not hesitate to look us up. You will always have a place to stay."

'I'll do that Mr. Kahane. Bye Edgar."

Dirk smiles at Ernest and they shake hands. Dirk and Edgar then turn and leave for town to send the message to the attorneys in

Charleston. Dirk and Edgar return home later that afternoon. Janine meets him at the door when they return. "Hello dear, have a seat," as she pours him a cup of coffee.

"What's going on?" says Dirk.

"I have something to run by you," says, Janine. "While you were out, my sister Jessica came over. Do you remember her son Timothy?"

Dirk replies, "Yes, Isn't he the one that if he went about life any slower he would be going backwards?"

Janine then says, "Well, yes and no. It isn't that he is slow, he just isn't so fast."

"What is the difference, it all has to do with speed?" Replies Dirk. "I just remember that his oars don't quite reach the water."

"Timothy is now twenty-four and he just needs a strong male figure in his life to give him some direction, influence, and an authoritative prodding in the right areas," Janine says. "Oh, and that is not all, he is also married to a gal named Stella. Jessica says that she has had a rather borderline nefarious past. When I told Jessica about our new life ahead of us she practically got on her knees and begged us to take them with us. I told her that I would bring it up at the dinner table. Well, what do you think?" Janine grins ear-to-ear.

"Well Hon, my mission in life is to bring you the maximum amount of pleasure and happiness in the shortest amount of time possible." Dirk replies with a like wide ear-to-ear grin and crossed eyes. "I know it would be good for both of them. More importantly for Timothy than Stella. Timothy probably wouldn't recognize it at first. They would be the only ones that we would know for a while. If I remember Timothy correctly, he is not going to enjoy life with me riding herd over him. In the long run, it will be good and worth it for him gaining self-respect and stability. Learning plantation life is going to be arduous and a constant learning experience for all of us," says Dirk. "Do Babs and Edgar know anything about Timothy and Stella?"

Janine replies, "Not yet, I wanted you to know first."

"Okay," Dirk says, "Tell the kids and tell your sister. Tomorrow, I'll book us passage on a ship going to Charleston. I want to meet Timothy and Stella as soon as possible to get to know what we're dealing with."

The next day Janine gives her notice at the accounting firm. They all love her and are saddened at her departure.

Two days later Jessica, Timothy, and Stella are at the Kahane's home. They all have dinner together, the kids, Dirk, Janine, Jessica, Timothy, and Stella. Dirk mostly listens more than he talks. He is just trying to figure what he has to deal with and the direction he needs move in more than anything else.

"Timothy", says Dirk, "What line of work are you in?"

Timothy replies, "I take wagon loads of freight from the railroad to the waterfront for the shipment of goods to Europe or other various factories and businesses."

Dirk asks, "How long have you been doing that?"

"Five years now Uncle Dirk, since I was nineteen."

Then Dirk asks Stella, "Stella, and what are you doing?"

Stella then replies, "Mr. Dirk, I just try to make a happy home for Timothy."

Dirk thinks to himself, "Bullshit, you lying hog".

"That's nice," says Dirk. Janine notices something amiss in Dirk's temperament.

"Timothy," says Dirk, "How do you like your job?" Timothy says, "Oh, it's okay Uncle Dirk. I've tried a lot of other things but they never seem to work out for me in the way I had anticipated."

Again Dirk thinks to himself, "That's because you are a dumb fuck Timothy." Then Dirk replies, "Things have a way of working themselves out."

With dinner over, Dirk again starts to help cleaning up the table. Jessica says, "I'll do that." "I'll help also." says Janine. Dirk looks out the corner of his eye at Stella who does nothing. She just sits there looking vacant.

Dirk says, "Well if you insist, okay then."

Dirk then says to everyone, "Our future is going to be new to all of us. We all need to learn new things. I don't know anything more about a plantation than any of you. We leave in about seven days for Charleston by way of ship."

They begin to pack their clothes and personal items. The plantation already has its own items for living, cookware, furniture, tools, etc. The seven days go by quickly. They are all excited to be going.

Eventually they are all loaded onto the ship and ready to sail with the tide out of Philadelphia. They get underway to Charleston. Babs and Edgar are having a good time. It is a new adventure for them and they get along great with the ships' crew. Janine doesn't fare as well. Out at sea she is sea sick a good part of the time. Timothy stays by Stella's side most of the time, so much that she gets a little perturbed at his constant presence.

"Timothy," says Stella," I need some alone time to think and be by myself. You are suffocating me." Stella has her alone time.

The ships' crew sure takes note of her and Stella enjoys all the attention and the excitement of being around so many men at once. This does not go unnoticed by Dirk. The trip by ship is 'old hat' to Dirk and just like old times. The wind is in their favor and the trip to Charleston is quicker than anticipated. As the ship is being tied up at the dock, the family notices a significant difference between Philadelphia and Charleston in the manner in which the blacks are treated. There is a lot of yelling and cursing by the whites directed to the blacks. The sounds of whips being cracked and a lot of screaming and yelling can be heard. Janine looks at Dirk and both shake their heads. Babs and Edgar don't know what to think.

Janine says to them,"I'll explain later, but for now just don't look." Timothy has 'the thousand yard stare in a ten foot room' look on his face. Stella, once again, she is just there. Charleston is a foreign country compared to Philadelphia.

Dirk says to Janine, "Honey, whatever the future holds for us is whatever we make of it. It can be good or bad. I pray the Good Lord gives us strength and wisdom to do what is right in his sight."

With their belongings stored for a short while they check into a nearby hotel for the evening. Dirk plans to pay a visit to the attorney's office tomorrow. They are all tired and weary from the voyage. They get something to eat and turn in for the night.

———

The next morning Dirk is up early and on his way to the attorney's office to sign paperwork and take official possession of his inheritance.

"Well Mr. Kahane", says his attorney, "you are now the official owner of 'Spanish Oaks'. That is the name of your plantation." They shake hands and Dirk goes back to the hotel. They get a bite to eat and then head for the plantation in a hired wagon. It is about a two-hour ride out of Charleston.

IV

As they approach the main gate for the plantation, they see a huge sign over it -- "Spanish Oaks". They see the most beautiful mansion off in the distance. The roadway approaching the mansion is lined with massive oak trees with Spanish moss hanging down from all the branches. As they get closer to the mansion they can see big white pillars on the front. They can see a porch that wraps around the mansion. The fragrances of the magnolia and honeysuckle blossoms permeate the air. The grounds are immaculately manicured. The roses are all in full bloom with every color in the rainbow. Dirk and Janine just look at each other in shock and amazement at their newfound fortune. They stop in front of the mansion and the whole family gets down from the wagon. The doublewide hand-carved wooden doors with stained glass panes are massive and as Dirk starts up the steps, the doors are opened. A black man greets him with a wide grin and pearly white teeth and gives a slight bow.

"Ah is yuh' house servant suh, and yo is Massa Kahane and Missa Kahane."

"That is correct," replies Dirk, "and you are?"

"Ma name is Jenson suh."

Dirk outstretches his hand to shake it. Jenson hesitates momentarily not expecting such a chivalrous first meeting prior to sticking out his hand.

"Jenson," says Dirk, "This is my family, my wife Janine, my daughter Babs, and my son Edgar. This is our nephew Timothy Conley and his wife Stella."

Jenson then replies, "Welcome to Spanish Oaks, we bin expectin' you." At that moment a black woman appears at the door. Jenson then says "This is ma wife Maybelle, yuh housekeeper and cook."

They smile at each other and enter the mansion. When Maybelle gets to Jenson, she whispers, "Ah dunno, they ain't like normal white foks' roun' heah. They is too nice."

Dirk says to Jenson, "We need to make arrangements to get our belongings that are stored in Charleston and this wagon returned. I assume the plantation has its own means of transportation."

"Yeh Suh, Massa Dirk, I'll get it done in no time at all."

They get shown around the mansion. The living room is massive with a huge fireplace that could burn five-foot long logs. The dining area could hold a small banquet. The kitchen area could cook for a small army. There is a walk-in storage pantry that can store enough provisions for a year or so. The master bedroom is bigger than some homes. The bedrooms upstairs are spacious. Timothy and Stella will have a guest house all their own separated from the mansion. Dirk had learned from the attorney that there was a separate carriage house that could be used as a dwelling.

Maybelle prepares the evening meal and Jenson serves it, then retires to the kitchen to be with Maybelle. It is a mighty fine meal of chicken, mashed potatoes and gravy, corn on the cob, greens and fresh baked bread. With the meal over, Janine and Dirk scrape and stack plates then pick them up and carry them to the kitchen. When Maybelle looks at them with the plates, she screams in horror. "Massa, Missa, what are yuh doing? Please have mercy on us fo not a getting out there sooner!" Jenson rushes over and starts to take the plates from them. "Please let us do that. Please don't be mad at us" says Maybelle.

"Jensen, Maybelle," says Dirk, "All is well. You're not going to be punished. This is what we normally do at the end of a meal."

Back in the dining room Dirk tells Janine "Tomorrow I want to look around on my own."

Dirk gets up at five A.M., steps into the kitchen and finds a quick bite to eat, straps on Sweet Thing, then steps out the back door to tour the plantation. Once out the backdoor, he sees a gate going through a tall hedgerow. Off he goes to look things over. Dirk steps through the gate to the other side. He sees a large well-kept barn. He walks to the barn and goes to the other side. Dirk is horrified at what he sees. Any semblance of the mansion's beauty and serenity come to an abrupt halt as he views the slave quarters where there is such squalor, filth, rundown, and wretched condition, that no one could call it living. Nevertheless, as he looks closer he sees small attempts to make it comfortable – a small pot of flowers, the beginnings of a latrine.

At that moment Dirk hears the crack of a whip and a blood-curdling scream. Not knowing where it came from, Dirk looks around again. Dirk hears the sound of the whip cracking again and the horrific scream. Dirks runs to where he thinks it is coming from. Dirk sees a large group of slaves, some are crying and weeping, some are hugging each other. Dirk runs toward them. The crack of the whip sounds again and the scream in painful agony. Dirk pushes his way through the crowd and sees one of the slaves tied to a tree. Dirk walks to the person with the whip. Just as the whip is ready for its next lashing out Dirk catches the arm as it starts its forward motion preventing it from doing further harm.

Dirk then says to the person with the whip, "My name is Dirk Kahane and I own this place. What is your name?"

He responds, "Mr. Kahane Sir," "I am Nash Snidley, the overseer of this plantation."

"Mr. Snidley, why is this person being punished?"

"He didn't show respect," says Snidley.

The slaves didn't know what to think of this confrontation.

"Mr. Snidley," says Dirk, "From now on all punishments are to be gone through me first, is that understood?"

"Yes sir Mr. Kahane," replies Snidley. The slave being whipped looked horrid. Gaping flesh wounds, blood running down his back, pieces of flesh were hanging by thin threads of skin. The flies were all over his back.

"Cut him down!" orders Dirk.

"Yes Sir Mr. Kahane."

Dirk motions to a couple of the slaves to pick him up and to tend to his wounds. The two picking him up make a slight bow as they pass by Dirk to pick up the lacerated and bleeding slave. A group of slaves mumble amongst themselves at what they had just witnessed and point at Dirk wondering who this person is. As Dirk looks towards the crowd he can't help but notice that one of the little girls, about four or five years of age is of a lighter skin tone than the rest.

"Mr. Snidley," says Dirk, "Please show me around the place. I was here once as a child and I don't remember anything at all about this place."

"Well Sir, Mr. Kahane," Says Snidley. "There are about seventy-five hundred acres here. The main crop is cotton with some coffee, sugar cane, corn, tobacco, and vegetables. The James River is over yonder. There is small waterfall complete with a swimming hole. Your uncle was going to drain the swamp to make more land available for crops. You can't see it from the swamp edge, but there is a ten-acre island out in the swamp. We was a gettin' close to that project till he got sick and died. We had a run-in with an alligator, but the slaves made short work of it and ate it. There are a lot of snakes out there also."

Snidley continues on with his tour, "With the extra swamp land drained that should give us another five hundred acres. You also have about two hundred acres of forested timber at the upper end of the plantation with all sorts of different trees. There are about seventy acres with a lot of rocks to be cleared. There are about fifty slaves here of various ages and many different skills many families and lots of children. The cotton is all hand-picked when the harvest comes in about four to five months."

Dirk and Snidley go to the barn. In the barn is one of the slaves tending to his blacksmithing jobs.

Snidley says. "This is Jasper our blacksmith. Not only does Jasper do the blacksmithing but he is also a first rate cobbler and repairer of leather goods."

Dirk nods to Jasper then turns to Snidley. "Mr. Snidley, show me where you live please."

"Yes Sir, right this way," says Snidley. "We have a lot of livestock and your uncle took great pride in his stallion over here. They look out into the corral where the stallion is. That is Rufus who tends and takes care of the livestock."

Rufus is combing and brushing the horse down.

"I am not a good judge of horse flesh, but that is one magnificent looking animal," Dirk says.

"That horse is a cross between an Arabian and a Quarter horse, speed, stamina, and strength. He is only about two years old." says Snidley.

"Does the horse have a name?" Dirk asks.

"Your Uncle named him 'Beaudandy', Beau for short." Snidley says.

"Appropriate name I'd say." Dirk responds. "Beau has an interesting color to him."

"Your uncle called it a 'blue roan'." says Snidley.

"Beautiful markings, I've never seen that in a horse before." Dirk says. "Now please show me your quarters."

They get to Snidley's quarters. A small home set apart from everything else. Once inside Dirk looks around and notices a lot of new and nice conveniences.

"It looks like you do pretty well for yourself from what I can see, Mr. Snidley."

Dirk notices some nice furniture, clothes, cookware, and other amenities. Dirk thinks to himself that he is living well beyond his means. With the afternoon getting late Dirk thanks Snidley.

"I'll see you Monday morning." "At what time does the day start?" Snidley replies, "I start rousting everyone up at around daylight and work starts at sunup and we work till the sun starts going down with a lunch break around noon time."

Dirk says that he and his nephew Timothy will be here.

Dirk makes his way back. On the way back he just can't get over the poor living conditions in which the slaves are forced to live in. Dirk stops when he notices an elderly woman in her rocking chair on her stoop of her 'run down not fit for living' shack. Dirk then goes up to her and says, "Hello maam. My name is Dirk Kahane and I am the owner of this plantation. What is your name please?"

"Massa Dirk, we all heard that you wuz a commin. Mah name is Mammy Em."

At that moment the rickety old door squeaked open and out steps an elderly old black man. Dirk introduces himself in an equally respectful manner as he did with Mammy Em.

"Your name is?"

"Suh, mah name is Georgie."

"Thank you Georgie", says Dirk. "How long have you two been here at Spanish Oaks?"

"Well Suh, I wuz born here and Mammy Em came here as a young chile. We bin here the longest of anybody."

"Do you two have any children here?" Dirk asks.

"We had one son, Franklin wuz his name, but yo' uncle sol' him off bout' five years ago," Says Mammy Em.

Dirk sort of hangs his head and says, "I'm sorry. What sort of jobs do you two do here?"

"We do jus' bout' anything no one else wants to do. Ah helps take care of the young uns' when the mommy is out in the fiels' a workin'. I also heps' with the birthin' and healin' and I can see things that nobody else can see."

Dirk didn't quite know what to make of that last statement, so he just let it go, then he asks, "What was the name of the young man that was being whipped this morning?"

"It was Jefferson Suh, his name was Jefferson," says Georgie.

"One more thing," says Dirk. "Who was that little girl I saw earlier that had lighter skin than the rest?"

"Well Suh, her is name Lulu Massa Dirk, her Daddy is Overseer Snidley. He don' have anything to do with her at all. Nobody else has much to do with to do with her since Massa Snidley so mean, hateful, an' full of the devil." Says Mammy Em.

"What about her mother?" asks Dirk.

Mammy Em says, "Her mommy died during childbirth, I did all I could but it was just too much for her and all. She was only about thirteen or fourteen at the time, a purty little thing."

Georgie adds, "Overseer Snidley took her against her will. We can still hear her a screamin' to this very day. Ever since she was birthed the chil' been passed around from one family to another."

"Didn't my uncle do anything about that?" asks Dirk.

"Overseer Snidley didn't tell your uncle anything but what he wanted to hear." Mammy Em says.

"Your uncle didn't really know what wuz a goin' out heah." says Georgie.

"Georgie, Mammy Em, I must go now. We'll talk some more real soon." Dirk shakes Georgie's hand and tips his hat to Mammy Em, then turns and leaves.

Mammy Em says to Georgie, "Ah has a good feelin' bout' this Massa Dirk." Georgie smiles and nods his head. All during their conversation there were several sets of eyeballs peering out of the shadows watching was happening at Georgie and Mammy Em's place.

Arriving back at the mansion, Timothy and Stella are awake and up too. The belongings have just arrived since Jensen had sent two drivers back with the wagon at the crack of dawn. Edgar and Babs are in their rooms still putting things away. Dirk finds his Marine Corps flag and hangs it on the verandah. Janine has found the ledger books for the plantation and is pondering them.

"Timothy," says Dirk, "We are going to be in the slave quarters at five AM Monday morning."

"Five AM!" says Timothy in horror, "Why so early?"

"Because that is when the day starts around here!" Dirk says. Dirk thinks to himself, "You worthless turd." "Enjoy your Sunday and get plenty of rest you'll need it. We have a long week ahead of and a lot to learn."

V

Monday morning arrives soon. Dirk straps on 'Sweet Thing' and puts a loose shirt over it. He then goes to the slave quarters area where the slaves are mingling about getting ready for the days work ahead of them. Dirk does not see Timothy anywhere. It is just starting to get daylight when Nash Snidley can be heard cussing and yelling at the slaves for no apparent reason. Dirk catches up to Snidley just as he was about to whip one of the slaves.

"Snidley," yells Dirk. "Have you forgotten our conversation on Saturday when I said that all punishment would be run through me first? If you would please, send someone over to roust my nephew Timothy up. He is obviously late."

"Yes Sir," replies Snidley. "I'll get right on it." Snidley yells at one of the slaves, "Rufus, go wake up Massa Timothy and be quick about it."

They all start to make their way out to the fields for their various jobs. Some had hoes, some had scythes for larger jobs. Men, women, and children of all ages work in the fields. Dirk thinks some look too young to be working in the fields. The slaves have been working for about two hours when Timothy makes his debut. Dirk looks at him in disgust and says in a harsh voice,

"Where in the hell have you been?" The slaves all look on in bewilderment.

"Sorry Uncle Dirk," Timothy says sheepishly.

"Get your ass out there and learn something," scolds Dirk. Dirk stays with Snidley in the attempt to learn the plantation business and more importantly to prevent any more beatings. Dirk learns a lot but feels deep inside that Snidley is purposely holding back on teaching him a lot of the information that he so desperately needs. Dirk looks around and does not see Timothy anywhere. "Where in the hell is that boy now?" Dirk says to himself. Dirk starts looking and in about a half an hour finds Timothy under a tree by the river.

Dirk roars, "TIMOTHY". Timothy jumps up in fright and hits his head on a low branch.

"Do you already know all there is to know about running a plantation? Are you an expert already that you can do whatever you want."

"But Uncle Dirk, it is so hot out here," says Timothy in his defense.

Dirk responds by saying, "Why don't you just go and tell someone who gives a shit. Now get your lazy ass back out in the field or we are both going to the doctor to get my boot removed from of your ass! Move it on out of here!" yells Dirk. Some slaves are nearby and can hear the entire ass chewing and are laughing themselves silly.

It is a typical hot July day in South Carolina. At noon the dinner bell rings. No one wasted time in getting something to eat in the common food line. Timothy is first in line. Dirk grabs him by the ear and pulls him to the rear of the line without saying a word.

"Ouch! That really hurts Uncle Dirk." Dirk then falls in line behind Timothy. The slaves look at each other in bewilderment. Jensen is worried because Dirk and Timothy should be in the dining room with the rest of the family but after the scene in the kitchen when they arrived, he is afraid to say anything. Snidley goes to his cabin for lunch. As the day wears on, the heat and humidity in the hot July sun is almost unbearable. Dirk thinks to himself, "How can anyone work in this heat." All throughout the day the slaves work and sing while they work. At one point Dirk asks Snidley about the singing.

"When they sing we know where they are. They call it "field hollers," says Snidley.

"I notice that some of the sing and the others answer. Is that usual?" asks Dirk

"Seems to be"

Dirk quickly determines that Jefferson is going to give him more information than Snidley, so he is out in the field chatting as Jefferson tends the plants. Jefferson glances up quickly toward the river, then after giving a low bird whistle, changes the song. The other slaves quickly pick up the tune. Dirk looks at Jefferson who just makes a sh-ing motion and whispers,

"Lata, Suh."

The Spanish Oaks slaves start to sing in unison:
Wade in the water,
Wade in the water children.
Wade in the water
God's gonna trouble the water
Who's all those children all dressed in Red?
God's gonna trouble the water.
Must be the ones that Moses led.
God's gonna trouble the water.

As Dirk walks toward Snidley, he sees that the overseer is fit to be tied.

"What's the matter?" Dirk says.

"It's that blasted song. They sing it every once in a while and I hate it," Snidley replies.

Dirk can see that he doesn't know what is going on and he decides to wait until talking with Jefferson before saying anything.

As the day draws to a close, everyone is dragging. The heat is taking its toll on Dirk. Timothy is the first one out of the field. Dirk just looks at Timothy as he heads out and just shakes his head. Dirk thinks to himself, "What have I gotten myself into with that idiot?"

Timothy gets to his house. Stella is sitting at the table drinking a cup of tea.

Timothy says, "What did you do today?"

"Not much. I just walked around and got to know the place." Stella replies. "What about you,"

"I can't get away with anything as long as Uncle Dirk is in the same field as I am." says Timothy. "I don't like this plantation life."

"Oh stick it out. I am sure once the money comes in you'll change your mind,"

"I sure hope so."

Dirk arrives at the big house. Janine, Babs, and Edgar all greet him at the back door. Dirk gives everyone a big hug.

Janine asks, "How did your first full day as the new plantation owner go?"

Dirk replies, "I'll tell you, I have a lot to learn. The heat and humidity here is almost unbearable and that Timothy is a real piece of work. I figured out why he has gone through so many jobs in the past. I have to keep riding him. He is a real challenge. What's for supper?"

Janine says, "Maybelle has prepared a fine supper for us."

Dirk looks at the kids and asks, "How was your day?"

"Fine daddy."

Jensen appears and announces that supper is served.

"Thank you Jensen." Dirk says. "Let us eat, I am famished ."

As they all sit around the table eating Dirk comments that he believes that Nash Snidley is not teaching him all that he should know. Dirk tells Janine about the little girl that Snidley fathered and how the young mother died during childbirth. Dirk also relates to Janine the personal history of Georgie and Mammy.

"Dirk," says Janine. "I have been going over the ledger book again and there is about a thousand dollars unaccounted for. I have gone over the books three times and I can't account for that at all. I just don't know where it is."

Dirk thinks back to his visit in Snidley's cabin and all the niceties he had.

Dirk asks, "What is Snidley's salary?"

"Thirty dollars a month plus his cabin and food," Janine says.

"Snidley has been getting more than offered, that little girl is proof to that," says Dirk. "I do believe that I have it figured out where the missing funds have been going."

Jensen is standing by should he be needed for anything.

Dirk says, "I need Snidley because I don't know anything about running a plantation. Timothy is as useless as tits on a snake. If brains were gun powder, Timothy couldn't even blow his nose."

Janine chimes in, "Now Dirk, just give him time."

"Time!" says Dirk. "Timothy should be a clock factory he has so much time."

Janine just smiles and tries to hold back from laughing.

Jensen walks over about that time and says, "Pardon me Massa Dirk and Missa Janine, I jus' cudn't hep' but hearing yo' problems. Georgie, Mammy Em , and Jefferson knows dis plantation better than anyone heah. They cud' run dis plantation with der eyes shut."

"Thank you Jensen for that information. That came just at the right time," says Dirk. Dirk then asks if Stella had been around at all today. Janine says, "No haven't seen her since last night." Mighty strange Dirk thinks to himself.

"Before I take a bath I need to go talk with Jefferson. Something strange happened in the field today and I want to find out what is going on. I don't want to talk to Snidley about it. Today about killed me, I'm not used to this." Dirk says. "As far as Timothy goes, I don't think he can walk and scratch his balls at the same time. I'll be back soon. Tomorrow is another day and I feel a change in the air."

Dirk heads back to the slave quarters and quickly finds Jefferson. He takes Jefferson aside and asks him about that afternoon. Jefferson is really scared and begs Dirk not to whip him.

"I'm not going to punish you, Jefferson. Just tell me what happened."

"I can't, Suh. It will just make trouble."

Dirk decides to think about this and follow up later after he understands more about the plantation.

———

The next morning, Dirk is up before sunrise. He straps on Sweet Thing and heads out to the slave quarters. As he walks he can hear Snidley yelling, screaming, and cussing at someone. At that moment Dirk hears the crack of a whip and a blood-curdling scream of pain. Dirk picks up his pace. Dirk sees Snidley readying his whip for another lashing.

Dirk roars at the top of his lungs, "SNIDLEY!" Some of the slaves scream at Dirks loud and overpowering voice. Snidley stops in his tracks.

"Snidley, I need to talk with you," says Dirk.

"Yes Sir, right away," says Snidley.

"I said twice that all punishments were to be handled through me, do you remember?" says Dirk. "I will not stand for insubordination by anyone."

The slaves are talking amongst themselves. They are still not used to the new owner nor have they figured him out yet. The sun is rising fast. Dirk looks around for Timothy and he is nowhere to be seen.

"Mr. Snidley, please send someone over to roust Timothy again."

"Yes Sir, right away. Rufus, go get Timothy again." says Snidley.

Everyone heads out to the fields again. About an hour and a half later Timothy makes his appearance.

"TIMOTHY', yells Dirk. "Who the hell do you think you are the Lord Jesus Christ or someone real important? Do you walk on water? I am getting sick and tired of babysitting you. Do you understand?"

"Yes uncle Dirk," replies Timothy. Some of the slaves are trying not to laugh out too loud at Timothy's plight.

The sun is about halfway to noon when the slaves start singing "Wade in the Water" again. This time, as Dirk looks toward the river, he sees a dark figure moving low along the bank trying to stay in the shadows. He immediately figures it is an escaping slave and decides to ask Jensen or Maybelle about it.

It is another hot and humid day in the South Carolina sun as the slaves toil in the fields. Dirk sees the little girl with the lighter skin again. Dirk also notices that Snidley sees her and goes in the opposite direction.

Dirk goes up to her and says, "Hi, what is your name?"

She replies, "Lulu Suh," and bows slightly.

"Oh that is a very pretty name Lulu. Who do you stay with?"

"Oh with different people every night."

"Okay Lulu, we are going to talk again real soon."

Then Dirk gives her a little hug. The morning turns into the noon meal time. The dinner bell sounds and everyone heads out to eat. Dirk notices Timothy wandering aimlessly about.

Dirk yells, "TIMOTHY". Slaves jump at the sound of Dirk's thundering voice again that can be heard from one end of the fields to the other. "Timothy, you are as useless as a fart in a wind storm." Dirk, in a raised voice says, "You are here to learn the same as I am and to lead. You cannot lead unless you know how to be lead. Every one of these people here are our teachers. I am going to make something out of you even if it kills you. Do you understand?"

Timothy cowers and quivers as he looks toward the ground while his ass is getting chewed out again.

Dirk says, "Timothy, stand up straight, look forward, suck in that gut, and stick out your chest. Show some pride in yourself for once. I'll not let you quit Spanish Oaks. You are here for as long as it takes." Dirk continues his tirade. "When you walk I want you to walk with purpose in each step. I want you to take pride in yourself and what you can become. Spanish Oaks and all the inhabitants are dependent on us and the decisions we make. Now go get something to eat!"

Dirk hears him quivering as he breathes and watches him as he walks away. Dirk yells, "Timothy, what did I say about the way you walk?" Timothy straightens up a bit. Dirk thinks to himself, "Try not to trip over your own feet." Some of the slaves are trying not to laugh as they cover their mouths.

Janine shows up to see Dirk about something in the slave area. Dirk has a singleness of purpose, get Snidley off of Spanish Oaks as quick as possible. With Janine at his side, Dirk hunts down Snidley.

"Mr. Snidley," says Dirk. "I need to talk with you." Snidley cannot take his eyes off Janine. Janine really feels uncomfortable in his presence.

Janine says, "I'll talk with you later." She leaves for the big house. Dirk would love to kick the shit out of Snidley.

Dirk then says, "Let us retire to your cabin."

"What is this all about?" says Snidley.

Dirk says, "Come on, I want to have a talk with you."

Once inside the cabin Dirk says, "Have a seat." Snidley sits at the table. Dirk notices a bit of nervousness in his countenance.

Dirk says, "What is wrong, why are you so nervous? Did you do something you shouldn't have?"

Nash Snidley replies, "Not that I am aware of."

"Well," says Dirk. "There are some discrepancies in the ledger book, inventory reports, and the accounting of monetary receipts."

Snidley is really squirming in his seat very noticeably.

"Do you know anything about that?" asks Dirk.

Snidley's mouth opens slightly and he says, "I don't know what you are talking about."

"We know that there is money unaccounted for in the receipts. As I look around here I can see that you are living well beyond your means." Dirk then adds, "In fact you are living so well that it is raising my suspicions that you have been skimming the profits for your own personal use. Your honesty is now in question and where your loyalty lies. Do you have anything to say in your defense?"

Snidley looks up at Dirk with a snarled look on his face, teeth bared, and his fists clenched. Dirk sees all the signs of a cornered beast about to fight for its life. Dirk eases his right hand to the small of his back should he need to use Sweet Thing.

Snidley then says, "I don't know what the fuck you are talking about."

Dirk then says, "I'll tell you what Snidley, all these new possessions you have, consider that your severance pay. You have two hours to get yourself and your shit out of here and I'll be back to check."

Dirk then eases himself backward towards to the door keeping his eye on Snidley and his right hand behind his back should he need to use "Sweet Thing." "Don't ever come back here," is Dirks parting shot as he steps out of the cabin backwards.

VI

~~~~~~~~

Dirk walks back to the big house. Babs and Edgar are there to greet him at the back door. Dirk gives them a big hug and kiss. Janine shows up and also gives him the same. Dirk smiles at them and says he loves them. They go into the dining room and Jensen brings them their dinner.

"Well" says Dirk, "I fired Snidley and gave him two hours to get out and never come back."

"Any problems," asks Janine.

"Oh! nothing that I wasn't prepared to handle." Dirk replies. "I feel that we have not seen the last of him though."

"Your uncle has quite a sword and gun collection." Janine says. "Lots of rifles and hand guns, with one strange looking one, a hand gun with six barrels within a solid big barrel."

"Oh, that is called a 'pepper box' hand gun. I'll have a look at all them." Dirk looks at Babs and Edgar.

"How was your day?"

They reply, "Just fine Daddy. We spent lots of time in the kitchen talking to Maybelle and Jensen. They like to hear about life up north."

"After awhile we'll go to the slave quarters and look around and get to know the others a little better and so that they can get to know us also. Not to mention checking to make sure Snidley got his ass out. I'll get Timothy and Stella to go along," adds Dirk.

Later that evening Dirk sends Edgar over to get Timothy and Stella to meet them at the slave quarters and work area. Upon arriving there, Janine gasps at the horror that is supposed to be living quarters and the rundown condition. Babs and Edgar just hug Dirk real close. Stella is just there physically, but without a thought in her 'pea-sized' brain and Dirk looks at her in bewilderment. Dirk sees Georgie and Mammy Em.

"Everybody follow me I want you to meet a couple of people." says Dirk. As they walk towards Georgie and Mammy Em, Dirk notices that Timothy has not joined them.

"Timothy, if it is not too inconvenient would you please join us."

"Oh sorry Uncle Dirk." replies Timothy.

Dirk says after they get to Georgie and Mammy Em, "This is my wife Janine, my daughter Babs, my son Edgar, my nephew Timothy, and his wife Stella." Georgie and Mammy Em bow their heads slightly not knowing what to make of all the politeness. Dirk then says that they need to move along. As they walk further, Dirks checks to make sure that Snidley is gone. Dirk feels the small of his back for Sweet Thing and proceeds to the cabin. Dirk approaches the cabin. The doors and window openings are all open. The cabin is empty and devoid of all his belongings. Dirk steps out and motions for everyone to come up. They all step in and look around.

Dirk says, "I would like for Georgie and Mammy Em to have this for their new home."

Timothy chimes in and says, "What about the overseer, Uncle Dirk? Where is he going to live?"

"Come outside Timothy, I have something to say to you in private." Timothy follows Dirk outside.

"You are the overseer you numb nut! That is your job. We are going to learn from these slaves. You are going to need to get your head and ass tied a little tighter from now on! Talk to them. Ask them questions.

Try to figure out what is going on." Dirk taps his hat brim on Timothy's forehead. They walk to the waterfall and swimming hole. There are several slave children having a good time there. On the way back they stop at the barn and admire how spacious and well kept it is. In the barn Jasper is hard at work.

"Jasper, you are doing a good job, thank you and keep up the good work," says Dirk.

"Thank you Suh." Jasper replies.

"Jasper, this is my wife Janine, my daughter Babs, and my son Edgar. This is my nephew Timothy and his wife Stella. We must go now, thank you Jasper. "

On the way out of the barn Dirk says to Janine, "Let's go and tell Georgie and Mammy Em about their new home."

"Oh that is a wonderful idea, I can hardly wait." As they walk to Georgie and Mammy Em's place, they see the older couple still on the stoop looking puzzled. They stand up to meet them.

Dirk says to them, "Can you two come up with us to where Snidley used to live, I want to show you something."

"Yeh Suh Massa Dirk and Missa Janine."

They all get up and proceed to the cabin.

Once inside Dirk says, "Georgie and Mammy Em, this is your new home to live in for the rest of your days for as long as you live."

Georgie looks at Mammy Em and Mammy Em looks at Georgie with their mouths wide open and tears running down their cheeks. Dirk looks at Janine and she too has tears running down her cheeks as well.

"Get as many as you need to help you." says Dirk. "Enjoy your new home."

Dirk could also be seen with tears welling up inside his eyes. Dirk looks at Stella and starts to say something when Janine looks at him and shakes her head no.

Dirk says to them, "I'll stop by tomorrow to see how things are going."

Georgie then says, "Thank yuh Massa Dirk and Missa Janine."

"Yes thank yuh." says Mammy Em also.

"One more thing, where can we find Lulu?" Dirk asks.

"Mose likely in duh barn Suh if she not in anyone's cabin."

"Thank you."

Then they all leave.

"Janine, I want you to see this little girl that Snidley fathered," says Dirk. When they get back to the barn Dirk calls out her name.

"Lulu," says Dirk.

"Yeh Suh, Ise ova heah." She replies. When Dirk, Janine, and the kids get to her they see that she was preparing a place to sleep in the straw for the night.

"Oh you poor little girl!" says Janine. "You come with us to the big house. We are going to have you live with us." Janine puts her arm around her and gives her a big hug and a kiss on top of her head.

"Mommy" says Babs, "I still have some of my clothes from when I was younger that Lulu can wear."

"That's good. The sooner that she is out of these rags the better. Come on let's get to the big house." Janine says.

As they are walking back to the big house, Dirk says, "Timothy, I'll need you to go into town for supplies on Monday. You will probably need to spend the night there so he can get an early start back the next morning. You can take Stella with you. Stop by and I'll give you some money and a list."

"Okay Uncle Dirk," replies Timothy. Timothy and Stella head back to their house while the others head for the big house with Lulu.

When they get there Dirk says, "Which room shall Lulu have?"

"I've already got it picked out," Janine says. "Lulu, you are going to love your new home."

"Thank yuh Massa Dirk and Missa Janine, thank yuh Missa Babs.

"Lulu, you are now in the family," says Janine. Dirk smiles at the little girl and pats her on top of the head. Edgar gives her a big hug. Lulu is very well mannered for such a young age Janine thinks to herself.

As the evening progresses, Janine says to Dirk that she wants to show him the books on some of the previous financial transactions that his uncle had made. Janine brings out a large ledger book and says, "Look at this! Here is where your uncle sold a male slave five years ago to a plantation owner in Lafayette, Louisiana. Your uncle received fifteen hundred dollars for this slave. Here is the man's name, sounds like it is French to me."

Dirk then says, "I wonder who the slave was that was sold?"

Janine says, "Your guess is as good as mine."

"I'll ask Jensen on Monday, maybe he knows."

———

On Sunday morning Dirk heads out to the slave quarters to get a feel of things on the day off. Dirk also wants to see how Georgie and Mammy Em are doing in their new home. Dirk goes to one slave woman who is relaxing on her stoop and says, "Hello."

She rises and says, "Hello," and slightly bows her head.

Dirk asks, "What is your name?"

"Mah name is Wanda, Suh," she replies. At that moment, a male slave walks over and stands by Wanda's side.

Dirk then says, "And who might you be?"

"Mah name is Rufus, Suh," he replies.

"Glad to know the both of you," Dirk says. "What is that you two do here?"

Rufus replies first. "It is mah main job to care and tend to the animals and livestock Suh. Ah also duz other things around here when extra hep' is needed Suh. Mah newest job is tah get Massa Timothy out of the house."

Dirk says, "That could turn into a full time position." Dirk then looks at Wanda, "And you Wanda, what is your job?"

"Mah job Suh, is to spin, weave, and card the cotton so that we can make clothes and ah also heps in the fiels."

"Very well," says Dirk. "Those are very important jobs for the both of you."

Another slave woman walks towards them with an armload of vegetables from the garden acreage.

As she nears Dirks asks her, "What is your name please?" She just looks and slightly smiles with a bow of her head. Dirk looks confused.

Wanda then says, "Massa Dirk Suh, she new heah and don' speak much too gud. But ahs gon' see what ah can do. Rufus, hep her wid duh food!"

Rufus takes some of the vegetables and lays them on the ground. Wanda then looks at her and then at Rufus and touches Rufus and says, "Rufus," then Wanda touches herself on the chest and says, "Wanda" then Wanda points to Dirk and says, "Massa Dirk." The slave woman then smiles and utters some clicking sound in the middle of some language that he had never heard. Dirk, totally bewildered at what he had just heard just blinked his eyes in confusion at and gives her a wide toothy grin. Dirk thanks Rufus and Wanda and just looks at the other slave woman and nods.

"I must be going now." says Dirk. Dirk then turns and continues his inspection. Dirk walks past many of the slaves. Dirk sees Jasper again with his woman and stops to talk. They smile and slightly bow to him.

"Jasper, what is your lady's name please? "

Jasper replies, "This is Rebecca."

Dirk asks, "What is your job here?"

"Ah heps in the fields and other things when others need hep."

"Thank you." Dirk says. "I must be going now." Dirk tips his hat. The slaves are watching from the shadows and have not quite got the new owner figured out yet. Dirk then goes up to another couple that he sees standing out in front of their cabin.

"Hello." Dirk says. "What are your names and what are your jobs here?"

"Mah name is Caesar and this is mah woman Beulah. Mah main job is the carpenter heah and Ah also heps with other things when mah hep' is needed."

"And you Beulah?" Dirk asks.

"Ah duz' jus' bout anything." Beulah says. "Ah works in duh' fiels', Ah heps with duh' spinning and weaving of duh cotton into cloth for clothes, an' jus bout anything Suh'."

"Those are all very important jobs and I thank both of you." Dirk says. Dirk sees another couple standing about talking to each other. Dirk goes over asks what their names are.

"Mah name is Zachary Suh."

"Mah name is Molly Suh."

"What are your jobs?" Dirk asks.

Zachary responds, "Ah am duh' grounds keeper Suh. Ah keeps duh grounds in an' around duh big house all in gud order and trimmed up alla' time Suh."

"Yes, we noticed that in our trip into the plantation on the day we arrived here. You do a very good job Zachary." Dirk says.

"Thank yuh' Suh." Zachary responds.

"You Molly, what is it that you do?"

"Ah duz' jus' bout' everything there is to do roun' heah. Ah heps wid' duh' cookin', Ah heps in duh' fiels', yuh name it Suh an Ah duz it." Molly responds.

"I thank you both.' "You both do real good work."

"Thank yuh Suh." They both say. Dirk tips his hat and leaves.

Little Willy, the six-year-old son of Jasper and Rebecca goes into his cabin. Rebecca is rolling out dough for biscuits. Little Willy sees all the flour on the surface and grabs a big handful and powders his face with it.

Willy then says, "Look mommy, Ise a white person."

Rebecca looks at him and smacks him on the buttocks and says, "You are a bad boy, now go and show your daddy what you have done." Rebecca gives him another smack on the buttocks. Little Willy doesn't know what to think.

He then goes up to Jasper and says, "Look daddy, ah is a white people." Jasper looks at him and picks up a kindling stick and hits him across the buttocks and says, "Now yuh go and show your grampa what yuh has duz' dun'." Little Willy now has tears running down his face.

Willy finds his grampa and says, "Look grampa, ah is a white people." His grandfather looks at him and starts yelling and screaming what a bad little boys he is. Little Willy then cries and yells back at everyone,

"Ah only been white fo' jus' a bit an' ah already can't stand you black people." Little Willy then goes off crying to wash his face clean of the flour.

Dirk gets to Georgie and Mammy Ems' cabin and knocks on the door. Georgie opens the door and gives Dirk a great big ear-to-ear pearly white-toothed grin and says, "Please come in Massa Dirk, please come in Suh." Dirk steps in the cabin.

Dirks says, "I see you two are about settled in."

Mammy Em then steps in and says, "Massa Dirk, we wuz jus a talkin' bout yuh Suh, how nice and different you is from the rest of the white folks roun' heah."

Dirk then replies, "I am what I am and I follow my heart. The Good Lord says, "Do onto others as would have them do unto you although there are exceptions that I have made. There are those that are in severe need of an attitude adjustment. I believe what you give out you'll receive back in abundance. Please don't be confused, I am not giving in order to receive, that is just the way I am and life just happens to work that way, in my opinion."

Dirk then says, "Georgie, I need some advice."

Georgie looks at Dirk and says, "Yuh wants advice from me? A black man giving advice to a white man? What is the world a comin' ta, Lawd have mercy. Yuh is one strange puppy Massa Dirk."

Dirk just grins. Dirk just looks at Georgie and says, "Georgie, I don't have a false puffed up pride. Successful accomplishments don't care what the source is. You two have been here the longest of anyone and pretty much know how things run."

"Yeh Suh." says Georgie. "That we have."

"Let's have a seat." says Dirk. As the three of them sit at the table Dirk then says, "Now that Snidley is gone and no longer the Overseer, who do you think would make a good foreman to help run this place. At the same time and in unison, Georgie and Mammy Em both say,"JEFFERSON."

"That was quick!" Dirk says. "Why Jefferson?"

"Jefferson knows this plantation inside and out. He started out as a young fiel' han'. Jefferson has done everything and knows everything there is to do on a plantation."

"How is he doing after the Snidley whipping?" asks Dirk.

"He is gon' be fine, a little slow on the move for a spell, but he is gon' be jus' fine." says Georgie.

Dirk asks, "Then why was Snidley whipping him?"

"Jefferson did something better than Massa Snidley and it made Snidley look bad in front of everyone. Thas' why Massa Snidley whipped him."

"Well then" says Dirk, "The problem is solved. I am making Jefferson the new foreman here at Spanish Oaks. Please let me tell him on Monday morning."

"Yeh Suh Massa Dirk, we won' say a thing."

Dirk then smiles, tips his hat and leaves.

Dirk walks around for a while. He stops and has idle chitchat with some of the slaves that are out and about. Dirk continues to walk around the plantation and finds himself at the swimming hole and waterfall. As he approaches the waterfall, Dirk can see through the foliage that there is the most beautiful Black Woman he has ever seen just swimming, bathing, standing up and diving back into the water. Dirk then says to himself in a low voice, "Good God, Jesus, Joseph, and Mary!" Then he hides behind a rock. "I've got to get out of here." "This isn't like me." Dirk says to himself, Dirk then takes another quick look and says, "Matthew, Mark, Luke, and John, Lord please forgive me for this lustful interlude." Dirk then turns to leave but then looks back at the beauty one more time and says to himself, "My Sweet Lord, I have run out of names." Dirk then leaves the beautiful Black Woman to her privacy.

Dirk gets to the big house. "Hi Janine" he says. "Let's go upstairs for a while." Dirk takes Janine by the hand and he hurries her up the stairs. As they go upstairs Dirk says to Babs, Edgar, and Lulu, "You guys stay here and play for awhile."

"Okay." They reply. Dirk leads Janine by the hand to the bedroom. Janine has a very puzzled look on her face when they get to the bedroom. Dirk just gives her a long hard and passion filled kiss. Janine returns the kiss in like passion as they hurriedly remove their clothes. They come downstairs just before dinner and have a terrific evening with the children who have been helping Lulu get accustomed to the house.

VII

Early Monday morning Timothy pulls up in the wagon. Dirk looks around and says, "Where is Stella?"

"Oh! She isn't feeling too well Uncle Dirk, so I'll go by myself."

"Okay," says Dirk. "I'll get you some money and the list. You should be back sometime late tomorrow afternoon. Bring back some whiskey and a box of hand rolled Cuban cigars."

Timothy then leaves for town.

Janine says, "Maybe we should check on her."

Dirk says, "Check on her after I leave for the fields. The less that I am around her, the better I like it. Stella is dingier than a ships bell."

"Okay says Janine, "Later on, I'll see how she is doing."

Dirk saddles up a horse and ties Snidley's whip to the saddle. Dirk gets to the slave quarters early and builds a big fire out in the open. The sun is starting to come up fast.

Dirk then says in a loud and commanding voice, "I want everyone to come here now. Get everyone out of the cabins and come here now in front of me."

As the slaves start to gather around they are all mumbling quizzically amongst themselves as to what this is all about. Georgie and Mammy Em are there also smiling and holding each others' hand.

Dirk then says, "Jefferson, come forward."

Jefferson sheepishly comes forward not knowing what this is all about. As Jefferson approaches, Dirk turns to the horse and retrieves the whip.

Jefferson sees the whip in Dirk's hand and starts a panic driven merciful crying and says, "Please Massa Dirk, Ah didn' do nuthin! Please Massa Dirk, don' whup me." Then Jefferson throws himself at Dirks feet crying bitter tears. The slaves are starting to cry and wail amongst themselves. Dirk notices the scars from previous whippings and the most recent wounds from Snidley's whipping.

Dirk then commands, "Jefferson, get your ass up and stand on your own two feet." Jefferson slowly gets up with tears running down his cheeks.

"Jefferson," says Dirk. "See that fire over there?"

"Yes Massa Dirk, Ah sees it."

"I want you to take this whip and go throw it in the fire." Dirk says. The slave community all gasped in unison and amazement as to what just happened.

"Go on Jefferson, take the whip and throw it in the fire. What are you waiting for?"

Jefferson takes the whip and goes and throws it in the fire.

"Jefferson," says Dirk. "I am not through yet, please come here."

"Yes Massa Dirk." says Jefferson as he gets to Dirk.

Dirk says, "Face towards everyone." Jefferson then faces toward everyone.

Dirk then says, "Jefferson is now the foreman of the Spanish Oaks plantation." Jefferson just opens his mouth wide open in surprise and looks at Dirk. "What Jefferson says is the same as what I would say."

Georgie and Mammy Em smile and hug each other. Dirk looks at Georgie and Mammy Em and gives them a wink.

"Well Jefferson, what is the First order of the day?"

With a big ear-to-ear grin Jefferson says, "It is time ta go ta work."

They all start heading out to the fields and Jefferson gets a lot of pats on his shoulders.

Rufus comes up to Jefferson and says, "Jefferson, Ah thought you was a gonna' git yo' ass beat again."

"Me too." says Jefferson.

It is another hot and humid day under the South Carolina sun. It is a normal yet better day now that Jefferson is foreman. All the slaves are more content than in the previous days, tired but content. Dirk keeps an eye on things as he has been doing, asking questions and trying to learn all he can. After the work day is over, Dirk heads for the big house.

Timothy has just arrived from town by the time Dirk gets there.

"Good, looks like you didn't have to stay overnight after all. Did you get everything? Why don't you go ahead and get home." says Dirk. "We'll get the wagon unloaded in the morning. Just take the horses back to the barn on your way."

"Okay Uncle Dirk, it wasn't any fun without Stella, so I came on back," says Timothy.

Dirk says, "See you bright and early tomorrow morning Timothy."

"Okay" responds Timothy.

———

With the evening meal over, Dirk and Janine retire to the living room.

Dirk says to Janine, "Did you check on Stella?"

"Yes I did and I didn't think she was sick at all." says Janine "I went over there around noon and she was still in bed sound asleep. There wasn't anything wrong with her at all."

"Mighty strange?" says Dirk.

"I've still been pouring over the books." says Janine. "Your uncle was a lot wealthier than what we thought. Not only has he gained more interest in his bank holdings but I also discovered that he is part owner of a lumber mill just outside of town. Also, he was part owner of a mercantile store and a hotel/restaurant. It is all here in the books."

"Well now," says Dirk. "That will give us something to do real soon. I wonder why those attorneys didn't see that when I was there? You know those lawyers. Get to the cigars and whiskey then pat each other on the back for a job well done."

Dirk smiles and says, "You know what you have with a hundred lawyers with just their heads sticking out of the sand?"

"No, what?" Janine says.

"Not enough sand." says Dirk.

Janine smiles and snickers. "I'm not done yet. Your uncle was also quite a connoisseur of wines. He has a lot of wine from Europe and a lot from California. Come here and look at all of these bottles."

Janine shows Dirk the collection of wines.

"No whiskey?" says Dirk. "I guess I could learn to like wine in a pinch." Dirk looks at all the wine bottles, Bordeauxs from France, Zinfandels from Germany, Merlots from who knows where, and a vast number of other wines.

"There is more." Janine says. "Your uncle also has a large stash of gold, silver, and currency in a box on the top shelf in the walk-in closet in our room. As near as I can figure, there must be about a half of a million dollars plus in that box."

Dirk then just falls back on the bed and says, "I just pray to God that we do the right with our new found prosperity."

After the shock wears off about the new found wealth and their nerves settle down, Dirk says, "Show me his sword and gun collection as long as we are here."

Janine takes him to another walk-in closet where all the swords and guns are. There are several Revolutionary cavalry swords and a couple of rapiers, fencing swords, and knives. There are several guns of various shapes, sizes, calibers, in both, pistols, rifles, and shotguns. There is plenty of shot and powder also.

"This looks like a small arsenal of some kind." Dirk says. "Wow, this is impressive." Dirk picks up a musket and examines it. "This is a .30 caliber smooth bore cap and ball musket converted from a flintlock. A .30 caliber is really small, rare, and not too many of them around. "Only good for rabbits, squirrels, and other small game. There is the pepperbox revolver, a .38 caliber." Dirk continues to look around the collection.

Dirk then says with excitement, "Oh look Janine, two .36 caliber Navy Colts. This piece is a six shot revolver with several extra cylinders. Look at this, a .40 caliber pocket derringer, and a .52 caliber Sharps carbine. Isn't this exciting? Calibers are measured in one hundredths of an inch." He takes it out to the window to get some better lighting. After looking down the barrel and taking a lever and opening it, Dirk then takes his thumb and places it at the breech opening to reflect sunlight off his thumbnail.

Dirk says, "Now here a piece ahead of its time. This is a rifle, not a musket. This has several spiral grooves down the length of the barrel, not a smooth bore. Even though you can only fire off one shot at a time, you have a self-contained cartridge, which you just stick here in the bottom end called the breech. A good shooter can get off about ten accurate shots in a minute as opposed to three with a smooth bore musket. The spiral grooves then give the bullet a spin by the time it gets out of the end of the barrel giving it more accuracy and a longer flight path. My uncle really knew his guns. Aren't you excited over all this?" Dirk asks. He looks at Janine whose eyes are now crossed and has a scarf shoved in her mouth in complete boredom and a total lack of understanding of what the hell he is talking about.

"Okay" Dirk says, "The gun lessons for the day are now over." He says with a smile.

"We have been thrust into everyone's lives here now and I just want us to do the best that we possibly can." says Dirk. "I detest slavery and what it does to the Black Race but there is also the little known gospel reality of 'divine retribution' that it has on the malevolent slave owner and 'like-minded people.'"

Janine says, "We have started something here that will eventually bear fruit for the betterment of all, us included."

Dirk says, "I believe you are right. Some things you can't put a price on."

"Yes," Janine says. "Just look at what has been done in the short while that we have been here. Look at the lives that we have impacted for the better. Lulu will have a better life now that we are here. It wasn't her fault that she was born."

Dirk says, "Lulu is a beautiful little girl in spite of the evil bastard that spawned her."

Janine nods in agreement.

"I had Jefferson throw the whip into the fire this morning. I almost think I should have saved the whip for Timothy's dumb ass."

"Now Dirk," Says Janine. "He'll come around I'm sure. Just give him some time."

"Time, if Timothy had any more time he would be a clock factory." says Dirk. "I don't know if I have the patience nor the years left in my life for him. The mold was broken when he was born, thank God! I wouldn't wish him on anyone. Tomorrow is another day." says Dirk. "I am tired and I believe I'll clean up and turn in early."

"Me too." Janine adds.

VIII

~~~~~~~

The next day arrives early as usual. By the time Dirk gets to the slave quarters, Jefferson already has things under control and everyone is already heading out in the fields to work. Jefferson gives Dirk a toothy grin and Dirk tips his hat and smiles back. Dirk looks around for Timothy. Timothy is nowhere to be seen. Dirk heads out to the fields and mingles with the workers. A couple hours go by when Timothy finally shows up.

Dirk looks at him in disgust and says, "Nice you could make it sweetheart! Now go learn something by following Jefferson around all day. fact, why don't you just climb into Jefferson's back pocket and maybe your pea brain will allow you to learn something by accident. Don't concentrate too hard, I'd hate for you to strain yourself."

"Okay Uncle Dirk." replies Timothy.

Dirk then asks, "How is Stella this morning?"

"Fine!"

Timothy then turns abruptly and heads out to fields to find Jefferson. Dirk hears a lot of a singing type of music going on throughout portions of the fields. "A happy lot'" Dirk thinks to himself. He walks among the workers and makes idle 'chitchat with them. Dirk happens upon two young workers that appear to be in their late teens or early twenties.

Dirk says, "Hello, what are your names?"

One says, "Mah name in Cornelius, Suh."

Dirk then looks at the other one and says, "And your name young man?"

"Mah name is Andrew, Suh."

Dirk then says to the both of them, "I am going to do my best to make life better here for everyone. But first, I have a lot to learn. I'm going to make life here a lot better than the previous administration."

"Thank you Suh." Cornelius and Andrew both reply.

Dirk then moves on. Andrew looks at Cornelius quizzically and says, "What is an administration?" Cornelius then looks at Andrew and says, "You big dummy, don't you know nuthin'? That's what women do every month."

Dirk sees Wanda out working in the field and goes up to her. "Good Morning Wanda and how are you today?"

Wanda replies, "Jus fine Massa Dirk, thank yah suh."

"And how is Rufus this morning?"

"Rufus is jus' fine Suh. Rufus has been real busy since y'all got heah. He leaves early and comes back late. I'm sure that he really wants to impress you, Suh."

Dirk squints his eyes and says, "I'm sure that must be the reason. We'll talk again soon real soon." Dirk tips his hat and moves on. Dirk sees Jefferson a couple hundred yards off and makes his towards him. As Dirk makes his way towards Jefferson he says hello to several of the workers and smiles politely to each of them.

Dirk gets to Jefferson and says, "Well, how is the new foreman doing so far?"

Jefferson replies, "Jus' fine Massa Dirk, jus' fine."

"Do you have any problems?" Dirk asks.

Jefferson replies, "None Suh. Everything is going jus' fine Suh."

Dirk then looks around and says, "Where is Timothy? I told him to stay with you!" Dirk is really visibly disturbed at not seeing Timothy anywhere.

Jefferson says, "Ah ain't seed Massa Timothy for quite awhile now Massa Dirk. The las' Ah seed of him was way back yonder that a way Suh." Jefferson points to another part of the field towards the river.

Dirk heads towards the river next to the tree line. He sees Timothy off in the distance and makes his way toward him. Dirk gets about ten feet from Timothy and yells in a very commanding voice,

"TIMOTHY! What the hell do you think you are doing? Did your mother have any kids that lived?"

At that moment the workers all raise their heads to see what is going on. Some start to laugh at Timothy's predicament. As Dirk approaches he sees that Timothy is not alone. With Timothy is the young maiden that Dirk saw at the waterfall on the previous day. Dirk smiles at her and forces himself to confront Timothy.

"Move it!" He says to Timothy.

The young maiden runs off toward the fields.

"Hold it" says Dirk. "What is your name please?"

"Mah name is Lucille, Suh."

"What is your job here Lucille?"

"Ah heps' in the fiels sometimes, wid duh cooking and other things Suh." Lucille replies as she leaves. Dirk admires her beauty as she departs.

Dirk then looks at Timothy very seriously and says, "Don't even think of it. The prejudice society that we are living in now is not ready for inter-racial relations yet, at least not in our lifetime living amongst the people that we are placed in. You will only make life unbearable for the two of you. Do you want to be like Snidley?"

Dirk knows that there is something amiss between Timothy and Stella.

Timothy then says, "But Uncle Dirk."

Dirk doesn't let Timothy finish his sentence and says, "Shut up! You talk too much."

Noontime has arrived and the dinner bell sounds. Everyone seems to be in good spirits as they head back to the living quarters for dinner.

Dirk looks at Timothy and commands, "In one hour I want your ass back out in the fields. Do you understand?" Dirk says sternly.

"Yes Uncle Dirk." replies Timothy.

Dirk sees Georgie and Mammy Em and heads their way. "Good afternoon Georgie and good afternoon Mammy Em. How are the two of you today?"

"Jus' fine Suh, real gud Massa Dirk." They reply.

Dirk notices them staring at Jefferson. "Why are you two staring so much at Jefferson?"

"Well Suh" says Mammy Em, "We stares at Jefferson a whole bunch cuz' he minds' us of our son when he wuz' that age. He wud be bout' thuty five now as far as I can recollect'." Georgie says. "Yo uncle sol' him. We don' know to who or where."

"I am truly sorry." says Dirk.

"It ain't yo' fault Massa Dirk," says Mammy Em. "Yo' had nuthin' to do with it."

"I know," says Dirk. "But I feel guilt by association. He was my blood relative."

"We understand, Massa Dirk," says Georgie.

"I am going to get something to eat." Dirk says. "We'll talk again soon." Dirk smiles and tips his hat.

Once at the big house, Janine greets him with a big hug and a kiss. Babs, Edgar, and Lulu are there also with their hugs. Dirk just smiles and gives everyone a hug back.

Dirk says, "My stomach is licking my backbone. My stomach swears that my throat is no longer in existence. What do we have to eat? I am famished."

Janine says, "I'll see if Maybelle has dinner ready."

A couple minutes later Maybelle and Jenson bring in the food. Dirk just smiles and grabs a piece of bread and some meat and starts eating.

As they are eating, Dirk says to Janine, "You know on that ledger book entry on the sold slave a few years back?"

"Yes," replies Janine.

"Well that was probably Georgie and Mammy Em's only son."

"How awful," replies Janine. "Breaking up a family like that."

"No argument from me." Says Dirk. "On our next trip to the city I'll confer with the brokerage firm and just maybe they can go back that far in their records to see what kind of help that they can give. Let us retire to the front porch and have some 'sweet tea'."

"I'm there." says Janine.

Dirk then says, "Oh Maybelle, would you be so kind as to bring Janine and I some 'sweet tea' on the front porch please."

Maybelle responds, "Yeh Suh Massa Dirk, right away."

As Dirk and Janine are relaxing with their drinks and enjoying each other's company, Dirk notices two little black faces peering at them through the bushes.

"Janine," says Dirk. "It would appear that we have company."

"Where, whatever do you mean? I don't see anyone." Janine replies with a puzzled look.

Dirk then points to the bushes, stands up and says, "Come here boys."

The two start towards him with fear and trembling in each step.

"Well come here guys," commands Dirk.

The two stand in front of Dirk and Janine not knowing what to do.

Janine says to one of them, "What is your name young man?"

He just looks at the ground and faintly mumbles something barely audible.

Dirk then says, "What? We didn't hear you. You need to stand up straight, look at us and clearly state your name."

The one little boy looks up and says, "Mah name is Benjamin Suh."

"Now what was so hard about that?" says Dirk.

Then Janine says to the other boy and says, "What is your name young man?"

The second boy gives Janine a wide toothy grin and says, "Mah name is Gabooti Missa Janine."

Dirk shakes his head and blinks his eyes several times and says, "What!"

"Gabooti Suh."

Dirk then gives him a long drawn out "Okaaay."

About that time Maybelle arrives to check on them and sees the two young boys and yells, "Now you two run along and git on outta heah!"

Janine then says to Maybelle, "That's quite all right."

Dirk says, "Maybelle, do you think you could scare up a couple glasses of lemonade for these two young gentlemen?"

"Yeh Suh, Massa Dirk." Maybelle says. As Maybelle turns and leaves she just sneers at the two boys.

Dirk says to the two boys, "Go ahead and have a sit."

Janine smiles and asks, "What do you two boys do here?"

Benjamin says, "We sometimes heps in the fiels' Massa Dirk."

Gabooti then says, "We also duz other things that need to be dun' when we is tol' to Suh."

Maybelle then arrives with the lemonade for the two boys.

"Drink up boys," says Dirk. "Why aren't you two out helping now?"

Benjamin says, "We jus' got tired and wore out and jus' didn't feel like a workin' no mo' today."

Dirk and Janine just smile at each and chuckle out loud very audibly. Dirk says to Janine, "These two have been hanging around Timothy too much." Janine just laughs and sips some more tea.

Gabooti says, "We needs to git along now Suh."

"Well okay then." Says Dirk. "You two be sure to come back and see us again now."

"We will Massa Dirk and Missa Janine." The two break out into a dead run and exit the yard. Dirk notices the grounds keeper at work.

"Come on, I'll introduce you to the grounds keeper." Dirk says to Janine. As they approach the grounds keeper, he stops what he is doing and wipes his hands.

"Hello", say Dirk and Janine.

"Good afternoon Suh." He replies back.

"What is your name please?" Janine asks.

"Mah name is Zachary Missa Janine and Massa Dirk."

Dirk then says, "We noticed right off what a great job you do in keeping the plantation grounds in good order."

"Thank yah Suh." Says Zachary.

Dirk then says, "We are going to have a look around, thank you Zachary."

Zachary nods. As Dirk and Janine look around the area they are amazed at their good fortune.

Janine says, "This is almost too good to be true."

"You are absolutely right. I can't believe it either," Dirk replies. "I just pray to the almighty God that we always do what is right in his eyes by our good fortune and that whatever we do we can make ourselves proud of each other because no one else will know. Eventually, I want Babs and Edgar to teach the workers some of their schooling. I want to start them out on the "milk" of education and then get to the "meat and potatoes" down the road."

"You know that's not legal here, Janine says.

"I don't care at all. They should know how to read and write," Dirk states.

Dirk and Janine continue their walk, hand in hand, out on the grounds. Dirk sees a very large 'Weeping Willow' tree with its thick leafy branches touching the ground in the full 360-degree circumference of the tree.

Dirk then says excitedly, "Oh look Janine, that is a special tree."

As they get nearer to the tree Janine says, "What is so special about this tree?"

"Well come on, I'll show you." Dirk says. They get to the tree and Janine just scratches her head.

"Well," Janine says, "I'm waiting."

Dirk parts the thick leafy branches and says, "Come on in."

Janine steps in and says, "What is so special about being under this tree?"

Dirk says, "This tree is extra special because nobody can see in here." He then pulls Janine close to him in a warm and passionate embrace.

"Dirk, not out here!" Janine says.

"Why not?" says Dirk. "No one can see in and we can't see out. That is why this tree is so special. Don't you just love it?" Dirk starts to unbutton her blouse.

"Dirk," says Janine, "Just last night." Before Janine can get another word out, Dirk has her blouse off and he lowers her to the ground with long passionate kissing embraces as she wraps her arms around his neck. About an hour later they both emerge from under the 'Special Tree'. Janine tries to fluff up her hair the best she can and brush off her blouse.

She looks deep into Dirk's eyes and says, "Thanks," Then gives him another big passionate embrace.

Dirk just looks back and says, "I'm gifted, it will be Christmas year round here." Dirk then gives Janine a wide toothy grin. Janine just smiles and hugs Dirk again. As they head back to the big house they walk hand in hand. Janine still is giving Dirk many passionate embraces and she gives him a bite on his cheek, another deep embrace and grabs his buttocks making him jump.

Janine says, "I just love that special tree."

"I am sure that there are more around, we just have to look," replies Dirk. Dirk then says that he needs to get back into the fields to see what is going on.

Dirk winks at Janine "and I know where you live."

Dirk drops Janine off at the house and says, "I'll see you at supper time."

Janine looks at him lovingly and mouths the words, "I love you." Dirk blows her a kiss, smiles then departs.

It is about an hour before quitting time when Dirk gets out to the fields. Dirk finds Jefferson and asks, "How is everything going?"

Jefferson replies, "Real good Massa Dirk, real good Suh."

"Where is Timothy?"

Jefferson replies, "Ah haven't seed him for quite awhile Suh. Ah don' know where he is."

"Okay, thanks." Dirk says. "Take care of things. I won't be back this afternoon."

"Yeh Suh Massa Dirk." Dirk looks all over for Timothy. He is not in the fields. He is not in the barn. He is not in any of the worker's area. Dirk finally heads to Timothy and Stella's cabin. As Dirk approaches their cabin, he can hear arguing and hot tempers.

Dirk yells, "Timothy."

The arguing ceases. Timothy comes outside and says, "Yes Uncle Dirk."

"What is going on?" Dirk asks.

"Oh nothing," replies Timothy.

Dirk says, "It is none of my business, but that was a lot of nothing the entire planet was just over hearing."

"Just some personal problems." Timothy says.

"There isn't anyone that does not have some sort of personal problem, me included. Our only problem is how we face it and overcome the problem." Dirk decides not to chew is ass out. "See you in the morning and be on time."

Timothy gives his standard reply, "Okay Uncle Dirk."

Dirk straps on 'Sweet Thing' and heads out to the field hand quarters. Dirk and Timothy get to the quarters at about the same time in the morning. Dirk blinks his eyes in amazement that Timothy is there on time. Dirk calls Timothy and Jefferson together.

"Janine, the kids and myself will be going to Charleston this morning. We should be gone only a couple of days. Jefferson," says Dirk. "You know what to do."

Dirk then looks Timothy square in the eyes and says, "Can I trust you to be here when you are supposed to be here?"

"Yes Uncle Dirk," replies Timothy.

"Okay then." says Dirk. "I'll see you when we get back." Dirk tips his hat and leaves.

IX

~~~

Dirk, Janine, Babs, Edgar, and Lulu are in the wagon headed for Charleston with their bags in the back of the wagon. Ever since Janine figured out their financial situation, they have been talking about what to do with the properties. They are concerned about their partners and the job of managing three enterprises at a distance from where they live. They decide that Dirk should investigate and check out the situation.

They get to Charleston in about two hours and check into the hotel that they partly own. The hotel clerk treats Lulu as if she is one of their servants and asks if they want her to sleep in the quarters.

"She stays with us!" Janine exclaims.

"She is not a servant," Dirk says. The clerk smirks but gives them their room keys. They get to their two adjoining rooms and freshen up.

Dirk heads over to the attorney's office to straighten out ownership of the hotel and the other enterprises that he has inherited from his uncle. The attorney informs him that the partner in the hotel venture wants to sell out now that Dirk's uncle is dead. He does not want to work with a Yankee. Dirk decides on the spot to buy the hotel, because of the trouble with the desk clerk.

"I'll buy out the other owner," Dirk says. "Please draw up the papers immediately. Here is a deposit. I will bring the rest of the money this afternoon. Please give me an ownership certificate."

"What do you want to do with the other properties?" the attorney asks.

"I'll check them out tomorrow. I want to meet the managers and assess the situation. I'll let you know."

When Dirk gets back to the hotel, he tells Janine what he has done.

"That's great," she says. "Now let's go get something to eat."

As they walk through the dining area Dirk and Janine cannot help but notice all of the stares that they get from the other guests.

Janine whispers in Dirk's ear, "People are sure staring at us a lot."

Dirk replies, "Yes, I noticed. If they don't like the color combination at this table, then the guys can all just go and piss into the wind and the women can all go and pound sand up their asses as far as I am concerned. I own this hotel!"

"And I'll hold the door open for all of them." says Janine.

Dirk just scratches his nose with his middle finger at everyone. As they are seating themselves, Dirk notices a young mustached gentleman wearing a suit and carrying a heavy-duty cane adorned with a big brass end on the handle, seated nearby looking at them. Dirk then stares back with a stern look. The young gentleman nods his head, smiles, and lifts his drink to them in admiration. Dirk then smiles back to him and nods back.

When no one comes to take their orders or bring them food, Dirk gets up and walks to the kitchen. He sees the staff looking fearful.

"What is going on here?" says Dirk.

"Massa, we can't serve a colored girl in the dining room. It agin the law, we all be whipped."

"This is my hotel and you will do what I say. If there is any trouble, have them speak to me." He shows them his deed. One of the staff looks at it and calls the manager. The manager looks at the document and bows to Dirk.

"Sir, we are please to meet you. I would like to talk with you later." He turns to his staff and orders them to serve the new owner and his family.

They all have a good meal. The young gentleman is finished with his meal and rises to leave. He again acknowledges Dirk and family with a smile and a nod of his head. Dirk gives a friendly smile back in return.

Janine says, "He was a nice person, sort of out of character for the rest of the clientele here."

"Yes," replies Dirk, "Any port in the storm for me."

Since it was still daylight and they are right across the street from the slave broker Dirk decides to pay him a visit.

"Janine, why don't you and the kids take in some of the sights while I have a talk with the slave broker across the street?"

"Okay." says Janine. "Let's go kids!"

Dirk steps into the slave broker's office and says, "Hello, I'm Dirk Kahane, I own the Spanish Oaks plantation about two hours out of town."

The broker, a balding overweight man in his mid-fifties stands and they shake hands.

He says, "Hello Mr. Kahane, I knew your uncle. My name is Josh Twindley and I am very happy to me you Sir. How may I help you?"

Dirk says, "According to his ledger book, about five years ago my uncle sold a slave through you to a French planter in Lafayette, Louisiana just out of New Orleans." "Would you by chance have any record of that transaction?"

"Five years ago, that was a long time ago," says Mr. Twindley. "I'll see what I can do for you Sir."

"Thank you," says Dirk. "I will pay you for time and effort. We are staying at the hotel across the street. I will check with you in a couple of days."

"I'll get right on it Mr. Kahane." says Twindley.

"I would very much appreciate it, Sir," says Dirk. Dirk smiles and tips his hat and leaves. Dirk meets up with the family. They go into a couple of the shops and end up in the mercantile store that they are partly own. Each of the kids gets some candy. Babs likes the lemon drops. Edgar gets some jawbreakers, and Lulu likes the peppermint sticks. Janine gets some Juju bees, and Dirk gets a couple pieces of jerky.

"Let's get back to the hotel," Dirk says. "It is getting late."

As they walk back to the hotel, they endure more stares from the townspeople that are there. Dirk and Janine could care less as they head back. The kids are too busy with their candy to notice anything. They get back to their rooms at the hotel.

"I have a lot of business to take care of in the morning." says Dirk. "I need talk with the manager of this hotel, to go to the bank, the lumber mill, and back to the mercantile to introduce myself." Dirk turns in early. Janine and the kids go to their room for a while before they turn in for the night.

In the morning, they all get ready to head down for breakfast. Dirk straps on 'Sweet Thing' and they go down to the dining room for breakfast. Like the night before, they receive a lot of stairs from the dining guests. Dirk and Janine overhear one husky voice saying, 'Mulatto'. Dirk stops to confront the asshole.

Janine squeezes his hand and just looks at Dirk and says, "NO, just leave him be. Don't pay any attention to him. Assholes are everywhere."

As they are lead to their table Dirk again notices the young gentleman with the brass knobbed cane from the evening before. Dirk smiles and tips his hat to him. The young gentleman replies in like manner back at Dirk and the family. They have a nice breakfast. Dirk then says, "Let's plan on meeting back here at five o'clock this afternoon. I have a lot to do and a short time to do it in." Dirk kisses Janine and hugs the kids, the young gentleman smiles and Dirk smiles back and tips his hat as he goes off to find the manager of the hotel and restaurant.

After a very informative discussion with the manager, Dirk is satisfied that things will run smoothly at the hotel and that he will be able to make some changes on his visits to the city.

Dirk then goes to the bank to sign papers and take care of his other affairs there. Next Dirk goes to the mercantile store where they were the night before and introduces himself. He shakes hands with the manager and asks how things are going. The manager is a middle-aged man who has been running the store for many years.

"Sir," he says. "I have been running this store a long time. I have always been honest, but very thrifty and I have set aside some money. Are you interested in selling your share in the store to me? I intend to buy out the other partner also."

"I certainly will consider it," says Dirk. They discuss the price and the finances. Dirk thinks this will solve one problem and leave good feelings all around.

Next Dirk goes to the lumber mill just outside of town. The smell of the freshly cut Southern Pine permeates the air. Dirk says to himself, "Ah the sweet smell of money." Dirk notices how busy everyone is and all the wagonloads of lumber leaving the mill.

"A very good sight indeed," Dirk thinks to himself. Dirk finds the mill office and introduces himself to the manager, a Mr. Sean O'Brian. Mr. O'Brian takes Dirk on a tour of the operation. Several hours later Dirk notices the time and politely excuses himself after saying thanks that he has to meet his family at five o'clock. "Thank you Sean for the tour. We'll be talking again real soon."

Dirk heads over to the attorney's office and gives him the rest of the funds for the hotel.

"The manager of the mercantile establishment wants to buy me out. I think it will be a good solution. He means to buy the other partner out too. Can you handle the paperwork and finances for me?"

"I'd be pleased," says the attorney. "What about the lumber yard?"

"I'd like to keep that and buy out the other partner. Investigate that for me, please. I think I have a good manager there."

"I'll do that." The attorney finishes up the necessary paperwork.

Dirk gets back to the hotel at about four thirty. He does not see Janine and the kids, so he waits outside the hotel. A couple of stray dogs are sitting on the boardwalk. Dirk says hello to the dogs and the dogs wag their tails. Dirk feels around in his pocket and comes up with a couple small pieces of jerky and throws a piece to each dog.

"Sorry pups that is all I have." Then he gives each one a pat on the head. Dirk then notices a young black couple loaded down with packages approaching the hotel on the boardwalk. At the same time Dirk also notices two white men watching them approach. It doesn't take much for Dirk to ascertain what is going to happen next -- trouble for the young couple. Dirk starts on over to where he knows what is going to happen.

As the young black couple approach close to the white thugs, one steps out in front of them and says, "Just what are your black asses doing on my boardwalk?" He then knocks the packages out of their hands. The young black woman screams. Their packages are all over the boardwalk. The other thug grabs the young black girls arm and she screams. Dirk gets there at that moment. Dirk grabs the one thug by the neck and slams him against the hotel wall in a resounding crash. Dirk looks at the other thug who is about to throw a punch at Dirk. Dirk catches his fist in mid swing and bends his fingers inward toward the palm of his hand bending and squeezing the fingertips rendering the thug useless and bringing him to his knees.

Dirk says to the young black couple, "Hurry and get your things and get out of here."

They do so without hesitation and are gone. Dirk hears a loud thud and scream and another loud thud and scream off to his side. The young gentleman from the dining room has come to Dirk's aid just at the right moment. The first thug was about to hit Dirk when the young gentleman took his brass knobbed cane and hit the thug on the foot and then hit him again in the forehead rendering him useless. The second thug is still screaming and cussing as Dirk still has a death grip on his hand.

The thug says, "Just who the fuck do you think you are? What the hell do you care about these 'Darkies' anyway?"

At that moment the thug pulls a knife out of his boot. Dirk had pulled 'Sweet Thing' out and was ready. A crowd had gathered by this time. As the thug starts forward with his knife, Dirk took the back edge of "Sweet Thing' and knocked the thug's knife loose from his hand.

The thug screams and says, "You Darkie lovin' son of bitch."

Dirk then takes 'Sweet Thing' in one fluid upward motion lops off the thugs left ear. As the ear is flying up in the air, Dirk catches the knife broadside and hits it out into the dusty street. The two stray dogs are there as the ear lands in the street. The fight is on for the ear. The one stray gobbles it up. The other dog sits up and begs for his snack.

The thug screams in horror, "You cut off my fuckin' ear you bastard." The blood is streaming through his fingers down the backside of his hand, down the side of his face, neck, and front side.

Dirk says, "Listen shit breath, you are lucky that is all I cut off." Dirk then wipes the blood off 'Sweet Thing' on the thug's shirt. "Next time I might really get pissed off and you might not be so lucky. Now you and your dumb shit friend get the hell out of here. If I ever see anyone of you two turds again, I am going to rearrange things on you." They run and hobble off in a daze.

Dirk then turns to the young gentleman and says, "Thanks for watching my back side sir."

The young gentleman replies, "Since last night at the dining table I have held you in great esteem because of whom and what you are in these adverse times."

"My name is Dirk Kahane." Dirk puts out his hand and shakes the young gentleman's hand.

"My name is Samuel Clemens," he responds.

At that moment a black waiter comes out and says, "Mr. Clemens, Suh, yo' table is ready now." Samuel smiles again and he and Dirk shake hands once more.

Janine and the kids were crossing the street now. Dirk gives Janine a big hug and kiss and hugs the kids.

Janine asks, "How was your day dear?"

Dirk replies, "Oh, just fine."

Janine raises her eyebrows detecting something amiss in Dirks reply.

"Let's go in and get something to eat." says Dirk. They are seated right next to Samuel's table. Samuel and Dirk smile at each other. Dirk then says, "Mr. Clemens, I would like to introduce my family to you." Clemens stands. "This is my wife Janine, daughter Babs, my son Edgar, and our adopted daughter Lulu."

Janine sticks out her hand to Samuel and he takes her hand and kisses it.

"Nice to meet you Sir," says Janine.

"Please, call me Samuel," he replies.

"And you Sir please call me Janine." She says with a smile.

Samuel then looks at each of them and says, "I am so happy to meet every one of you. You do not know how lucky you are to have such a fine, honorable, and upstanding husband."

Dirk says, "Samuel, I see that your dinner has not arrived yet. Please honor us with your presence at our table."

Janine adds, "Please do Samuel, it would be a pleasure to have you sup with us."

"The pleasure is all mine." says Samuel as he is seated. They are all seated when Dirk orders drinks for all. The kids have sarsaparilla, Janine has a glass of wine, Samuel and Dirk have bourbon.

Samuel looks over at Dirk and says, "I have great respect and admiration for you Dirk for interceding for that black couple who were complete strangers to you. You put your safety and well being on the line for two unknowns."

Dirk looks a sideways glance at Janine.

Janine has a puzzled look on her face and says, "Oh please do go on with your story Samuel." Janine says sternly giving Dirk a very puzzled look. "Dirk won't tell me a thing."

Samuel then proceeds to go on with the sequence of events that transpired. Janine gasps in horror as Samuel explains the situation.

Janine looks at Dirk and says, "I thought you said your day was okay."

"It was," says Dirk. "Samuel about beat a guy to death with his cane and I fed a guy's ear to a dog. Neither Samuel nor I was harmed. When you and the kids showed up, everything was just fine." Dirk gives Janine a wide toothy smile. Dirk says to Samuel, "Let's order dinner before she asks anymore questions."

"You got it," says Samuel. They all have a good dinner and good conversation. Everyone laughs and has a good time.

Samuel looks at his pocket watch and says, "It is getting late. I take a train to New Orleans in the morning. I have many stops and transfers before I get there since there are not any direct routes from here to New Orleans. I am going to take a 'paddle wheeler up the Mississippi River. I have some ideas on a book or two that I am thinking about writing sometime in the future."

Samuel, Dirk, and Janine all stand. "Samuel," says Dirk, your dinner is covered."

"Thank you very much, I appreciate that."

Janine shakes his hand and thanks him again for helping Dirk.

Dirk says as they shake hands, "Samuel, you will always have a place to stay if you are ever out 'Spanish Oaks' way. Please don't hesitate to stop by."

Samuel looks at the kids and says, "Good bye." They in unison say good-bye back to him. Samuel then heads up to his room.

"Tomorrow," says Dirk, "I want to stop by the lumber mill to place a large order for lumber to build new living quarters for the workers and for other big structures."

Janine says, "Oh yes, please do, they deserve much better than what they have."

"It is getting late let's turn in." says Dirk.

———

The next morning they get ready for the two hour ride back to Spanish Oaks. Dirk straps on 'Sweet Thing'. As they are checking out, Dirk is informed that there is a note for him with the desk clerk. The clerk hands him the note.

"Who is it from?" Janine asks.

"It is from Josh Twindley, the slave broker from across the street," says Dirk. "You all wait here, I'll be right back."

Dirk steps into Twindley's office. Josh looks up and says, "I see you got my note."

"Yes replies Dirk. "Talk to me."

"Good news," says Twindley. "The slave in question is still outside of New Orleans in Lafayette. The same French planter still owns him and would be willing to part with him if the price is right. One thing," Twindley adds, "He is recovering from a broken leg and has been out of commission for awhile."

"That is not a problem," says Dirk. "Please find out his price. We are on our back to Spanish Oaks now. Would you please get word to us on his price and I'll make arrangements for transportation. Thank you very much Mr. Twindley." Dirk then hands him a five dollar gold coin.

"Thank you Mr. Kahane, Thank you very much." says Twindley. "I'll get working on this right now."

Dirk says, "Thanks." Then tips his hat and departs. Dirk crosses the street to the hotel where the family is still waiting. "I'll get the wagon and tell you everything on the way home," says Dirk. Dirk tells Janine of the impending transaction and waiting to hear the price that the Frenchman wants and of the recovery from the broken leg. Dirk stops at the lumber mill and hunts down Sean O'Brian, the manager. Dirk places the order for the lumber, then heads back to the wagon for the trip home.

As they are going down the road, Janine says, "You know something hon?"

"What's that?" Dirk replies.

"We have only been here a short time and just look at lives that we have improved," says Janine.

"I know." Dirk adds. "We have turned their lives upside down in a good way from the only lives that they knew."

Janine says, "And it is only going to get better."

"If not by the Grace of God, there go I," says Dirk. "I feel that I am on a mission from some unknown source."

Janine says, "I feel the same way also."

Dirk adds, "If I ever go astray or do anything wrong, I just hope and pray that a gentle hand slaps me on my ass and sets me straight, gently of course."

Janine smiles as they continue on.

X

They arrive at Spanish Oaks mid afternoon. Everyone is tired. Dirk helps unload the wagon then heads out to the plantation. He heads to where the livestock and other animals are but does not see Rufus. Dirk sees Georgie and Mammy Em taking care of some of the children and carding some of the cotton to get it ready for spinning.

Georgie says, "Good afternoon Massa Dirk."

"Good afternoon Georgie. How are you and Mammy Em doing?"

"Jus' fin' Suh."

"Everything going well?" says Dirk.

"Yeh Suh, Mammy Em an' me is jus fin' Suh. The chilluns is jus' fin'."

"That's good. I am going to see how Timothy and Jefferson are doing. You two have a good afternoon." Dirk tips his hat and leaves.

Dirk heads out to the fields and hooks up with Timothy and Jefferson.

"Oh hi Uncle Dirk." says Timothy.

Dirk asks, "How are things here?"

Timothy replies, "Oh pretty good."

Jefferson says, "Things is runnin' jus fin' Suh. Yeh Suh, jus' fin'."

"Well good," says Dirk, "I am going home. I'll see you two tomorrow." Dirk leaves.

On the way back Dirk sees Rufus. "Hello Rufus, I didn't see you when I came by earlier."

"Oh ah had ta catch me a couple of chickens got loosed Suh." Rufus replies.

Dirk tips his hat and continues on to the big house. Dirk gets back and settles in for the evening. Jenson serves the evening meal to them.

Janine just looks at the food and says, "I'm not very hungry right now. I might have something a little later on. Thank you Jenson."

"As you wish Missa Janine," says Jensen.

Dirk reaches over and holds Janine's hand and says, "Are you okay hon?"

Janine replies, "Yes I'll be just fine. It was probably the trip and all. I'm sure that I'll be fine in the morning."

Saturday morning arrives early as usual on the plantation. Since Dirk has taken over, Saturday is half a workday for everyone. Everyone is mulling about readying for the day's work. Timothy comes strolling in also. Dirk just looks astounded that Timothy is there.

"Good morning Timothy," says Dirk. Timothy just passes by still looking half asleep. The field hands are all singing as they head off to the fields. "That is a good sign." Dirk thinks to himself.

As the morning wears on, the workers quietly notice some another slave running and hiding along the river trail. They all start singing their field hollers again directing the runaways where to go. After the runaway is out of sight they return to their singing. This time, Dirk sees the fleeing figure and decides to get to the bottom of this.

Dirk goes to the barn and gets the pack mule and two water barrels and fills them with water. Dirk then heads back to the fields. Dirk finds Benjamin and Gabooti.

"Hi guys," says Dirk. "The mule and I are going to work. Would you two like to help?"

"Yeh Suh Massa Dirk," they reply in unison.

"This is what we are going to do." Dirk says. "We are going to give everyone water in the fields so that everyone can have a drink. I'll lead the mule and you two can take water to everyone. Okay, let's get started. Next week, we are going to do this three or four times a day."

Benjamin and Gabooti are eager to help and please Dirk. Timothy is with Jefferson. The field hands are singing happily. Dirk, Benjamin, and Gabooti are just about finished with the water. They head back to the living quarters.

Dirk says to them, "Thank you, you two did a fine job." Dirk reaches into his pocket and retrieves two shiny ten-cent silver coins and gives one to each of them. They look at the coins and break out into a wide ear-to-ear grin and take off running. Dirk just smiles and takes the mule back to the barn. Dirk notices that Rufus is riding the prized gelding doing some fancy horsemanship the likes that he had never seen before. Rufus was doing some quick stops and turns and a lot of other remarkable feats that really impress him.

Dirk wants to talk with everyone at the end of the day about an upcoming change that will affect everyone. Dirk also wants Janine and the kids to be there. Dirk goes to Timothy and Jefferson and informs them. He asks to have everyone together and to quit work an hour early. Dirk leaves for the big house. On the way Dirk stops by the barn to talk to Rufus and check on things. Rufus is not to be seen anywhere. Dirk continues on to the big house again. Dirk sees Janine and the kids and informs them of what is to transpire and that he wants them all by his side at that time. Dirk also says to Janine that he would like Babs and Edgar to teach the workers how to read, write, and do basic math.

Dirk says to Babs and Edgar, "How would you two like to become teachers?" Babs and Edgar just look at each with mouths wide open.

"Well!" says Dirk. "I believe you two are up to the task or I wouldn't have said anything."

Janine smiles at the kids and says, "You two shouldn't have any problems. You can start with Lulu." Janine then runs outside and throws up. Janine returns to a stunned Dirk and says, "I tried to eat something but I just throw it up."

"I wonder what is wrong with you?" says Dirk.

"I wonder." says Janine with a sideways glance to Dirk. "I feel well enough to go with you to the workers area. Let's go kids."

As they near the workers quarters, the slaves are just returning from the fields. Georgie and Mammy Em are there also.

Mammy Em has a hard look at Janine and says, "How are yuh a feelin' chil'?"

"Just a little ill," replies Janine.

"Let me have your hand Missa Janine," says Mammy Em. Mammy Em then takes Janine's hand into hers.

Mammy Em holds her hand for a long while and looks into Janine's eyes and says, "Chil' you are a gonna' have a baby. "Missa Janine, yoh' is a gonna' has to take extra special care of yo'self. Duz' yuh understan'?"

Janine replies, "Why yes, but whatever do you mean?"

"Jus' be real careful wid' yoself'."

About that time Dirk is approaching and Mammy Em releases her hand. The rest of the field hands gather around. Timothy and Jefferson are there. Janine and the kids stand by Dirk.

Dirk looks at Janine and asks, "What is wrong dear?"

"Oh, nothing! Janine replies.

Dirk just frowns, he knows that something is amiss.

Dirk starts his talk to the throng of gathered field hands. There is a lot of mumbling and low talk amongst them as to the nature of this.

Dirk clears his throat and says, "This is what is going to happen here. have ordered enough lumber to build everyone new cabins. Plus enough for another building for activities, barbeques, or whatever we want."

Jaws then drop wide open as they can get. The workers are dumfounded and don't know what to say.

"Is that okay with all of you?" Dirk says.

"Oh yeh Suh Massa Dirk, yeh Suh!" they reply.

"But first, I need to find carpenters." Says Dirk. "I might have to borrow some from other plantations and loan some of you out till the construction is completed."

Wanda chimes in and says, "Ah volunteers Rufus. Where is that Rufus anyway?" as she looks around.

"The lumber should be here in three to four weeks." Dirk says. "Oh! And that is not all." Babs and Edgar are going to teach those of you who want to learn reading, writing, and mathematics."

A loud and audible gasp can be heard throughout the throng of field hands.

Dirk says. "I could care less what others elsewhere would say about that. If you want education, then you'll get it the best way we know how. Now enjoy the rest of your weekend."

There is a sudden blood-curdling scream coming from the crowd. The workers all turn towards the scream and more screaming can be heard. The crowd parts like the Red Sea. Coming through the masses is one huge behemoth of a slave. Muscle upon muscle. He looks like an upside down pyramid with a bucket on it he was so muscular. He is obviously an escaped slave that made to Spanish Oaks. As he approaches Dirk a knife can be seen in his left hand.

Janine screams, "Dirk lookout, he has a knife."

"I see it, " says Dirk as he pushes Janine and the kids away from him. Mammy Em's eyes roll back in her head and she raises her hands skyward as she starts to pray something Dirk has never heard before.

"What do you want?" Dirk says with authority.

The slave responds, "Ah hates white men."

Dirk just looks back straight into his eyes and leans forward and says, "Well you can start by telling someone who gives a shit." The crowd gasps and Janine and the kids start to cry as they hug each other. Dirk then asks, "What is your name you walking pile of shit!"

The crowd is nervous, panicky and most fearful.

Janine cries out, "Dirk, just turn and run."

Dirk holds his left hand up and says, "I'll handle this the only way I know how." Dirk then says again to the escaped muscle bound slave, "Hey fuck head, I asked you what your name was?"

The escaped slave then responds and says, "Mah name is Orthaniel an' ah don' likes white men and ah am agonna' stick this heah knife in you."

Dirk looks at him and says, "Well fuck you Orthaniel, I don't see any anchor tied to your dumb black ass. Do your worst."

Janine yells, "Let me go get a gun."

Dirk just holds up his hand again. There is crying and weeping from the crowd, Mammy Em still has her eyes rolled back into her head praying something indiscernible.

Dirk looks back at Orthaniel and says, "You are going to make one hell of a splat when you hit the ground."

At that moment Orthaniel takes a running lunge at Dirk. Everyone screams in horror. Dirk side steps away from his knife hand. As he gets near, Dirk knocks his right hand away with his left hand and spins himself 360 degrees. Then with his right hand gives him an open hand blow to nape of the neck and trips him up.

"Git im' Massa Dirk." Someone yells from the crowd. Orthaniel then goes careening to ground face first. Janine and the crowd are screaming, crying, and yelling. Orthaniel is slow to get up. He is obviously stunned from his dirt diving. Orthaniel gets to his feet slowly. His mouth is bleeding, a couple of missing teeth, and a lot blood coming from his nose. This time, Orthaniel races toward Dirk. Dirk parries the knife hand away from him. Dirk grabs his collar and falls backward to the ground flipping him over on his backside. By this time Dirk is sitting on Orthaniel's chest, has him pinned, and his knife hand subdued.

"Thank you Tanaka," Dirk says to himself. 'Sweet Thing' is in Dirk's hand at Orthaniel's throat. "Drop your knife!" commands Dirk.

No response. Dirk then pushes the blade a little harder against Orthaniel's neck and then blood can be seen trickling down his neck. "Listen asshole, I said drop the knife or I'll feed your head to the gators. This is your last chance." More pressure is added to the knife and more blood starts to flow a little faster where the blade is touching his neck. "Okay, you are gator food."

At that moment Orthaniel releases the knife. Dirk yells to the screaming horrified crowd, "Get me some rope."

"I'll get it Massa Dirk." says Rufus. Dirk just looks at Rufus and says, "Nice you could make it here."

Rufus returns with a length of rope.

"Tie his hands," Dirk says. "What am I to do with you? Should I feed you to the gators or cut you up for hog feed? Stand up you maggoty bucket of puss!" Dirk yells in his face.

Janine and the kids are crying bitter tears as are many of the field hands.

"I think what I'll do is take you to the highway and let the patrollers have you," Dirk says, "Get your dumb ass moving! All of you, go ahead get your weekend started while I take care of this little pussy girl."

As Dirk is taking Orthaniel out to the road Dirk says to Janine, "I'm hungry. I'll be home in a bit."

Janine and the kids are still bawling their eyes out. They wipe away their tears as Georgie and Mammy Em comfort them.

"Come on Missa Janine, come on kids." says Georgie. "We'll walk you to the big house till Massa Dirk gets back."

"Thank you George, Thank you Mammy Em, we appreciate that." Janine says.

Mammy Em says, "Missa Janine, now you member' what ah says bout' a takin' care of yosef' with that new life in yuh. Yuh unerstan' now, yuh heah! Now ah means it, chile."

They all get to the big house.

"Bye now Missa Janine, bye kids."

Janine says, "Thank you Georgie, Thank you Mammy Em."

On the way back to their cabin Mammy Em says to Georgie, "Ah fears for the little one aformin' inside of her."

"Oh, she should be okay." says Georgie.

"Ah hopes so." Mammy Em adds.

About an hour later Dirk shows up at the big house. Janine rushes to him and hugs him like there was no tomorrow.

Janine says, "Honey, I just don't know what to say."

Dirk replies, "Sweetheart, you have just witnessed a side of me that I hoped you and nobody else would ever have to see."

Janine then says, "Well, I'm glad you had that side. It kept you and most likely several others from getting hurt and possibly killed. Where on Earth did you ever learn to fight like that? I have never seen or heard of anything like what you just did, especially since that escaped slave outweighed you by at least one hundred pounds."

"Oh, it was just something that I picked up in my Marine Corps. travels." Dirk says. "The runaway's fate is now unknown. I don't know what kind of treatment he'll get once the patrollers get a hold of him. Anyway, how are you feeling?" Dirk pours himself a glass of sweet tea.

"Oh, about the same." Janine says. "Guess what?"

"What?" replies Dirk as he takes a large drink of tea.

"I'm pregnant," she replies.

Dirk then spews tea all over the place. Dead silence. "Well how the hell did that happen?" Dirk asks.

Janine crosses her arms and gives him a stern look and says, "Well, I wonder if that 'Special Tree' had anything to do with it?" More dead silence.

Dirk faces his head towards the floor and gives Janine a sideways look and says, "Nah, I don't think so."

"Well then!" Janine says sternly. "Do you think it must be the water?" As she moves her hands clenched to her hips. Dirk looks at her clenched hands on her hips and gives her a wide toothy smile.

Dirk then goes to Janine and gives her a deep embrace and a passionate kiss and embraces her again and says, "I love you Janine and our baby inside of you."

Janine returns the kissing and the embrace and says, "I love you too Dirk. You are the love of my life."

Tears start to well up in Dirks eyes. "I don't know what to say anymore other than I love you." Dirk and Janine embrace again longer and more passionate.

Dirk then adds, "In my opinion, this was meant to be." Janine just gives Dirk another deep embrace. Dirk continues, "The baby will have two parents that will love it and that love each other. Not to mention an older brother and sisters." Tears run down Janine's face. Dirk just kisses the tears away as they continue to embrace. "Our baby will grow up and be taught to treat others with respect and dignity as well as to love the Lord Creator God."

Dirk then yells, "Babs, Edgar, Lulu, come here." The kids all come running.

"Yes Daddy, what is it?" says Babs.

"Sit down, Mommy and I have something to say." The kids all take a seat on the sofa.

"You guys are going to have another brother or sister sometime next year." Janine says, "Probably around March or April."

The kids just smile at each other.

"The next time we are out, we'll try to find us a Doctor." says Dirk.

"We need to meet some of our neighbors and introduce ourselves anyway, " Janine adds.

"Good idea." Dirk replies.

Janine doesn't say anything about Mammy Em's words of caution concerning this pregnancy.

Dirk says, "Tomorrow is Sunday, we should all go to church."

"Good idea." Janine says.

Jensen appears and asks, "Will Massa an' Missa be a'needin' supper today?"

"Jensen," says Dirk, "Why don't you and Maybelle take the rest of the today and tomorrow off and we'll see you Monday, but first I want to ask you something. Let's go to the kitchen."

"Yes, Suh, Thank you Suh, " replies Jensen.

"Edgar, I want you to go over and tell Timothy and Stella that we are all going to church in the morning. If they want to go tell them to be here at eight o'clock." says Dirk.

"Okay Daddy." Says Edgar and off he goes.

Dirk takes Jensen into the kitchen. Now that he has seen one of the escaped slaves, he figures out what the field hands were singing.

"Jensen, when the field hands start singing different songs, is that because there is a runaway down by the river?"

"Oh, Suh. You not sposed to know about that. If they git caught, they whipped mos to death, sometimes branded or have a foot cut off."

Dirk is horrified and decides to let things go along for a while. He doesn't want to stop the escapees.

XI

～

Later in the afternoon, Cornelius and Andrew are on their way to the river to do some fishing. They have their cane poles over their shoulders and a sack of bait. They are idly just chitchatting away with not a care in the world other than catching some fish. They are walking along the trail next to the river. Leaves, sticks, and small branches litter the trail. They are oblivious to their surroundings.

Cornelius takes a step and a snake rears up and bites him between the legs right in the crotch. Cornelius screams bloody horror.

"What's wrong Cornelius?" screams Andrew.

"A snake bit me, a snake bit me," yells Cornelius.

"Where?" asks Andrew.

"Right on my dingus."

Andrew gasps in horror.

"Quick Andrew! Run like the Devil is after you and ask Mammy Em what to do." Cornelius screams between the tears.

Andrew drops everything and starts to run.

"Quick, quick, before I die!" screams Cornelius.

Andrew is gone in a flash. Cornelius is crying bitter tears knowing that his life is fading fast and that death is just moments away. Andrew is running as fast as he can. Andrew hurdles over fences as though they weren't even there. He runs through the fields dodging obstacles all the way.

As Andrew nears Mammy Em's cabin he starts yelling, "Mammy Em, Mammy Em!"

Mammy Em steps out on the stoop and says, "What is it chile', you are all out of breath."

Andrew says between gasping for air, "What do yuh' duz' for snake bite?"

Mammy Em says ,"Oh' that is easy. Fust' thing yuh duz' is to take a rag and tie it above the bite marks so that the poison don' go to the rest of the body."

Andrew just gives her a grimaced look.

Mammy Em continues, "Then what yuh duz' nex' is to take yuh a sharp knife and hold where the snake bite is."

Andrew's eyebrows start to crinkle up.

"Yuh takes the knife and cuts a little 'X' on the bite marks." Mammy Em continues.

Andrew looks as though he is going to cry.

Mammy Em then says, "Where each of those little 'X' cuts are yuh then sucks the poison out and spits it on the ground."

Andrew starts to get the dry heaves at the prospects of even the thought of that.

"Then," Mammy Em continues, "Yuh has to do it all over agin' to make sure the poison is all gone."

At that time Andrew is crying and bitter tears are streaming down his face. Before Mammy Em could ask any questions Andrew was off and running again still crying. Cornelius was just sitting there waiting at death's door and still feeling the pain between his legs. Cornelius was looking at where the snake was. In fact the snake wasn't even moving. He picks up a stick and hits the snake. The snake didn't move. Cornelius takes the stick and hits the snake again. The snake still didn't move. He just gives it a very puzzled look. Cornelius scratches his head and starts to poke at the snake and it still does not move. He gets up and steps toward the snake and pokes at it again and again, no movement.

"This is not right." Cornelius thinks to himself. As he examines it closer and continues the poking and prodding he then realizes that it is not a snake after all. Cornelius thinks to himself, "I must have stepped on the branch and it hit me and I thought that it was a snake." A smile and a deep sigh of relief can be seen all over his face. About that time Andrew shows up all out of breath.

Before Cornelius could say a single thing, Andrew says, "Cornelius, yuh' is a goin' to die."

"Andrew," shouts Cornelius. "It wasn't a snake at all, it was a stick that ah stepped on and ah thought it was a snake."

Andrew gets on his knees and puts his hands together, looks up and says, "Thank yuh Jesus."

Andrew hugs Cornelius and they jump for joy. Andrew looks up again and says, "Thank yuh agin Jesus."

Andrew wipes the sweat off his forehead and says, "Let's go a fishin'." Off they go just like nothing ever happened idly chitchatting away.

Timothy shows up Sunday at the big house.

Janine says, "No Stella today Timothy?"

"No Aunt Janine, she isn't feeling too well again." Timothy replies.

"Okay." says Dirk. "Let's be off." Dirk gives Janine a sideways glance looking skeptical about Stella's health. They pull into the churchyard, just about a half hour buggy ride away. Dirk sneaks something from his left coat pocket and puts it underneath the buggy seat. Dirk introduces themselves to the first couple they see. Some are taken 'aback' at the presence of Lulu. Dirk and Janine just ignore them. Dirk and Janine meet several other plantation owners and even a Dr. and Ruth Holden, a couple that look to be in their mid fifties. Dirk and Janine smile at each other at the introduction of Dr. Holden.

"Dr. Holden," says Dirk. "We need to talk after the service."

"Oh, certainly," replies Dr. Holden. Dirk and Janine introduce themselves to the preacher and his wife, Pastor Merle Clavin and his wife Joyce. The service is long winded but finally over. Dirk shakes pastor Clavin's hand. After some idle conversation Dirk finds out also that the pastor is also a veteran of the War with Mexico.

Dirk says, "Sometime we'll have to swap war stories."

Pastor Merle says, "That could be arranged in short order." Other plantation owners had brought some of their slaves with them. The slaves tend to the horses and have their church service under a big tree. It is led by their own black preacher.

Dirk and Janine talk with Dr. Holden and his wife Ruth about Janine's pregnancy.

"Congratulations," says Dr. Holden, who gives her a big smile.

"Before the summer is over we would like to throw a big party at Spanish Oaks," Dirk says. "We need to meet our neighbors and get to know them. You and your family are all invited."

Ruth says with a big smile, "We would like that very much."

Dr. Holden then says, "We'll be looking forward to very much."

Dirk asks, "Where is your home?"

"Well we are just about half way between you and here." replies Dr. Holden.

"Great!" says Janine. "We would like to have you for our family Doctor."

"It would be my honor to be your doctor and friend," Dr. Holden replies.

"Oh yes indeed," replies Ruth.

"We need to introduce ourselves to others," says Dirk.

"Anytime that you are out our way, please do stop in." Janine says.

"I certainly will." says Dr. Holden.

Ruth waves as they leave. Dirk pulls the item out from underneath the buggy seat and returns it to his left coat pocket without anyone noticing it. On the way home Timothy doesn't have a lot to say as the trip to church was new for him. The kids just chatted and giggled most of the time. Dirk wonders what is going on with Timothy and Stella.

Once back at the big house Dirk says to Timothy, "Let's grab something to eat and go for a walk." As they walk and eat Dirk asks, "What is going on with you and Stella?"

"Oh nothing Uncle Dirk," Timothy responds.

"Don't think for a moment that you can hide things. It is very noticeable to Janine and to me," Dirk says.

"It isn't anything that I can't handle," replies Timothy.

"Suit yourself." says Dirk. "If your Aunt Janine or I can be of any help, even if it is just talking about things, please don't hesitate one moment."

"Thank you Uncle Dirk. I'll be going now." says Timothy.

Dirk just looks at him as he walks away and shakes his head in sympathy. Dirk gets back to the big house. They spend the rest of the afternoon enjoying each other's company. Dirk waits on Janine every chance he gets and gives her hugs and kisses every chance he gets. Dirk acts as though he has fallen in love with Janine all over again and Janine is eating up every minute of it. Dirk relates his and Timothy's conversations.

XII

≈

Mundane Monday morning arrives in all of its boring splendor. Dirk straps on 'Sweet Thing' and heads out to the field hands' area. All the workers are already at it by the time Dirk gets there. Dirk decides to go to the barnyard to talk to Rufus.

"Rufus!" Dirk says.

"Yeh Suh Massa Dirk," replies Rufus.

"Where were you on Saturday before I had the fight with that runaway?" Dirk asks.

"Oh, I wuz a chasin' some loose chickens that got out agin Suh," replies Rufus.

Dirk then says sternly, "Repair the break and don't let anymore get out again."

"Yeh Suh, Massa Dirk," replies Rufus.

"Also," Dirk adds, "I want you to show me around here and explain exactly what your job is."

Rufus replies, "Yeh Suh, Massa Dirk, right away Suh." Rufus then takes Dirk around the barnyard and the surrounding area.

Rufus says, "Ah takes care of the feeding of all the animals. Ah milks the cows, slops the hogs, tends to the cattle and the sheep. Ah also heps' in the vegetable garden, heps' grow the feed for the animals. Ah also heps' Jasper the blacksmith whenever he a needin' extra hep'."

"Very impressive," says Dirk. "Whenever do you find the time to chase down loose chickens?"

Rufus just looks at Dirk and smiles.

"Thank you Rufus," says Dirk.

"Yeh Suh Massa Dirk," says Rufus.

Dirk heads out to the fields again. Dirk finds Benjamin and Gabooti. "Hi guys." says Dirk. "Do you two remember last week when we took water around to everyone?"

"Yeh Suh, Massa Dirk." Gabooti replies.

"Okay then, from now on that, will be your jobs. Do you two think that you can do that without any trouble?" Dirk asks.

"Yeh Suh Massa Dirk," says Benjamin.

"Okay then," Dirk says. "You are now on your own. Four times a day give everyone water. I'll see you two later."

Benjamin and Gabooti take off on a dead run for the barn. Dirk just smiles as he watches them run off.

Timothy is out in the fields with Jefferson. Jefferson is doing a lot of talking and pointing things out to Timothy. Dirk walks amongst the field hands. They all smile at Dirk and wish him a good morning. Dirk smiles back, and tips his hat back to them and asks how they are.

Dirk goes up to one of the women and says, "Wanda, am I correct?"

She replies, "Yeh Suh Massa Dirk."

"How are you today Wanda?" asks Dirk.

"Jus' fine Suh." "Ah is a doin' real gud Suh." Wanda replies.

A couple of figures can be seen scurrying along the trail by the river. The field hands start into their field hollering and singing again. But this time their tune has changed somewhat. They start to sing:

You can keep on a runnin' to freedom
If yuh wants ta. Our Massa loves us
and treats us kindly. It is all up to you
if yuh' wants. We all got our freedom
right here. Run if yuh' wants ta, or stay here."

One of the runaways comes to a screeching halt and listens. The other just keeps on the trail. Dirk looks around and sees Benjamin and Gabooti with the mule and the water. Dirk is proud of them and smiles to himself.

Dirk heads back to the big house to eat. Janine is there waiting for him. They give each other a hug and a deep kiss.

Dirk asks, "How are you feeling today?"

"Okay," Janine replies. "I ate a little something earlier and I'll have a bite with you."

As Jensen is serving them, Dirk notices a dispatch rider approaching the big house.

Dirk points and says, "I wonder what this is all about?"

Janine responds, "I think that we are going to find out real soon."

Dirk goes out and meets the rider. "Afternoon." Says Dirk to the rider.

"Good afternoon Sir," responds the rider. The dispatch rider says, "I have a message from a Mr. Josh Twindley for you Sir."

Dirk smiles and raises his eyebrows in anticipation. "Thank you very much." Dirk says. Dirk reaches into his pocket and gives him a ten-cent piece for a tip.

"Thank you very much Sir." says the rider. He then turns to leave.

Dirk says to him, "If you step around to the kitchen, Maybelle will find you something to eat and drink. It is a fair piece back to Charleston."

"Thank you Sir, I would be much beholden to you for that." replies the rider.

"I'll be right back." says Dirk. Dirk goes inside and Janine says, "Who is it from?" "It is from the slave broker in Charleston. He says that the French planter just outside of New Orleans is willing sell back Georgie and Mammy Em's son. We just need to figure out a price and make arrangements for transportation. I need make sure the dispatch rider gets some food. I'll be right back." Dirk goes to the kitchen and sees that Maybelle has already given the rider some turkey meat between a couple slices of bread, an apple, and a slice of pie.

"Thank you very much Sir," says the rider and he turns and leaves. Dirk returns to the table to finish eating.

"How much does he want?" asks Janine.

Dirk says, "Since he is recuperating from a broken leg, the planter only wants nine hundred dollars."

"He paid fifteen hundred for him five years ago according to the books." says Janine.

Dirk says, "I believe we should get him back here where he belongs."

Janine smiles and gets the dry heaves and tries to throw up but falls short of it. Dirk just gives her an ear-to-ear grin.

"I'll send Timothy into Charleston in the morning with the money and have him spend the night. He can take Stella with him if she has had a miraculous healing, that is."

"Maybe the trip will do her some good," Janine says. "If need be, Timothy and Stella can go on into New Orleans and pick him up if all the paper work is in good order."

Dirk finishes eating and heads back out into the fields. Everyone is singing and seems to be content. Timothy shows up and Dirk tells him about the impending trip for him and Stella in the morning. Benjamin and Gabooti are at it again with the water detail. The day passes quickly. The field hands are returning from the fields. Everyone smiles at Dirk and Dirk returns the smiles.

Dirk looks at Timothy and says, "I need for you to go into Charleston in the morning and possibly on into New Orleans for a few days. You can take Stella with you if you want. See you in the morning."

"Okay Uncle Dirk," replies Timothy.

———

Timothy pulls up in the buggy alone the next morning.

Dirk asks, "Where is Stella?"

"She is not feeling well again," Timothy says.

"Okay then, here is some money for the transaction transfer, food, lodging, railroad fare, and a little extra," says Dirk. "See you in a few days."

"Okay Uncle Dirk," says Timothy and off he goes.

Dirk says to Janine, "Why don't you stop by and see how Stella is doing later on."

"I think I should," replies Janine.

Dirk heads off to the fields but first stops by Georgie and Mammy Em's cabin. Georgie and Mammy Em are both on the front porch watching some of the field hands' children while the parents are working.

"Good morning," says Dirk to them. "How are things today?"

"Jus' fin' Massa Dirk, things is jus' fin'," replies Georgie.

"Massa Dirk, things sho' have changed since y'all got heah Suh." adds Mammy Em.

"They sho' nuf have Suh." adds Georgie. "Everyone is so happy, more than ah has ever see'd."

Dirk just smiles and says, "Well, I'm sure things will continue to get better and better everyday."

"We hopes so Massa Dirk an' we all thank yuh very much." says Mammy Em.

Dirk smiles and says, "I need to be getting out into the fields now." Dirk tips his hat, turns and head towards the fields. Jefferson has things under control. Benjamin and Gabooti are on their water detail. The field hands are singing their field hollers and performing their various duties. Dirk walks to the waterfall and studies the lay of the land. He crosses his arms and is deep in thought. Dirk walks to the top and looks with deep intent. Dirk has an idea about how to bring running water to the living quarters of everyone, including the big house instead only having a community well.

Dirk heads for the big house. Janine is walking back from Timothy and Stella's at about the same time he gets there. Janine has a puzzled look on her face.

Dirk asks, "What is the matter?"

Janine says, "I went to check on Stella. I knock on the door and I could swear that I heard whispering from inside and a door creaking. Then Stella says, "just a moment." About a minute later she opens the door and lets me in. I say to her that Timothy says that she wasn't feeling well and that I came over to check on her. Stella says she is just tired all the time. I asked her if I could do anything or get her something, but she said that she would be fine. I told her to come over for supper if she wanted to."

Dirk says quizzically, "Whispering, you say you heard? I am curious as to why she is so tired? I wonder what sort of tiring activities she's been up to?"

Stella does show up at the big house for supper. Dirk does not have much to say to her. If it weren't for Janine and the kids, things would have been totally silent. Dirk is at the point of loathing her and it shows no matter what Janine does to Dirk under the table. Dirk only manages a half-hearted smile.

Four days go by and Timothy returns with Georgie and Mammy Em's son Franklin. Dirk, Janine, Babs, Edgar, and Lulu are all there to greet them. It is still early in the afternoon. They all head over to the field hand quarters. Dirk drives the buggy over with Franklin sitting next to him and the rest of the family sitting in the rear. As the buggy heads into the living quarters, Dirk can see Mammy Em on the porch with some of the little ones still. From a good distance, Mammy Em stares and shades her eyes as they get nearer. Mammy Em stands to her feet. She notices a shape of something that she hadn't seen in several years. Tears start to well up in her eyes and her lips start to contort and quiver.

Mammy Em screams, "Georgie come here quick get out here now!"

Georgie gets outside as fast as his tired and aged legs will carry him. "What is it Mammy Em, what on Earth is it?" Georgie asks.

Mammy Em's hand is shaking uncontrollably as she just points to the wagon. Georgie looks and his jaw drops wide open as tears flood his eyes. He and Mammy Em just hug, sob, and wail tears of happiness and joy as the wagon with their only son gets nearer and nearer.

Georgie says, "Is it?"

"Yes!" screams Mammy Em, "It is our baby boy Franklin. My baby, my baby, my baby! He has come home to us." Georgie and Mammy Em hurry as fast as they can to meet the wagon. Dirk helps Franklin out of the buggy and hands him his crutch. Georgie and Mammy Em are screaming, crying, and running as fast as they can with open arms to Franklin. Georgie , Mammy Em, and Franklin are all crying as they embrace each other. Dirk and Janine are crying also.

"Oh Franklin honey, we thought that we would never see you again. Thank you Jesus." Mammy Em says.

"Oh, you can call me Dirk." replies Dirk.

"Welcome home son," says Georgie.

Janine says to Babs, "Go up to the porch and keep an eye on the little ones till we get there."

Dirk hugs Edgar and Lulu close to him.

Timothy says, "I think I'll head home now."

"Good job, take tomorrow off," says Dirk.

"Thank you Uncle Dirk," replies Timothy.

They all start to the cabin. Franklin hobbles along with his crutch and Mammy Em says, "What is wrong with your leg?"

"Oh I broke it a couple of months ago when a bale of hay fell on my leg." says Franklin.

The field hands are returning to their quarters at that time. They all smile and pay their respects to Franklin.

"Come on Babs, let's go home," Janine says. They all get in the buggy with Dirk and Janine still drying their eyes.

On Sunday morning they all go to church again. Dirk again takes something out of his left coat pocket and puts it secretly underneath the buggy seat. There is a lot of talk about what had happened on the highway the night before. Dirk and Janine say their hellos. Dirk overhears the conversations and asks quizzically about what had happened.

"Oh, didn't you hear?" says one of the ladies.

Dirk and Janine just look at each other.

"Hear what?" asks Dirk.

"Whatever are you talking about?" Janine inquires.

"Well," says one of the ladies. "The patrollers caught this big runaway slave, the biggest muscular one they had ever seen. A fight ensued, and before the patrollers knew what was going on the runaway killed one of the patrollers with his bare hands. They say it took five shots to bring him down."

"Oh! Is that so?" Dirk says.

Janine just hugs Dirk's arm real close and looks him in the eyes lovingly. Dirk and Janine talk for a while with some of the other plantation owners before church starts. They say hello to Merle and Joyce. Dirk strikes up a deal with some of them for their carpenters in exchange for labor from Spanish Oaks and some financial remuneration. The lumber delivery is to be next Saturday. Construction is to start on the following month. Handshakes and smiles are made and into church they go. The blacks are having their own service under a tree with their own preacher again while some of the others are watching out for their Masters' horses.

With church service over they have a conversation with Dr. and Mrs. Holden.

Janine says. "Why don't we all get together some afternoon for dinner at our place?"

Martha smiles and says, "Oh! That is a wonderful idea."

"We'll make plans as soon as our new construction is finished," Dirk says. "We have a major project starting this next month."

"We'll see you next Sunday." Janine says. As Janine is talking Dirk removes from underneath the buggy seat something and puts it in his left coat pocket. Off they go home again for a leisurely day of relaxation.

Monday morning Dirk is at the field hands' quarters.

Dirk goes up to Jefferson and says, "Next Saturday the lumber is to be delivered here for the new living area. We will need to exchange some of our hands for the carpentry work loaned to us. There are two different plantations that we need to send workers to."

Jefferson replies, "Yeh Suh Massa Dirk. We have some that can be spared for a short while."

The sun is starting to rise higher. Dirk looks around and scratches his head.

"Jefferson" "Did we have a bunch of kids grow up here overnight? There seem to be a few extra here, or is it my mind playing tricks on me?"

Jefferson just smiles and laughs. Jefferson then turns and shouts, "It's go to work time. Let's go y'all."

Off they all go to the fields singing as they go. Dirk just tips his hat and smiles as they all pass by. The field hands smile with their big pearly white teeth on their way. The hot and humid South Carolina sun is at its best in August. Benjamin and Gabooti are at their assigned tasks with the water. Suppertime, the field hands are meandering back in from the fields. Dirk heads to the big house for his meal by way of the barn and livestock area. Dirk sees Rufus tending to the animals.

"Hello Rufus," says Dirk.

"Good mornin' Massa Dirk," replies Rufus. "No Massa Timothy today?"

"No. I gave him the day off," Dirk says. "It is nice to see that you are not off chasing chickens again."

"Yeh Suh," replies Rufus. "Ah gots that taken care of."

Dirk gets to the big house. Timothy and Stella are both there also for supper.

"Good afternoon you two," says Dirk.

Stella manages a smile and Timothy waves as he is chewing a big mouthful. Dirk gives Janine a big hug and kiss. Dirk joins them for a fine meal. Jensen finishes serving the meal. He and Maybelle clean things and retire to the rear of the big house.

"As long as we are all here, there are some things that I want to run by everyone," Dirk says. "As you know, next weekend the lumber will be here for the new living quarters and a pavilion for barbeques, parties, and whatever. After the hands are all moved and settled in their new homes, I want to treat them like paid employees, complete with regular income. They will have their garden plots, new living quarters, and, I want to give them their freedom if they want it. They will have it better here than being free outside the gates of Spanish Oaks."

Janine says, "Why that is a wonderful idea. They'll have new homes, regular income, and food year round. Why would anyone want to leave?"

Timothy adds, "I think that is a good idea Uncle Dirk."

Stella manages to crack another faint smile.

Dirk then adds, "At least I'll offer it all to them and let them make their own decisions. I'll make that announcement after the new buildings are up and everyone has moved in. I just wanted to run that by all of you first. Okay then. I'm headed back out now."

Timothy gets up to go with Dirk. Dirk tells Timothy to come back tomorrow.

"Oh, that's okay Uncle Dirk, I just want to have a look around," Timothy replies.

"Okay then," says Dirk. When Dirk gets there the field hands are all on their way back to work.

Dirk says to Jefferson, "I am going to walk around and look at things and try to come up with some ideas."

"Yeh suh Massa Dirk," replies Jefferson.

Timothy is walking around the barn and livestock area. He then walks into the barn and sees Rufus working.

Timothy says to Rufus, "Good morning."

Rufus turns around with a surprised look on his face. "Good mornin' Massa Timothy," replies Rufus. "Ah didn't spect to see yuh heah. Yuh scared me Suh."

"Sorry," replies Timothy. "How are things going for you

"Jus' fine suh," replies Rufus.

Timothy continues, "How is Wanda?"

Rufus is starting to get a noticeable worried look on his face. "Miss Wanda jus' fine, Suh," says Rufus.

"Rufus," says Timothy, "I have been wanting to ask you something."

Rufus thinks to himself, "Oh shit, I am in for it now." Beads of sweat start to roll down his face.

Rufus then says with a cracking voice, "Yeh Suh Massa Timothy, what is it?"

Timothy then says, "You seem to do pretty good with your woman keeping her happy and all. Do you do anything special, any tricks, or secrets you can share?"

A sigh of relief envelopes Rufus and he smiles at Timothy.

Rufus then says, "Well Suh, Massa Timothy, what I duz at night when the lantern is way down low an' barely throwing any light, and my woman is in bed, ah strolls over to the bed an' Wanda has the covers pulled up over her head, Ah just takes my dingus an slaps it against the bed post two or three times and she jus' gets all excited and worked up and can hardly wait for me to mount her." Rufus says with a big smile.

"Thank you Rufus," says Timothy. "I'll be running along now."

Dirk finds himself at the waterfall. Dirk walks around examining the area intently. He crosses his arms walks around some more and re-crosses his arms again and again. An idea is taking form within him. The waterfall has a twenty-foot drop to the bottom. There are trees, shrubs, grasses, and rocks of various sizes and shapes all over. A couple of ideas take shape. Build a water flume to the living quarters, the barn and livestock areas, the big house, and the guesthouse. From the flume would come several lines for each of the new cabins, the barn, and the two houses. This would take care of everyone and they wouldn't have to use a community well. Another idea for the future is to dig a cave next to the waterfall and have a portion of the creek's water diverted into the cave on a hand-made rock bed and flowing back into the main creek. The water cave would then be made cooler for perishable food storage. Dirk smiles within and thinks, "I must make plans for both of these projects."

Dirk looks at his pocket watch. It is about noon so he starts heading back to the big house for his noon meal.

Dirk sees Franklin on the front porch and stops by and says to him, "How is the leg doing today?"

Franklin replies, "Getting betta' Suh. Momma put some home-made salve on it las' night. Mah leg feels that it is a doin' real gud, Suh."

Dirk responds, "That's great. Tell me Franklin, what did you do in Louisiana?"

"Massa Dirk," responds Franklin. "Ah wuz' owned by this man jus' outside of N'awlins. a place called Lafayette. Ah heps' wid' the cotton, sugar cane, backy, an' a lot of other work also. Ah also learned how ta play the fiddle. They got a lot of different and strange soundin' music from that part of the country. The likes that ah neva' heard befo' and music makers that ah neva' seed . Ah learned ta love the music and play it real gud on the fiddle."

Dirk adds, "I believe that I also have heard that type of music and grew to like it when I was down there in my military days. That music has some catchy tunes and it is hard to keep your feet still when they play it. When you feel up to it why don't you play some out in the fields? I am sure that we would all enjoy it."

Franklin smiles and says, "Ah can hardly wait Suh."

Georgie and Mammy Em come out to the porch. "Massa Dirk, we jus' can't thank yah enough for a bringin' our baby back to us." Mammy Em says.

Georgie chimes in, "Yeh Suh Massa Dirk, thank yuh so much."

Dirk can see tears starting to pool up in Georgie's eyes.

"You both are quite welcome." says Dirk. "I'll be going now. You all have a good afternoon."

They all smile at each other as Dirk tips his hat.

Mammy Em looks at Dirk as he is walking away and says, "That Massa Dirk is a gud, kind hearted, loving, and caring person. Massa

Dirk be a needin' ta be extra careful. Ah can see danger down the road for him." Mammy Em then looks up into the sky and raises her hands to the heavens. Mammy Em closes her eyes and prays, "Gud Lawd, if yah please, watch over Massa Dirk an' his family. Please Lawd, make Massa Dirk wary and careful. Please Lawd, give Massa Dirk wisdom, strength, knowledge, and the ability to see danger afor' it happens. Please almighty Lawd God, guide his each and evry step. We are a thankin' Yuh already Lawd, Amen."

Together, Georgie and Franklin say Amen.

Dirk sees Jefferson while on his way to the big house.

Dirk says to Jefferson, "I'll be gone the rest of the day."

"Okay Massa Dirk," replies Jefferson.

Dirk gets to the big house and has a bite to eat with Janine. While they are eating Dirk goes over the waterfall ideas. Dirk goes over his ideas on running water for everyone and the cave idea. Dirk looks at Janine and gives her a big smile and tells her that he loves her and gives a loving embrace.

That evening Timothy is in his home about ready to turn in for the night. Stella is already in bed with covers over her head. The lamp is turned way down low. Timothy goes up to the bedpost, "slap", "slap," "slap," goes the sound of the dingus being slapped against the bedpost.

From underneath the covers Stella says with an alarming tone in her voice, "Rufus, what are you doing here? Now you get on out of here before Timothy gets home!"

Timothy turns the lamp up brighter. Stella just looks at him without saying a word.

———

The next morning Timothy meets Dirk as he is leaving the big house. Timothy says that he is taking Stella to Charleston to get a train back to Philadelphia. Dirk opens his mouth and raises his finger as though he is going to say something. Before Dirk could say anything, Timothy turns and leaves. Dirk thinks to himself, "Good riddance Stella." Dirk goes back to the big house and informs Janine of the good news.

Janine says, "It was only a matter of time before Timothy wised up. Maybe he can get his life in order now."

"I hope so," says Dirk. "I'll let Timothy volunteer any information if he wants. Otherwise, I'll not say a thing." Dirk then heads out to the field hands quarters to talk with Jefferson and the hands before they head out into the fields. With everyone gathered around Dirk praises them all for their good work and how good the crops are coming.

Dirk says, "The cotton crop is coming along real good. The corn crop is going to be a bumper crop this season. The vegetables and tobacco are doing excellent. Thank you all for doing a good job. Rufus, you are doing a great job with the livestock. The livestock are rapidly putting on the pounds and are fattening up nicely. We shouldn't have to worry about food this winter."

As Dirk looks around at everyone he has a puzzled look on his face and says, "I swear that I see new faces here every day. Have I not been paying attention to my own affairs? I can't figure out where all the new faces are coming from. I swear some of you grew up overnight on me. Okay Jefferson, take over."

"It's go to work time," Jefferson says with a great big smile. As they all head out to the fields, one stays back, a thin bony looking young fellow. Dirk just looks at him with a puzzled look on his face. Dirk walks toward the young fellow.

"Do I know you?" says Dirk. The young fellow doesn't say a word. He just makes a squealing sound and breaks out in a dead run to the fields with everyone else. Dirk just scratches his head and says to himself, "What in the hell was that?"

Dirk finds Jefferson out in the fields.

"Jefferson." says Dirk.

"Yeh Suh Massa Dirk," replies Jefferson.

Dirk then says, "I've been thinking, since we have so many more workers than I thought we had, what do you think about running things by setting up groups who can rotate in the fields and let everyone have some rest time throughout the day?"

Jefferson replies, "What duz' yuh mean Massa Dirk?"

Dirk continues, "This is what I have in mind. In the shade trees we'll have some food and water. Every couple of hours we'll have five, six, or maybe even seven workers give breaks and rest time throughout the day. When the one group is done, they will then go out and give rest and break time to another group and when they are done they can go out and the same for another group. By the end of the work day everyone will have been rotated in and out of the fields throughout the day and their asses won't be dragging the ground at quitting time. Everyone will have eaten and rested throughout the day and have had their noon meal. No one will have been overworked. What do you think about that?" Dirk asks as he looks at Jefferson.

Jefferson looks back a Dirk and says, "Massa Dirk, Ah believes that would work out real gud Suh."

"Great! We'll start tomorrow and I'll have Benjamin and Gabooti help with that being their new job. We'll get the food and drink set up in the shade trees tomorrow. The first group can get things set up before they start to give the first rest breaks. One more thing, here is my pocket watch, you will need it."

Jefferson looks with his mouth agape and says, "Thank Yuh Suh, thank Yuh Massa Dirk."

Dirk just smiles as he hands him his pocket watch. Dirk then looks around again and says, "I swear, I don't remember all these faces we have. I must have fallen asleep at the reins is all that I can figure out." Dirk just scratches his head as he walks away. As Dirk walks away he sees Benjamin and Gabooti and calls them to him. They come over to him with the mule and the water barrels.

"You two have been doing an excellent job taking care of everyone with the water. We are going to start doing something different tomorrow. Jefferson will fill you in on that. You two did such a good job with the water I am going to give you both something."

Dirk reaches into his pocket and produces a shiny silver dollar coin for each of them. Their mouths drop open and eyeballs about pop out of their sockets as they stare at their newfound wealth and off they run.

Dirk yells to them, "I'll put the mule and the water barrels up." Dirk just smiles.

As the next Saturday arrives, the lumber order shows up. A whole wagon train of Southern Pine in various sizes, lengths, and dimensions arrives to be unloaded. Everyone pitches in to help with the unloading process, even Dirk, Timothy, and Edgar. The wagons are unloaded and spacer strip is placed between the layers to allow for air drying and seasoning prior to construction. It is an all day job of unloading the wagons and stacking the lumber.

Dirk says to Jefferson, "In one month after the lumber has had a good chance to season in this weather, we'll need to send some workers to a couple of other plantations in exchange for their carpenters. "

"Yeh Suh Massa Dirk, I'll take care of that." Jefferson replies.

The Kahanes and Timothy all go to church the next morning. Again arriving at church, Dirk takes something out of his left coat pocket and quickly puts it under the buggy seat. Dirk makes the needed arrangements for the carpenters and the exchange of labor to begin in one month. Dr. and Mrs. Holden exchange pleasantries with Dirk and Janine.

Dr. Holden asks Janine how she is feeling with her pregnancy.

"Oh, as well as can be expected I guess," Janine replies.

The blacks are all under a tree with their own black preacher. There is talk amongst the churchgoers about some British folks in town talking sedition against the federal authorities. Dirk just pays it no never mind and just chalks it up as the British mind set. Dirk and Janine notice that Timothy has struck up a conversation with a young lady. The church service is over and Dirk reconfirms the arrangements with the carpenters from other plantations and the workers in exchange.

"See you in one month." Dirk says. They bid their goodbyes to Dr. and Mrs. Holden. Dirk hurriedly pulls out from under the buggy seat an item and puts it back in his left coat pocket. They head home.

XIII

⁓

The month goes by fast. The carpenters from the other plantations arrive and start right in on the new construction. The first building to go up is the pavilion. A big fireplace with a roasting spit, a small stage platform, shelving, and tables. The next day, the first cabin is emptied and contents moved to the pavilion. The old cabin is dismantled and the new one built on the same plot of ground.

As soon as one cabin is complete, the field hands move in on the same day. This is repeated throughout the entire week and continues on into the next week. The carpenters are really fast and efficient and know their trade well. The last carpentry project is a small military style barracks-looking structure that can hold up to about thirty people complete with cooking facilities, large den, shelving, a half a dozen bed frames, and a couple of tables to boot. Everyone is in awe of their new cabins and the other buildings.

Dirk is so happy that he gives each one of the carpenters a five-dollar bill before they leave. Everyone is very happy.

Dirk says to everyone, "As soon as the pine seasons a bit longer, I'll get some white wash and you can paint your cabins."

Wanda is bent over in front her new cabin picking something up. All of the sudden one of the pine boards breaks loose with a loud pop and smacks her right square on butt. She screams loud enough for all the hands to be heard out in the fields.

Cornelius says to Andrew, "I guess Rufus got home early today."

Andrew covers his face and laughs.

Dirk then says, "There could still be a few boards that are in need of a tad bit more additional seasoning."

The field hands laugh at the situation. Timothy is there throughout the entire construction project lending a helping hand wherever he could. Dirk notices the positive change in ever since he got rid of Stella. Dirk even feels a small sense of pride in Timothy.

As the summer wears on and nears fall, the corn needs to be picked, husked, and stored for winter. Other vegetables need to be picked also. The hands start in on the harvesting of the corn. In three days time the crop is brought to the barn. There is a lot of corn. The next day the corn husking starts and everyone pitches in to help. The field hands are singing and having what seems to be a party. Franklin shows up with his fiddle and adds to the festivities. Janine, Babs, Edgar, and Lulu also help in the husking. Janine is starting to noticeably show her protruding stomach with her new life inside. The corn husking continues until it is complete.

About mid-week, Dirk has Jefferson call everyone together in the pavilion so he can make his announcement about their freedom and employee status. Dirk also has Janine, Timothy, and the kids there.

With everyone gathered about Dirk asks, "Is everyone moved in okay?"

"Yes Massa Dirk," come several replies.

"You all have nice wood floors now and not those old dirt floors. This fall, before winter sets in, I'll have the white wash here so you can paint your cabins. What I really called you all together for is this."

Dirk steps up onto the stage area and addresses everyone en masse. "I have called you all here for a special reason. From the very first day that Janine and set our feet on Spanish Oaks, we have never considered any of you slaves. You probably figured that one out for yourselves months ago. We have learned a lot since we have arrived here. We have learned so much from each and every one of you and we will continue to learn daily. What we really want to say is this. You are no longer slaves and you are all free to do as you wish. I will have the papers drawn up by my attorney in Charleston. As far as we are all concerned, you were all free the day we set foot on Spanish Oaks."

Tears could be seen rolling down some cheeks and several embraces could be seen among the couples. There is a lot of low murmuring and talk amongst the workers.

"Each of you will be given your freedom papers," Dirk then says, "That is not all. You all are employees and will be treated and paid as such. Janine, Babs, Edgar, Lulu, Timothy, and myself consider you to be more family than anything else. That being said, each of you can decide for yourself on what you want to do. You have new cabins, we all have plenty to eat, barring any events beyond our control. Plus, each household will be paid twenty dollars a month cash money. If any of you want to leave, we will respect your decision. We do not want to lose any of you at all. This coming Saturday is payday. Have a good evening."

Dirk and his family start to leave. Several come up to Dirk and Janine and shake their hands.

"Massa Dirk, Missa Janine we all neva' had so gud till y'all got heah." Wanda says.

Jasper says, "Ah may be dumb but ah ain't stoopit. We is a stayin' right heah."

Another chimes in and says, "New cabins, lots to eat, and we is agonna' git paid too. We neva' had it so gud. No Suh Massa Dirk and Missa Janine, we all is a stayin' put."

One of the ladies come up to Janine and clasps both her hands with tears rolling down her cheek.

She looks up at Janine and says, "Me an' mah family luvs yah Missa Janine and Massa Dirk. We ain't a goin no place!"

Others pass by and you can hear them say that aren't going anywhere. Spanish Oaks is their home. Tears can be seen welling up in Dirk and Janine's eyes.

"Jefferson," says Dirk. "Now that I have you off to the side, you are going to be paid twenty five dollars a month since you are the foreman. Tomorrow, you and Timothy are going to be here by yourselves. I am going in to Charleston tomorrow for supplies and order some white wash and a lot of paint brushes. Timothy, you and Jefferson are going to run things while I go into town."

"Okay Uncle Dirk," replies Timothy.

Dirk and Janine head for the big house. "Do you want to go tomorrow to Charleston?" Dirk asks Janine.

"No. I just don't feel up to the trip," says Janine.

"Okay then, I'll take Edgar and Lulu. Babs can stay and keep you company while were gone."

"They would like that," Janine replies.

Dirk and Janine hold hands as they walk to the big house. Dirk tells Jensen and Maybelle what he told everyone else.

Dirk, Edgar, and Lulu leave early in the morning for Charleston. They make it there in a couple of hours. Dirk stops by the attorney's office to pick up the papers for legalizing and granting freedom before they get to the hotel. The attorneys just look at Dirk in disgust as they hand him the papers. Dirk just gives them a stern look back and says thanks.

Dirk and the kids get a room for the night and freshen up. After a short rest they head out to the mercantile store. Dirk places an order for a hundred gallons of white wash and a couple dozen big paintbrushes. Dirk also places the order for needed daily supplies for the plantation and the field hands.

"Pick out some candy." Dirk says to Edgar and Lulu. "Don't tell mommy that I let you have candy before breakfast."

"Okay Daddy." They say in unison.

Dirk picks out a couple pieces of jerky for himself and puts it in his shirt pocket. They head back to the hotel to get a bite to eat before the next order of business. They get inside and get a table. Dirk senses a lot of stares being directed them because of Lulu, but the manager remembers who he is and orders the waiters to serve them. Dirk pays them no heed and could care less. They have a good time. After the meal they take a walk along the boardwalk and just look in windows till they see something they like and go in and look at it. Dirk is holding Lulu's hand. They look at cloths, dresses, shoes, pants, and whatever strikes their fancy in their ramblings.

As they round the corner of stores on the boardwalk Dirk almost runs into the two thugs that he had a run in with on the previous trip. The one that Samuel Clemens hit with the cane was walking with a limp and there is the one that Dirk modified his left ear. They just stop and stare at each other. Dirk puts the kids behind him and places his hand on Sweet Thing's handle. Dirk then gets a mean look about himself and a 'don't mess with me' look on his countenance.

Dirk then says with bravado, "Well if it isn't 'one ear' and the 'gimp'."

The two just look in fear and hurry to the opposite side of the street. Dirk watches their every move until they get of sight.

Edgar says, "Daddy, do you know those guys?"

"Not really," Dirk replies.

As they continued on with their walk, Dirk sees the dog that he fed the ear to on his last trip. Surprisingly, the dog remembers Dirk and sits up on his hind legs begging. Dirk reaches into his shirt pocket and gives the dog a piece of jerky. They pass by a show house advertising a musical event that evening.

Dirk says to the kids, "A group of Creole musicians from South West Louisiana will be here to play a style of music mainly found in that area. I have heard this music before when I was in the Marines with a stopover in New Orleans. We'll go to that tonight if we can get tickets. Right now, I need to get to the bank and retrieve some funds from our business holdings."

The afternoon wears on. Dirk buys the kids some clothes and things for Janine and Babs. They get back to the hotel room and freshen up before dinner. They go to the restaurant again for supper. Again more stares of contempt are directed in their direction. The kids don't pick up on that but Dirk does. Dirk just scratches his nose with his middle finger at everyone. After they eat they go back to their room clean up and change clothes.

"Let's go! We'll get our tickets to the music tonight."

They get to the music hall and there is a 'Sold Out' sign on the poster.

"Oh! too bad." Dirk says. "All is not lost. I am going to try and get this group to come to Spanish Oaks and play. You kids stay here while I try to get these guy to come to Spanish Oaks."

Dirk is gone for about a half an hour before he returns.

"It is all set. They will be out in about two weeks to play for us. Come on kids. I am tired anyway. We have to load up the wagon in the morning and we need to get an early start. I also have to stop by the lumber mill and place another big order on the way back."

The next day, Dirk gets his business taken care and heads out to the lumber mill and places the order for two hundred one by twelve by twenty foot long boards to be delivered whenever they get them cut. They are on their way back home.

They arrive at Spanish Oaks about noontime. Janine greets them with a great big smile and hugs for everyone.

"How was the trip?" Janine asks.

"Oh, great!" Dirk says. "We went shopping and were going to take in a music show but tickets were all sold out."

"I'm sorry." Janine says.

"I did the next best thing. The group will be here in two weeks to do a show for us. It is a type and style of music that you'll just love and I am sure the hands will love." It is called Sarico, or syreco, or Zydeco or something or other. I remember the music from my Marine Corps. days with New Orleans being one of the ports of call. They use fiddles and wash boards. Some even use a guitar and a drum. This group has a new instrument. They call it an accordion, came from Germany or Italy. There is another group down there called Cajuns. They also have a similar style of music all their own. They have some food down there that will make everyone want to dance. Some of the hottest and spiciest food that I ever ate was down in that part of Louisiana. I found out the hard way that I don't have a cast iron stomach like I thought I had. One time I shit molten lava and fireballs for three days. Oh that was some good eating."

Janine chuckles, "Yes, It sure sounds like it."

"We'll have us a big barbeque and the group can stay in the new big building. We'll invite Doc and Martha Holden and throw out the invite to a couple of other plantation owners that helped us with the construction."

Janine says, "Oh, it will be our first party here."

They just smile at each other.

Dirk takes the wagon to the barn to unload the white wash and brushes. Jasper is there to help him. The workers are on their way in from the fields. Dirk sees Jefferson and Timothy.

"The white wash and brushes are in the barn. If anyone wants to get started white-washing their cabins Saturday or Sunday, tell them to get started. Monday we'll have a couple start white-washing the pavilion."

By that time several had gathered around so Dirk decides to tell them about the upcoming musical group that is coming.

"Jefferson, we'll butcher a hog and some chickens." Dirk says. "Rufus, can you handle that? Yeh Suh Massa Dirk. Ah can take care of that."

"What about wood?" asks Dirk.

Jasper says, "We has a lot of hickory already split and seasoned."

"That's great." Dirk says, "Barbeque sauce. What about barbeque sauce?"

Rebecca chimes in, "Massa Dirk Suh, Lil' Ray makes the sweetest barbeque sauce."

"Well that's great." Dirk says. "All is taken care. In two weeks, we have a party."

Dirk starts to head back to the big house when Wanda confronts him.

"Massa Dirk, Massa Dirk," Wanda says.

"Yes Wanda, what is it?" Dirk replies. "

Ah be a wantin' a devoce from Rufus."

"You two have been together for several years. Whatever could cause you to want a divorce from Rufus?" Dirk asks.

Wanda replies, "Rufus don' be a wantin' nuthin' from me no mo'. I think Rufus is a 'Hobo Sexual'."

Dirk tries not to laugh but just breaks out in a smile.

"Miss Wanda," Dirk says. "I don't think you quite understand the vernacular of the words that you are choosing to describe your situation. You see Wanda, sexual is the intimate relations between a man and a woman in a private situation. A hobo, is like, well how shall I say it, a transient, a homeless person, a beggar, or a bum."

Wanda then says, "That's right Massa Dirk, that Rufus ain' nuthin' but a fuckin' bum!"

Dirk couldn't contain himself any longer and breaks out in laughter.

"Miss Wanda, I'll have a talk with Rufus. I'll see what I can do." Dirk says still smiling.

"Thank yuh' Suh," says Wanda.

Dirk continues on to the big house. On the way to the big house, Dirk sees Jefferson and Lucille conversing out in the open. Lucille can hardly look Jefferson in the eyes and is acting like a little girl embarrassed.

"Good afternoon," Dirk says to them.

"Afternoon Massa Dirk," they reply.

"Jefferson" says Dirk, "if anyone wants to get started with the whitewash tell them it is in the barn and that they can start anytime they want."

"Yeh Suh, I'll have some get right on it."

"You two have a good weekend."

"Thank yeh Suh," they reply.

Dirk gets to the big house and has a bite to eat with Janine and the kids.

"Janine," Dirk says. "It would appear that you are starting to show a little more each day."

"How observant of you," Janine replies sarcastically.

Dirk just smiles picks up her hand and kisses it. "School should be starting next month I believe."

"Lulu, we'll take care of you when the time comes." Janine adds.

"Yes," says Dirk.

"Remember Babs and Edgar, you two are to become teachers right here." adds Janine. "Also, this is going to be something that we are not to talk about to others in any way, shape, or form. That is very important right now."

"Okay, we understand," Babs says.

Dirk says, "Tomorrow we'll go to church. We'll invite Dr. and Mrs. Holden to our party and maybe a couple of other deserving plantation owners that we see fit to invite."

"Good idea," Janine adds.

"Edgar" Dirk says, "If you would go tell Timothy that we are all going to church in the morning. Just tell him to show up if wants to go."

"Okay daddy." Edgar replies and off he goes.

XIV

O ff they all go to church in the morning with Timothy. They arrive at church and Dirk very quickly pulls something out of his coat pocket and places it under the buggy seat. They see Dr. and Mrs. Holden and invite them to the upcoming barbeque and music festivities. Dirk and Janine see a couple of other plantation owners that they feel are not prejudiced and adverse toward the negro race and cordially invite them also off to the side. Everyone looks forward to the festivities at Spanish Oaks in two weeks.

Dirk looks around for Timothy. He notices him talking to a young lady that he had conversations with the Sunday before. Dirk nudges Janine and points in his direction.

"Why don't we ask Timothy if he wants to invite his young lady and her family to the music and barbeque?" Janine asks.

"Good idea," replies Dirk. "We must let them know in advance of the situation that they will find themselves in."

They all file into the church for the service. Timothy is sitting with his lady and their family. When the service is over Janine calls Timothy to the side to extend the invite to his lady and her family and be sure to inform them that the field hands will be mingling with us also because it is for them.

"Oh, thank you Aunt Janine, I'll ask them right now." Timothy responds excitedly.

Dirk asks Janine, "What do you think about inviting the black preacher to Spanish Oaks for the workers some Sunday afternoon for their spiritual needs."

"Good idea, why didn't we think of that before?" Janine says.

"I'll ask him right now for next Saturday afternoon."

While Janine is talking with the Holdens, Dirk goes over and talks with the black preacher.

Dirk says, "Hello, my name is Dirk Kahane and I own the Spanish Oaks plantation down the road a piece." Dirk holds out his hand.

The black preacher also extends his hand and says, " Yeh suh, Ah knows where Yeh is Suh. Mah name is Roscoe Bell and this is mah wife Martha."

"I am happy to meet the two of you." Dirk says. "What I would like, if it meets with your schedule, is for you to come to Spanish Oaks and preach to my people next Saturday afternoon."

"We would love to, wouldn't we Martha?"

"Oh yeh Suh, Mr. Kahane." Martha says.

"We'll feed you and put you up for the night and make sure that you are not late getting out in the morning."

"We is a lookin' fowud to it suh and we'll see you next Saturday aftanoon."

"Thank you very much." Dirk says as he tips his hat. Dirk returns to Janine and the kids and says, "He'll be there next week. We must go now. I want to take a walk out in our forest land for some special trees when we get home."

Janine just opens her mouth to say something when Dirk realizes what he had said.

"These special trees will be supports for a water flume that is going to be built in the near immediate future." Dirk just looks at Janine and smiles. Janine tilts her head to one side and smiles back.

"Private joke, I assume." says Dr. Holden.

Dirk and Janine just smile back. Dirk, Janine, and the kids all head for their buggy.

Dirk then says, "Well I don't think that we are going to get out of here as quick as I thought."

Dirk and Janine see Timothy who is talking with his lady friend and her family and go over to him.

Timothy says, "Uncle Dirk and Aunt Janine, this is Marlene Simone and her parents Alejandro and Marguerite."

"I am very happy to meet you," Dirk says and puts out his hand to shake Alejandro's hand. Janine smiles and does a little curtsy.

Janine says, "We are looking forward to having you over for the festivities and be sure to bring your appetites."

As they are conversing, another plantation owner shows up and joins in on the conversation. "

Mr. and Mrs. Webster," Dirk says.

"Please, call us Woodrow and Christine." Woodrow says.

"We were just telling the Simone's to be sure and bring a good appetite."

"I don't see any problem there," Christine says.

"Great, we need to get going, see you in couple of weeks." Dirk pulls something out from under the buggy seat and quickly puts it in his left coat pocket without anyone noticing it. The all load up in the buggy and head out.

They are having a good ride. Edgar says that he is hungry. Babs and Lulu are too.

"I am kind of hungry myself," says Dirk.

Timothy chimes in and says, "Oh, I had a big breakfast before I left the house, I'm not hungry at all."

They are about twenty minutes from Spanish Oaks when they round a corner in the road. Two highwaymen stop them and one fires off a shot into the air. Dirk pulls hard on the reins and the horses rear up in the air and come to an abrupt halt. Needless to say, Dirk is startled and scared. Janine screams and the kids are crying at the new found danger that has been thrust upon everyone. Timothy just stares.

One of the highwaymen then says, "All your money, now!".

The other highway man then says, "But first, let's have a closer look at the women. They sure are pretty." He gives a toothless grin.

"Which one do you want?" asks the other.

"It don't matter to me," says the first one. "The darkie, we'll just toss on the roadside."

Janine puts Lulu close to her side along with Babs and Edgar. Timothy is still sitting there with his mouth agape. Dirk just gives a hard stare back at them. Dirk waits for a few moments.

The one highway man then says again, "Your money now you son of a bitch!"

"Are you hard of hearing?" Dirk says, "I'll give you all the money I have, just don't hurt any of the family."

One of the highwaymen then says, "Hurry so we can get to your women."

Dirk hesitates for a few more moments and says, "Let me come down and I'll see what I've got."

Janine is still crying as are the kids. Timothy doesn't know what to do other than just sit there with his mouth wide open. The highwaymen dismount to confront Dirk.

Janine says hysterically between tears, "Dirk, do whatever they want."

"Yes dear," Dirk replies.

They are just a few feet from Dirk. The highwaymen still have their guns trained on Dirk.

"Let me see what I have available for money," Dirk says. He reaches into his right pants pocket and produces three silver and one gold coin. The highwaymen see this and are fixated on the money. Dirk throws the coins up in the air over their heads. As the highwaymen focus on the coins, Dirk reaches into his left coat pocket. Dirk then pulls out the .40 caliber Derringer, has it cocked and fires at the one highwayman shooting him right square between the eyes. The ball leaves a neat bloody hole going into his skull, tears through the brains and leaves a fist size hole as it exits out the top and rear of his head taking brains and skull fragments with it. While this is happening, Dirk already has Sweet Thing in his right hand. The sunlight flashes on Sweet Thing's blade as Dirk makes a wide sweeping motion toward the second highwayman's neck. Sweet Thing catches the second highwayman at the top of his neck just below the skull. Sweet Thing makes a clean cut, severing the esophagus and partially severing the vertebrae at the base of the skull. On the backward swing with Sweet Thing, Dirk finishes the job with the backside of the blade tip finishing the severing of the vertebrae except for a small piece of skin and flesh causing the head to hinge backwards and flop on his back. There is a column of blood that geysers out into the air as the bandit's knees fold and his body falls backward to the ground.

Janine and the kids are crying hysterically as they hug each other. Timothy is awe-struck and can only hold his mouth open. Everything is over and done with in less than one second, as the coins fall back to the ground. Dirk breathes a sigh of relief, then wipes Sweet Thing's blade clean on one of the highwayman's clothes.

Dirk looks down at the still quivering bodies and says, "Say whatever you want to me. This is what happens when you try to fuck with my family." Dirk then says, "Timothy, come here."

Timothy just sits there with his mouth still wide open and in a daze.

"Timothy," Dirk says louder. Timothy blinks his eyes a few times and shakes himself back to reality.

"Huh," says Timothy.

"Come here," Dirk says.

Timothy slowly gets off the buggy and immediately throws up his breakfast.

Dirk looks at him and says, "As soon as you are done bragging about your breakfast, get their horses and we are going to tie their bodies to them."

"Okay," Timothy says still in a daze.

Janine and the kids get down from the buggy and go to the rear and wait. Dirk picks up his money and puts the guns, powder, and shot in the buggy. Dirk and Timothy tie the bodies on their horses. With the bodies securely tied to the horses, Dirk then slaps the horses on the rump and off they run. Dirk goes back to Janine and the kids.

"Is everyone okay?" Dirk asks.

"Yes, were fine, just shook up quite a bit." Janine says.

Dirk then gives them all a hug and kiss and starts to tear up. "Come on, let's go home, but first, I need to load up the gun again."

"Please do." Janine says.

When they arrive at Spanish Oaks, Timothy immediately heads for his house.

Dirk then says to everyone, "Let's all go up to the front porch and talk. Have a seat. Once again, you have witnessed a side of me that I had hoped none of you would ever have to see again. I had to take two lives in order to save all of our lives and Timothy's. The good Lord was with us and gave me the strength to carry out an act of preservation. Right now, we need to put those thoughts behind us and think of things that are beautiful, pretty, cute, nice, and cuddly. We need to think of what could have been and where we are now. We are safe with nothing wrong and our whole lives ahead of us. Let's all have a family hug."

They all hug and embrace, tears running down their faces.

"I imagine that we will find out more next Sunday morning at the gossip sessions prior to the service." Dirk continues. "I'll look for those trees tomorrow."

They all go inside.

"Edgar," says Dirk. "Tomorrow you and I will go look for those special trees after everyone goes out into the fields. I'll come back and get you."

"Okay daddy," Edgar replies.

"Let's get something to eat."

"I'm not hungry," Janine says.

"Neither am I," says Babs.

"I'll get something later," Edgar says.

"Okay then, I'll grab a bite to eat." Dirk eats and then takes a nap.

XV

═══

It is Monday morning again. Dirk straps on Sweet Thing. He gets to the cabins just as Jefferson and Timothy both get there.

"Jefferson," Dirk says, "Pick out a crew for the whitewashing of the new construction, if you would please. But first, please call everyone over to the pavilion, I have something to say to all."

"Yeh Suh Massa Dirk."

Dirk goes over to the platform and steps up. In a few minutes everyone is gathered inside the pavilion.

"Now that I have you all here I just wanted to tell you that next Saturday I invited a black preacher to come here for all of you to hear the Word of God. Those of you that so desire to hear the Word, this will be your chance. I'll try to get him to come here as often as he can. If you could take turns feeding him and his family that would be great." Dirk looks around and says, "Little Ray, how is the barbeque sauce coming along?"

Lil' Ray answers, "Jus' fin' Massa Dirk, Ah gots a big batch a makin' raht now Suh."

"Good job Lil' Ray. One more thing before we start the day." Dirk says. "After the music and barbeque party, on the following Saturday, Babs and Edgar will start teaching those of you that wish to learn to read, write, and do arithmetic. Classes will be in the afternoons on

Saturdays after work. I'm sure I don't have to tell you not to talk about this to outsiders." The workers all smile and gasp. "Okay Jefferson, they are all yours."

Jefferson then says, "Its go to work time y'all."

They all smile and give Dirk a slight bow as they file by.

Dirk sees Rufus and calls him aside. "Rufus, Stella is no longer here and is not going to come back ever again. Your Wanda is a pretty woman. Take care of your homework or someone else will be more than happy to take care of it for you."

"Yeh Suh Massa Dirk," Rufus replies.

Dirk heads for the barn to see Jasper.

"Jasper," Dirk says.

"Yeh Suh Massa Dirk."

Dirk asks, "How are we fixed for nails and hammers?"

"We has a gud supply of all different kinds for mos' any job that comes along an' we gots five or six hammers." Jasper replies.

"Excellent," Dirk replies. "Bye"

Dirk heads out to the fields. Dirk makes idle conversation with the workers. They all smile, laugh, and are having a good time even though they are all working. Everyone seems to be happy. Dirk sees Wanda and goes to have a word with her.

"How is Wanda this morning?"

Wanda looks up and manages to crack a smile in spite of her obvious displeasure.

"Wanda," Dirk says. "I had a talk with Rufus earlier. I believe things will get better."

Wanda looks up and says, "Thank yuh' Massa Dirk."

"I'll talk to you later," Dirk says. A couple of hours go by when Dirk sees Benjamin, Gabooti, and one of the other woman setting up under the shade trees the food and drink. Jefferson and Timothy are bringing in a group of six workers for their first break of the day. Dirk then heads back to the big house to Edgar to go look for the special trees in the forest land.

Dirk goes in the house and Edgar is waiting for him.

"Let's have a quick bite and we'll be off."

The forest land is about a twenty minute walk from the big house.

Dirk says to Edgar, "The kind of tree that we are looking for is called a cedar tree. These trees have a stringy bark and can come off in long strips. The cedar tree has a fragrance when cut like no other tree. But, the main reason I want this particular tree is because of a natural oil that preserves it just about forever. Let's take a walk inside the forest and see if we can locate a few of these."

As they are walking they notice that there are lots of trees of all different types. Lots of pine that can be sold to the sawmill later on.

"Oh, there is one of those trees now," Dirk says excitedly. "This is what we are looking for, a tree about this size, a good three to four inches across. Let's look around for some more. We are going to need a lot of them."

They walk about for a good hour or so finding more cedar trees, some too big and a lot of the desired sizes.

Edgar says, "Daddy, I need to pee."

"Go behind a big tree somewhere over there."

Edgar walks to a nearby tree and steps behind it to relieve himself. Edgar is just about done when he smells smoke and hears people talking. He hurries back to Dirk and tells him. They walk to the direction of the smoke and talking. Dirk and Edgar approach cautiously being careful not to make any noise or step on any branches or twigs. The talking is getting louder and the smell of smoke is getting stronger. They walk a little slower. Dirk and Edgar can see movement through the undergrowth.

Edgar whispers, "Daddy, I am scared."

"Do you want to stay back while I go in?" Dirk whispers back.

"No way!" Edgar whispers back.

"Well come on then." Dirk gets on his stomach and tells Edgar to do the same. Dirk starts to do a low crawl toward the smoke and talking. Dirk looks over at Edgar and pushes his butt down which was sticking way up in the air. They see the source of the smoke and talking. It appears to be a family of runaway slaves that have made camp in the woods. Dirk makes a quick visual reconnoiter before making his move. Dirk sees a flintlock musket leaning against a tree but nothing else to be overly concerned about. Dirk and Edgar then step out into a clearing and surprise the group of runaway slaves that have made camp. One of the slave women screams in horror at their discovery. One of the men starts toward the flintlock musket.

Dirk then yells as he pushes Edgar to safety behind a tree, "Stay away from the weapon."

The runaway stops. Dirk has his derringer out but not cocked for firing, but his thumb is on the hammer if needed. The women are crying and the men are most fearful. Dirk then tells the would be protector to return to the group. He does so nervously.

Dirk then says with his hand raised in the air, "Please do not be afraid, I'll do no harm to any of you." Dirk returns the derringer to his coat pocket. The runaways' tension eases quite a bit at the return of the derringer to the pocket.

Dirk then addresses them, "My name is Dirk Kahane and this is my son Edgar." Dirk motions for Edgar to come out from hiding. "I own this plantation that you are on." Dirk and Edgar approach them a little closer. The runaways don't know quite what to think of these white people that have invaded their space.

"Continue on with whatever you were doing and stay as long as you want. We will not bother you." Dirk adds, "You are all safe here from whatever you are running from. I would like to take a look at your musket."

Dirk picks up the musket and looks at it with much scrutiny. Dirk then says to the runaway slave husband, "What did you intend to do with this? You don't even have any powder in the pan. Do you even have powder, wadding and a ball rammed down in the barrel?"

"Yeh Suh, Ah runned outta powda' for the res' of it," he replies.

Dirk pulls out his powder flask and charges the flash pan with powder.

"Try not to hurt yourself," Dirk says as he returns the musket to its resting place. One of the women gets up and approaches Dirk and Edgar.

She goes up to Dirk and gives him a bow and says, "Thank Yuh' Suh', we are much beholdin' and will be a movin' on afta' it gits dark."

"So be it," Dirk says. "I hope you find what you are looking for." Dirk tips his hat then he and Edgar depart. Dirk and Edgar head back to the big house since it is getting late in the afternoon.

"Daddy," Edgar says. "I was sure scared back there, weren't you?"

"Well, not so much scared as I was overly cautious," Dirk replies. "You see, we had the element of surprise on our side. After making a careful observation of what we were up against, I decided that the situation wasn't going to be bad or dangerous at all. They were just people willing to risk all for a better life."

They arrive at the big house. Edgar goes in the house first and excitedly tells Janine of their experience in the woods.

Janine just looks at Dirk as she hugs Edgar and says, "What are you a living magnet or something that attracts dangerous and potentially life threatening situations?"

Dirk just looks back and says, "Aren't you glad it was me and not you or one of the kids by themselves?"

"Well yes, I guess so," replies Janine.

"What's for supper?" Dirk asks.

———

The next morning Dirk is at the pavilion with Jefferson and Timothy.

"Jefferson," Dirk says. "There are more than enough of the cedar trees that we'll need for the water flume supports. What are now needed are three people, saws, axes, ropes, the flat bed wagon, and a horse. Pick me out the three people that you feel that would be good for the job and I'll get them started."

"Yeh Suh Massa Dirk."

"I am going to the barn to get the tools that we will need. Have the crew meet me there." Dirk turns and leaves. Dirk is in the barn hitching up the wagon and loading up the tools. In walk the three that got volunteered.

"Morning guys," says Dirk. "Lil' Ray, not only do you do barbeque sauce but you are also going to be a logger for a few days. You two, what are your names?"

"Mah name is Ambrose, Suh," says the one worker.

The other one says, "Mah name is Harlan Suh."

Dirk says, "Very well, let's get started." They get to the woods.

Dirk says, "We are only to cut one kind of tree, the cedar. I'll show you what they look like." Dirk says. "When we find these trees always leave at least one growing so that more will grow in the spaces that we make. Also, only cut trees that are four to six inches in diameter."

Dirk notices the thousand yard stare in a ten foot room look on their faces. Dirk then says, "Let me rephrase that, cut trees that are this big around to this big around." Dirk makes a couple of circles with his hands. "Anything bigger and we'll have to split them by hand. No use making any more work for ourselves. Tie the horse up and grab the tools. Let's go."

Dirk finds some of the trees, a group of five in about a thirty foot area. "Here are five trees. We'll only cut four of these leaving the biggest one sort of in the middle so that it will produce more all around it. See how big one tree is as compared to the smaller ones around it. That is the seed tree that will produce more of these cedar trees. I'll show you how to properly cut one of these down without getting your asses killed. First, figure out where you want the tree to fall and then make sure that when it does fall you can get the hell out of the way. These are small trees and real easy to fell."

Dirk continues with his lessons. "As the tree is about to fall you need to give out a loud holler to alert anyone else that might be near that the tree is falling so that they will be aware of the danger that is present. No matter what the size is, we are going to be real careful anyway you look at it. Lil' Ray, bring the saw and you and I will get started. Ambrose and Harlan, you two stand clear, watch and listen."

Dirk goes to the first tree, a nice cedar about four inches in diameter.

Dirk says, "We want this tree to fall in that space over there. To make this tree fall where we want it to, we first have to go on the front side and make two cuts, called the face cut and the undercut. Lil Ray, take the other end of this saw. We are going to make this upward cut at an angle to just over the half way point and then make another cut straight back to meet up with the first cut and remove the cut piece. Let's do it."

Dirk and Lil' Ray start to saw in unison. They make their angled cut and then make the next cut. Dirk then takes the axe and knocks out the cut piece. Then he takes the axe, head first and sticks it in the cut with the handle sticking out.

"This tree will fall in the direction that the handle is pointing. This next cut is real important. We are going to come in from the back side. This is called the back cut. Here you have to be really alert. When we start in on the back cut, watch for the tree starting to slowly move as we are cutting. As it starts to move, give it a couple more good cuts and get the hell out of the way. This tree is only about eighty feet tall, but it can kill you the same as one that is two hundred feet tall."

Dirk and Lil' Ray start in on the back cut. Ambrose and Harlan are listening and watching intently. The sawing is going good and Dirk notices the tree starting to lean. The give it a couple more good sawing cuts, they leave the saw and move out of the way to a safe location. Dirk then gives a loud and resounding holler as the tree is falling. The tree creaks and groans as the wood is stretched and the tree falls forward with a resounding crash to the ground. Branches continue to fall after the tree comes to rest.

"Next," Dirk says. "We are going to cut the limbs off and then cut this tree into twenty foot logs. Ambrose, Harlan, bring the axes. As small as these trees are' you still need to watch out so you don't kill yourself or someone else. Since these are small trees, stand on the opposite side that you are cutting on with the axe. Observe please." Dirk then takes the axe and starts to cut off the limbs.

"Next," Dirk says, "We are going to make this tree into logs." Dirk goes to the bottom of the tree and steps off twenty feet.

"Lil' Ray, bring the small saw and cut this tree right here."

Lil' Ray cuts the tree into its first twenty foot log.

Dirk then puts his boot on the log and says, "This is what we want right here. We still have some more of the tree here to use." Dirk steps off another twenty feet.

"Lil' Ray, make the next cut right here."

Lil' Ray does so.

"One tree, several logs, one log slightly smaller than the last; however, it all is usable. Let's go on to the next tree." Dirk says. "We'll make this one fall right next to the last one."

Dirk and Lil' Ray observe their surroundings and start in on the sawing of the undercut. They remove the cut piece and start in on the back cut. The tree starts to move they give it a couple more quick cuts and move to safety. The tree comes crashing to the ground just as the last one did. They start the cutting off of the limbs and cutting into logs.

"Two trees and several more logs, not bad," Dirk says. "Let's get these other two trees and then we'll head back and get something to eat."

Dirk and Lil' Ray cut the other two trees down while Ambrose and Harlan observe. They limb the trees, and make more logs.

"Let's go get something to eat," Dirk says. They get back to the cabins.

Dirk says, "I'll see you after we eat."

Janine meets Dirk at the back door. "Hi Hon," says Janine. "How was your morning so far?"

"Oh, pretty good," Dirk says. "We cut down a couple of trees and made them into logs. We'll do more after we eat."

Jensen brings in a fine meal for Dirk and Janine.

"Thank you Jensen," says Dirk. "Most of the morning was showing Lil' Ray, Ambrose, and Harlan how to cut down a tall tree without killing themselves and how to fall it where you want it to fall."

Janine then asks, "Where did you learn all these skills in cutting down trees?"

"Oh, that was something I picked up in my Marine Corps. days when I was in the Oregon Territory. I wasn't always fighting Indians and exploring with John C. Fremont. I do know that I would hate to do that for a living, no matter where I was. Out on the Oregon coastal area the mountains are so steep and the brush is as thick as a jungle. That part of Oregon would make a stud monkey cry for its mommy. The coast of Oregon has the most beautiful sand dunes about the mid part of the territory. There was this one river we sailed up right between this stretch of sand dunes. It took us three attempts to get into this river, the water was so rough. We had to wait for the tide to settle down before we could try to get into the river again. The ship started to broach sideways in the mouth of that river but corrected itself thank God."

Dirk continues on with the story, "The chief Bo'sun's mate remembered that river from a previous trip he had made years earlier. He said it was still just as scary as his first trip. We finally made it in and sailed up river. There was a big island around this big bend in the river. Opposite this island on the port side of the ship, that is the left side, was a small settlement below the ridge. There was a lot of low lying land upriver another mile or so and another small settlement there as the river made about a ninety degree turn to the port. On the starboard side of the ship, starboard is on the right side."

"Well duh!" says Janine. "A ship only has a right and left side."

Dirk just smiles. "The ship continued on for a ways up river a bit more. There was this other river that emptied into the river that we were on. One of the Navy crew thought that river was the one that the explorer Jedediah Smith mapped out. I guess he had some problems with the local Indians there and barely escaped with his life. His men probably got drunk and let their powder get wet. We continued on up river for a bit longer. We noticed this long stretch of pasture-like land below a long mountain ridge on the 'starboard' side of the ship. In this stretch of land were hundreds of elk just resting there without a care in the world. Needless to say, we spilled the wind out of the sails and dropped anchor, rowed to shore with our muskets and shot a couple of those animals. We had fresh meat for quite awhile after that. I could live on elk meat. While the ship was at anchor, a couple of the sailors managed to catch several salmon. It was good eating for a long time after that."

Dirk finishes his meal with Janine.

"Well enough of the sea stories. I need to get back out there and cut down more trees." says Dirk. Janine gives Dirk a big kiss.

"See you later on." Janine says.

Dirk gets to the workers' cabins. Lil' Ray, Ambrose, and Harlan are already there and waiting on Dirk.

"Who is ready to cut down a tree with me?"

Ambrose raises his hand.

"Good," says Dirk. "Let's get in the wagon and get it done."

They get to the woods and go to where the cut up trees are.

"Lil' Ray, you can unhitch the horse and pull these logs out of the woods and get them stacked close together while we find some more trees."

"Yeh Suh, Massa Dirk." says Lil' Ray.

"Ambrose and Harlan, let's pick up the tools and find the next group of trees." They move a good safe distance from Lil' Ray. Dirk locates a group of six trees. One of the cedar trees again is larger than the rest. Dirk looks at Ambrose and asks.

"Which tree are we not going to cut Ambrose?"

"The big tree in the middle Massa Dirk," says Ambrose.

"Why?" asks Dirk.

"So the big tree will make little trees." Ambrose says.

"Correct, let's get started cutting," responds Dirk. "Harlan, you watch us and then you and I will do the next one."

Harlan gets back a safe distance.

Dirk says, "We'll fall this one right over there in that direction."

Dirk and Ambrose make their undercut and move to the backside to make the back cut. The tree starts to move and they make a couple more quick cuts and move back. Dirk lets out a loud holler as the tree starts its journey to the ground. Lil' Ray could hear Dirk from where he was. The tree hits the ground with a resounding crash. They wait a few moments for the rest of the debris to quit falling before moving in to remove the limbs and buck it into twenty foot logs.

"Okay Harlan, your turn." Dirk says. They move on to the next tree. Ambrose gets clear of any danger. Dirk and Harlan make their undercut and then the back cut. The tree starts to move and they give it a couple more quick cuts and move back. Dirk gives out a loud holler and the tree crashes to the ground. They move in remove limbs and buck into twenty foot logs.

"Okay Ambrose, you and Harlan cut down the next." Dirk says. "I'll be right here next to you."

Ambrose and Harlan make their undercut and move to the backside for the back cut. The tree starts to move they give it a couple more quick cuts and move back.

"Ambrose," Dirk says loudly. "Give us a holler!"

Ambrose hollers out as the tree is falling. The tree hits the ground. They wait a few seconds for the remainder of the debris to fall. They go in to remove the limbs and buck it into twenty foot logs.

"Do you think that you can handle the next ones by yourself?" Dirk asks.

"Yeh Suh Massa Dirk." replies Harlan.

"Just because you cut down a few trees already does not make you an expert, I am not an expert." Dirk says. "I just want you to be careful every time no matter what. I am going to check on Lil' Ray now and I'll be back after awhile."

Dirk walks back to where Lil' Ray is. A loud holler and a crashing tree can be heard out in the woods. Dirk gets to where Lil' Ray is.

"Looks good," Dirk says. "We'll just keep bring them out of the woods into the clearing before we haul them out of here. We need to let Ambrose and Harlan get ahead of us so as we don't get too close the falling trees."

More hollering can be heard as more trees are felled.

"We'll finish up here and see about the next group of logs to be pulled out into the clearing." Dirk says.

Dirk and Lil' Ray finish up and head towards Ambrose and Harlan. Dirk lets out a holler to let them know that they are close. A holler in return is answered.

"Coming in," Dirk yells. Dirk looks at the fallen trees and bucked up logs. "You are doing a good job guys."

"Thank yuh Suh," they reply.

"Ambrose, you take the horse and pull out some logs and Lil' Ray and Harlan can fell some more trees. We'll work a little while longer then it will be time to go in," says Dirk.

Work progresses smoothly for the remainder of the day then they all head in. They get back to the living area.

Dirk says to the crew, "Tomorrow, you will all be on your own. You know what to look for, how to cut the trees, how to be safe and careful about it. Take the long wagon in the morning and start bringing in a load of logs with you each time you come in. I'll show you where to unload them when you get here

Dirk finds Jefferson and Timothy.

"Jefferson, we'll need to get a couple people started nailing the 1 x 12 boards together tomorrow morning for the water flume."

"I'll take care of it Massa Dirk."

"Good," Dirk replies. "I'll see you two in the morning."

"Good night Uncle Dirk." Timothy says.

Dirk tips his hat and departs for the big house.

Dirk gets to the big house and Janine is there to greet him with a warm embrace and a passionate kiss. Dirk responds in like manner. They sit down at the table for a good supper with the kids. Jensen delivers the meal that Maybelle has prepared.

"Thank you Jensen," Janine says.

"Yuh welcome, Missa Janine," Jensen replies.

Dirk smiles back. Dirk looks at the kids and asks, "Well what have all of you done today?"

Babs says, "I was reading in one of my books today."

"Oh, which one?" Dirk asks.

"I was reading 'The Last of the Mohicans'." Babs says.

"That is a good book," Dirk says.

Janine says, "The author of that book, James Fenimore Cooper, is the very first North American author."

"Really?" Dirk says. "Edgar, what did you do today?"

"I was looking at your gun collection," Edgar replies.

"Well I guess you are old enough that you should know something about firearms and how to properly handle them," says Dirk. "Maybe next week we'll go out and get you started on how to load, aim, shoot, and to be safe with firearms."

Edgar smiles and says, "Oh boy that would be great daddy."

Janine looks at Dirk and puts her hand on his arm and gives him a worried look.

Dirk looks back at Janine and says, "Don't worry, all will be fine. Edgar is old enough and mature beyond his years and I want to be the one that introduces him to guns before someone else does in the wrong way."

"Okay," says Janine with a long sigh.

"Lulu, your turn to tell us what you did today," Dirk says.

"Oh, I was looking at pictures of little baby animals in one of Babs' books. I really like the little baby bunnies." Lulu says.

Janine says, "Yes, little baby animals are really cute, aren't they?"

Lulu smiles from ear to ear and says, "Oh yes, they really are, I just love them." Dirk and Janine just smile at each other. With dinner over, Jensen comes in and cleans the table.

"Thank you Jensen and please thank Maybelle for the excellent supper." Dirk and Janine say.

Dirk and Janine retire to the front porch and the kids are off playing again.

"Tomorrow, I am going to let Lil' Ray, Ambrose, and Harlan go out by themselves and cut the trees." Dirk says.

"Do you think that they are ready to do that without you there?" Janine says.

"I believe so," replies Dirk. "The trees are small, the terrain is mostly flat, and there isn't much undergrowth to worry about. My only worry is that of the unexpected and I don't have any idea what that could be."

"I'm sure everything will be just fine," Janine says.

"I hope so," says Dirk .

Dirk is at the workers' cabins in the morning.

"Jefferson," Dirk says, "Lil' Ray, Ambrose, and Harlan can go out by themselves today. Pick out a couple of men to start nailing the 1x12's together and send them down to the barn."

"Yeh Suh Massa Dirk, I'll get right on it." Jefferson says.

"I just need to have a word with them before they go. I'll be out with you and Timothy later on." Dirk says.

"Yeh Suh, Massa Dirk." Jefferson says.

"Lil' Ray," Dirk says. "You three are going out by yourselves today. You know enough that you all can handle things alone. Take the extra long wagon and start bringing in a load of logs each day and drop off three logs starting at Timothy's house and working back to the big house then work your way back to the forest. Lil' Ray, drop off the three logs each every eight paces, Ambrose and Harlan make it every six paces." says Dirk.

"Massa Dirk." says Lil' Ray.

"Yes" replies Dirk.

"Ah don' know how to count and what is a pace?"

"No problem, let's go to the barn and I'll explain it," Dirk says with a smile. "A pace is your stride, your step, the distance with each footstep. To count your steps, just do this. With each one of your fingers, one finger at a time, just touch your leg as you make a step." Dirk demonstrates by taking one step and touching his leg with one finger each time.

"You do that with this hand and with this many fingers on the other hand." as Dirk holds up three fingers on his other hand. "Let me see you take eight paces now." says Dirk.

Lil' Ray does so. "Ambrose and Harlan will only need to do six paces because they are taller." Dirk holds up six fingers.

"I wish that ah was ah bit taller Massa Dirk." Lil' Ray says.

"Lil' Ray, you have to play the cards that the good Lord dealt you," Dirk says.

"Ah understan' Suh," says Lil' Ray.

"You can teach Ambrose and Harlan on how to count their paces." says Dirk. "Okay, you guys will be on your own till the job is done."

"Yeh Suh Massa Dirk," replies Lil' Ray.

"Okay then, let's hitch up the long wagon so you can get going." Dirk says.

Lil' Ray and the others leave for the woods. The two other workers show up at the barn to nail the 1x12s together.

"Hi guys." Dirk says. "What are your names?"

"Ma' name is Nathan Massa Dirk."

"Mah name is Marcus Suh."

"Great, you two are going to nail these boards together like so." Dirk takes two of the boards and puts them at right angles and starts the nailing process. "You just keep doing this till they are mostly gone and stack them up outside of the barn till we are ready to use them." Dirk says.

"Yeh Suh Massa Dirk," they say.

Dirk then leaves for the fields to be with Timothy and Jefferson.

Dirk is with Jefferson and Timothy out in the fields. Everyone is happy and singing. Franklin is playing his fiddle to every one's approval. The workers are very friendly and cheerful. Work progresses very smoothly and the crops are doing well. The summer is quickly moving into the fall harvest season. Dirk walks around the fields making idle conversation with the workers. Benjamin and Gabooti and one of the adults are setting up their station for the breaks. Dirk looks around with a sense of pride and accomplishment. Dirk is also experiencing an inner feeling deep within his soul and spirit that he cannot identify, a good feeling, a job well done, a guiding and prodding from an unknown benevolent force.

Dirk removes his hat and holds the opening up as to let the air cool it off, closes his eyes and lifts his head skyward and lets a cool breeze coming off the river caress his face and hair. At that moment a white plumed feather, about eight inches in length, floats from the sky as if it were guided by some unknown force and it lands directly into Dirk's hat. Dirk looks around for some sort of birds flying and sees none. Dirk smiles and says thank you in his thoughts and places the feather in his hat band.

Dirk heads to the barn to see how the flume board project is progressing. Dirk continues on with his conversing as he makes his way to the barn.

"Nathan, Marcus, how are things going with the boards?" Dirk asks.

"Jus' fin' Massa Dirk. We dun' a whole bunch of them and stacked em up outside Suh."

Dirk looks outside and is very impressed. "Good job guys, you are doing very well."

Dirk goes over to Jasper and says, "Jasper, we are going to need as many strips of leather to be cut and put into a salty brine solution for a couple of days of soaking. Show me our leather supply to see if we have enough."

Jasper shows Dirk a couple pieces of tanned hide.

"This won't be enough for the job. I'll have to pick some up next time I'm in town. It is getting close to dinner time, everyone go ahead and knock off early and get something to eat."

"Thank yuh suh," say Nathan and Marcus .

Dirk steps out of the barn, he sees Lil' Ray, Ambrose and Harlan on their way in with a load of cedar logs.

Dirk meets them. "You have done very well guys. Looks like you have done real well. Take three each," Dirk holds up three fingers, "and start from the big house, then towards Timothy's house with the pacing, making sure that the logs are close to the same size in each group. Then work your way back toward the living quarters, but go eat first and then get started. See you after dinner."

"Thank Yuh Massa Dirk."

Lil' Ray, Ambrose, and Harlan are already at the unloading and placing the cedar logs in place when Dirk returns from dinner.

"How is everything going guys?" Dirk asks.

"Jus' fin' Suh." says Harlan.

They have the logs in place to Timothy's house and up to the big house. Ambrose is pacing off for the next drop.

"Okay then," says Dirk, "You know what to do. I'll see you at the end of the day."

The week grinds on and the work projects go better than Dirk had expected. The workers appear to be mostly content. Dirk heads for the barn to check on the flume boards. Nathan and Marcus are well at it.

Dirk sees Jasper and says, "Jasper, you might as well get started on cutting the hide into strips, then we'll be that much ahead by the time the rest of the leather gets here."

"Yeh Suh Massa Dirk." replies Jasper.

"I'll be back later onto see how things are going," Dirk says.

Dirk first goes over where Benjamin and Gabooti are with the food and water. Lucille is there with them to help.

"How are things going?" Dirk asks.

"Jus' fin' Massa Dirk," replies Lucille.

Benjamin and Gabooti give Dirk a wide grin each.

"See you all later." Dirk says.

Dirk heads out to the fields with Timothy and Jefferson. Dirk, Timothy, and Jefferson converse out in the middle of the field. They hear a commotion on the dirt road going to the forest land. A plume of dust can be seen of in the distance.

"I wonder what the hell all that is about?" Dirk queries.

"I don't know uncle Dirk," Timothy says.

"Let's get up there. Whatever is going on, he is in a big hurry and his shadow can't even keep up with him," Dirk says.

They get up to the workers cabins. It is Lil' Ray. Lil' Ray is crying and all hysterical.

"What is it Lil' Ray?" Dirk asks.

"It's Harlan Massa Dirk."

"What, what, come on speak up!" Dirk says.

"Ambrose and Harlan was a cuttin' this heah tree when alla' sudden it started to split up the middle instead of falling over like it should have."

"Oh shit, a barber chair," Dirk says.

"The tree come back an' hit Harlan in the head, Ah think he is dead."

"Jefferson, go to Mammy Em and tell her what is going on. Timothy, go get Janine and tell her to come over to Georgie and Mammy Em's to help if need be. Lil Ray, let's go," Dirk says.

Dirk and Lil' Ray are off in a flash. The horse goes as fast as it can with Dirk and Lil' Ray in the wagon. A few minutes later they pull up to the forest.

"Lead the way," Dirk says.

They run into the forest and reach the accident site a few minutes later. Ambrose is holding Harlan's head in his lap. Dirk sees the tree that split up the middle.

Dirk says, "Let me see him. Lil' Ray, get those two smallest logs, we are going to make a stretcher."

Dirk looks at Harlan's face. He is pretty well tore up and bleeding bad. "He's not dead because he is still flowing blood."

Dirk takes off his coat and tells Ambrose to do the same. They button up their coats and run the two pieces up inside the coat making a stretcher.

"Lil' Ray, grab the tools. Ambrose you take the back and I'll take the front." Dirk says. "Okay, lift."

They lift and they are all headed out of the woods with Harlan on the stretcher. They get to the wagon and load up. The buggy goes off at a fast pace. They get to the cabins. Mammy Em and Janine are there waiting.

Mammy Em takes a look at him and says, "He's a gon' be alright. Right now he is jus' knocked out cold and a lookin' real ugly an' all. Ah duz' have sum' work cut out for me right now."

"Do you want me to get Doc Holden?" asks Dirk.

"This ain't nuthin' that ah can't handle Massa Dirk," replies Mammy Em. Mammy Em then looks up at Dirk and notices the white feather in his hat band.

"Massa Dirk, wherever did yah git that white feather?" asks Mammy Em.

"I was out in the field with my hat off and it just fell right into It." says Dirk.

Mammy Em smiles and says, "Massa Dirk, yah has found favor wid' the Lawd an' has given yah a gift of the 'White Feather."

Dirk smiles and says "Oh, that's nice."

"Dirk," Janine says. "What happened out there in the woods?"

Dirk says with a big sigh, "The unexpected thing that we never know about happened. it was going to happen. They were cutting on this tree when it split up the middle instead of falling to the ground. That is called a 'barber chair' because of the way it split. The tree kicked back and hit Harlan on the side of the face knocking him out cold. It could have been worse. Luckily all the trees are real small."

"Oh thank God," Janine says.

"Yes indeed," replies Dirk. "Mammy Em, what more do you need from us?"

"Nuthin' Massa Dirk. We can put him up in our place till he gits betta'"

"Janine, why don't you go ahead and head for the house. Timothy and I are going to put the horse up and the tools away."

"Okay hon, I'll see you in a bit," Janine says. They hug and then Janine heads for the big house.

On the way to the big house Janine is confronted by one of the young adolescent girls.

"Missa Janine, Missa Janine," she says frantically.

"Whatever is wrong child?" answers Janine.

"Ahs a bleedin' from between mah legs an' have real bad cramps an' my mommy is still out in duh fiels'. What is happenin' ta me? Ah dun' know what to do." she says.

Janine smiles and puts her arm around her and says, "Oh darling this is a perfectly natural thing that is happening to you. You are having your first menstrual period and all is okay. First off, what kind of flow do you have?" The young girl just looks at Janine with her mouth contorted and squints her eyes as if she doesn't know what she is talking about.

She then says, "It's made of wood like all the oders."

Janine just looks at her in wonderment and says, "Huh." Janine is dumfounded and then realizes what she thought she said and breaks out in hysterical laughter.

"Come on in your cabin and I'll get you fixed up."

Janine is still laughing all the way. They get into the cabin and Janine says, "Find me some cotton and a piece of rag." Janine is still smiling. Janine fixes her up and says, "Change this twice a day at least or more if needed and all will be okay with you."

"Thank yuh Missa Janine," she says.

"You are quite welcome," Janine replies. Janine leaves again for the big house. Janine smiles to herself and says, "flow," and starts to chuckle again. Janine arrives at the big house and waits for Dirk to show up. Dirk shows up about a half hour later.

Dirk says, "That was the unexpected that happened. I am going out there and help finish the job with Lil' Ray and Ambrose."

Janine then relates 'the flow' incident to Dirk. He breaks out in hysterical laughter and doubles over.

"Thanks, I needed that," says Dirk as he wipes a tear from his eye. "I've had enough excitement for one day. The next trip to town we need to pick up some leather so Jasper can cut it into strips for soaking them in a brine solution."

"What is soaking them in a brine solution going to do?" Janine asks.

"When the strips of leather dry, they will shrink and constrict around whatever they are fastened to like iron clasps."

"And where did you pick up that tidbit of leather working knowledge?" asks Janine.

"Well," says Dirk, "The Marines weren't called Leathernecks for nothing."

"Point taken," Janine says.

"What are the kids doing?" asks Dirk.

"In their rooms when I left the house," Janine says.

"Tomorrow is Friday and I hope to get most of the tree cutting finished. The flume boards are coming along just great."

Jensen shows up and says, "Supper will be ready shortly Suh."

"Thank you Jensen," replies Janine.

Jensen gives a slight bow and exits the room.

Dirk says, "I'll get the kids ready for supper."

At that moment Janine gives a little startled jump and a gasp as she puts her hand on her stomach.

"I just felt a small kick or something," says Janine.

Dirk smiles and pats her stomach lovingly. Dirk then hollers up at the kids that supper will be ready pretty soon. A resounding "okay" is heard.

It is Friday morning and Dirk is at the pavilion mingling with Timothy, Jefferson, and the workers. Dirk has everyone gather around.

"Tomorrow afternoon the preacher is going to be here to give you the word of God. He and his wife will be spending the night in the long house. Who will feed them?" Dirk asks.

Beulah says, "Jasper an' me will take care of them Massa Dirk."

"Thank you Jasper and Beulah." Dirk responds. "Nathan and Marcus, how is your project coming along?"

Nathan responds, "Jus fine Suh, we is doin' jus' fin'."

"Lil' Ray and Ambrose, I'll be going out with you till the project is over. A week from tomorrow, the group from Louisiana will be here to play for us, eat barbeque, and spend the night." Dirk says. "Rufus, are we all set for the meat?"

"Yeh Suh, we has a hog all ready to roast, lots of chickens, corn on the cob, fresh tomatoes, cucumbers, okra, watermelon, apple cider, and sweet tea. Rebecca says that she and one of the other woman is a goin ta make fresh biscuits and have fresh butter." responds Rufus.

"Oh!" says Dirk, "I can feel stretch marks forming on me already," As Dirk rubs his stomach. "I can hardly wait. Okay! Let us knock off an hour early tomorrow so we can get ready for the sermon. One more thing, tomorrow is payday. Let's go to work. Lil' Ray and Ambrose, get the wagon and tools then pick me up at Georgie and Mammy Em's cabin. I want to see how Harlan is doing."

"Yeh Suh," says Ambrose.

He and Lil' Ray head for the barn. Mammy Em is on the front porch with some of the little children when Dirk gets there.

"Mornin' Massa Dirk." says Mammy Em.

"How is Mammy Em this morning?" Dirk asks.

"Jus' fin' Suh." responds Mammy Em.

"How is the patient this morning?"

"He be a doin' jus' fin' Suh. He is a goin' ta have a bad head ache for a day or so, but he is a goin' to heal up real good with sum' of mah the poultice Ah made for him. He a goin ta be a eatin' afore the day is dun'."

"Outstanding," Dirk says. "Have a good day."

"Thank yuh suh." Mammy Em says.

Lil' Ray and Ambrose pull up in the wagon and off they head for the forest.

Timothy and Jefferson are out in the fields with the field hands. The sun is up and bearing down with a vengeance on anyone out in it. Lucille, Benjamin, and Gabooti are setting up the food and refreshments in the shade of the trees.

Jefferson says, "I'll go over and see how things are going over there before the first crew shows up."

Timothy smiles and says, "Have fun."

Jefferson just smiles back. Lucille sees Jefferson approaching and fluffs up her hair and straightens out her dress and acts nervous as though she has forgotten to do something.

"Mornin' Lucille," Jefferson says.

Lucille giggles and hides her face and says real shyly with a big wide grin, "Mornin' Jefferson."

Jefferson smiles back and says, "How are you today?"

Again Lucille giggles and hides her face and shyly says, "Jus' fin', thank yuh."

Benjamin and Gabooti are enjoying the show and laughing at Lucille's giddiness. Lucille just glares at them with her hands on her hips. That just makes them laugh even more.

Jefferson says, "Tomorrow is the when the preacher will be here. Can I sit with you?"

Lucille says in a barely audible voice, "Yes please."

About that time the first group of workers are headed in for a break.

Jefferson says, "I'll talk with you later," He then gives her a big smile.

"Okay," Lucille smiles back sheepishly. Benjamin and Gabooti are still laughing when Lucille starts chasing them. All three of them are laughing.

Jefferson says with a big smile to the field hands coming in, "How y'all doin'?"

"Jefferson," says one of the field hands, "What yuh been up ta? Yuh looks like a little kid that jus' stole a piece of candy."

Jefferson just gives a wide ear-to-ear grin then continues on. Jefferson finds Timothy and just smiles.

Timothy just smiles back and says, "Lucille is a very good looking woman that any man would love to have for his own wife."

Jefferson just looks up at the sky with a tear in his eyes and says, "Ah knows that an' ah am a workin' on that right now. We is a goin' to sit together tomorrow when the preacher is heah. Ah gits butterflies in mah stomach whenever ah gits close to her."

"Jefferson," says Timothy, "you are sick, 'love sick'." The first group of field hands are on their way back out to fields and the next group are on their way in for a break.

Jefferson continues on, "She is all ah can think about everyday from sunup to sundown."

Timothy looks at him and says, "You got it bad. The worse case I've heard of."

Jefferson just gives a big sigh and says, "Ah knows it."

They turn and head back out into the fields. Everyone is singing while doing their work. Timothy looks towards the river and sees some blacks running along the trail, crouching under the trees.

Timothy asks, "Who are they?"

Jefferson says that they are runaways.

"Oh!" Timothy says as they continue on in the fields.

As the noon hour approaches, Dirk, Lil' Ray, and Ambrose are on their way in with a wagon load of logs. They stop at the living quarters and unhitch the horse to give it water and feed.

Dirk says, "Let's eat and we'll unload the wagon after dinner."

"Yeh Suh, Massa Dirk," they say.

"See you guys in an hour."

Dirk heads for the big house. He gives Janine a big hug and kiss.

"Supper is almost ready. The kids and I are all waiting for you to come in so we can eat together."

"Oh thank you," Dirk says.

As they are eating Dirk says, "Tomorrow is payday for them and I told everyone that we are going to quit a hour earlier than normal to get ready for the preacher and to pay them. Babs and Edgar, since most of them don't have any conception of money and how to handle it, you two will be the ones to teach them when the lessons start in a couple of weeks."

"Okay Daddy," Babs says.

Janine says, "This is exciting, our own little world getting better and better for all every day."

Dirk smiles and nods his head. Jensen brings in the food and they all enjoy a good family meal together.

"I got to go," Dirk says. "See you in a few hours."

Dirk gives Janine another hug and kiss. Then lovingly pats her protruding stomach.

Janine smiles and says, "See you at supper."

Dirk smiles and leaves.

Lil' Ray and Ambrose are waiting for Dirk at the wagon with the horse already hitched up. The field hands are making their way back out into the fields. Timothy and Jefferson are already out there.

Dirk says, "We'll drop off these logs at the proper intervals then assess how many more we'll need to finish the job. We are going to use the smallest parts that we left out in the forest. We'll go back later for those when the time comes."

They drop off the logs then head back to the forest for more.

Dirk says, "I think about another half morning of work and we'll have this tree cutting project over and done with. With the water flume boards that Nathan and Marcus are nailing together, you two can load up the wagon with as many as it will hold and drop them off on each side of the dropped of logs. We'll stop when we get to the waterfall. You two can start on that Monday morning."

They get to the forest and resume cutting the trees that are needed and bring out a load on the way back and start to drop them off in the direction of the waterfall. With that done they head in for the remainder of the day.

At the supper table Dirk says to Janine, "I am going to have the workers all come in an hour early so that we can give them their first pay. This will be a momentous occasion for all of them. We just need to get Babs and Edgar started on the education process so that they don't get cheated out of their hard earned cash."

Dirk looks over at Babs and Edgar and says, "Maybe you two should be thinking of some lessons plans."

Janine adds, "Now remember, these folks have no education at all so you will have to keep it very simple and easy for them to understand."

"We know mommy," says Babs.

Edgar just nods in the affirmative with his mouth full of food.

"Lulu, you too can sit in on these lessons," Janine adds.

"Okay." says Lulu.

With dinner over, Dirk and Janine retire to the front to relax.

Dirk grabs a quick bite and heads out to the field hands' quarters.

Everyone is mingling when Dirk gets to the pavilion. More are making their way in. Dirk goes up to the stage to get every ones attention.

"Jefferson", says Dirk, "Get everyone over here so that I may speak to everyone."

"Yeh Suh Massa Dirk," says Jefferson. Jefferson turns and says, "Hey y'all, Massa Dirk wants ta talk at us."

They all quiet down. Dirk clears his throat and says, "Today, every household will make history. Today is your very first payday. Jefferson and Timothy will make sure that we all come in an hour early to get paid and get freshened up for the first church service this afternoon held at Spanish Oaks. I don't know about you, but I am excited for every one of you."

"Massa Dirk," says Wanda, "We bin' a talkin' all week long out in duh fiels bout' this day, an' we all is cited' ta boot."

"As well you all should be." Dirk adds. "Okay Jefferson, they are all yours."

Timothy and Jefferson and the field hands all head out to the fields. Dirk, Lil' Ray, and Ambrose head out for the forest.

Dirk says on the way out, "We should have a short morning of this. It won't take long to finish up and drop off the remaining logs ending up at the waterfall."

They get to the forest and commence working. After a couple of hours they load up the wagon with logs and the tools and proceed to where they ended up with the dropping off of the logs on the previous day. They end up at the waterfall with a couple of logs to spare.

Dirk pulls out his pocket watch and says, "Oh hell it is ten o'clock. By the time we get back it will be almost time for everyone to be back anyway. Let's get out of here."

They get back with time to spare.

"You guys go ahead and put the wagon and tools up while I go and see if Janine is ready."

"Yeh Suh Massa Dirk." Lil' Ray says.

Dirk gets to the big house. Janine has her ledger book ready and a tin full of cash and coin. Janine has everyone's names pre-written down in the book.

"Where are the kids?" asks Dirk.

"They were here just a minute ago," Janine says.

"I'll holler at them," says Dirk. "Kids!"

"Yes Daddy," comes a response.

"Let's go, we are all going to the pavilion to pay everyone and I want you all to be there to witness this event."

"Coming," they say. The kids come down stairs.

"Lulu, tell mommy that I had to go upstairs and get something and that I'll be right back. Babs," says Dirk, "tell Jensen and Maybelle that we are just about ready to go. Edgar, you go help mommy and I'll be right back."

Dirk goes upstairs into the bedroom to where the guns and the money are. Dirk puts four silver dollars into his pocket. He then loads up the Derringer and sticks it in his left pocket then returns to Janine and the kids.

"We all ready?" Dirk says.

"Yes," says Janine, "Let's go."

Jensen and Maybelle are waiting by the back door. They get to the pavilion and Janine sits at a table, puts the ink and quill down next to the ledger book. All the workers mill about with big smiles on their faces.

Janine stands up and says, "As promised, the head of each household will be paid twenty dollars each for the family. You all have new cabins and food year round. You are going to be educated, and things are going to get better for all of you as time progresses. When I call your name please step up to the table. Georgie, step up and make your mark next to your name."

Georgie puts an 'X' next to his name and Janine initials it. Janine gives him twenty dollars in currency and coin.

"Rufus, step up and make your mark," Janine says.

Rufus also puts an 'X' and Janine initials it.

"Jasper, step up and make your mark." Janine initials it.

All the while this is going on Dirk keeps a watchful eye out for anything that would be out of character or out of the ordinary because of all the money out in the open. Janine continues to call the heads of each household up to make their marks and be paid their twenty dollars in currency and coin. They all mingle about and Jefferson is the last to be paid. Jefferson makes his mark and Janine initials it. As promised, Jefferson receives twenty-five dollars in currency and coin.

It takes about an hour to get everyone paid.

Dirk calls over Benjamin and Gabooti and says, "I am proud of you two for the work that you are doing. You don't have to be told to do anything, you just do it. I don't believe Lucille could do that without the both of you."

Dirk then shakes their hands reaches into his pocket. He pulls out four silver dollars and gives two each to the both of them. Benjamin and Gabooti just look and stare with their mouths wide open. Janine then stands next to Dirk and smiles with a tear in her eyes as she clutches Dirk's arm.

About that time Roscoe and Martha arrive. Dirk shakes his hand and smiles.

"Have you two had anything to eat yet?" asks Dirk.

"We ate earlier, Mr. Kahane." says Roscoe.

"Come with us up to the big house and have a bite anyway." Dirk turns to the people and says, "We'll be back in an hour for the church service for those of you that wish to attend."

Dirk, Janine, Roscoe, Martha, and the kids all head for the big house.

"Edgar," Dirk says, "Run ahead and tell Jensen and Maybelle that we are coming with a couple of guests for dinner."

"Okay daddy," Edgar says and takes off in a run.

Jensen meets them all at the door and greets every one with a smile and a nod of the head.

"We has two more settings in place, Suh." says Jensen. "Maybelle has a mighty fine supper prepared for all of yuh."

They all sit at the table then Jensen and Maybelle bring in the food. Fried chicken, sweet potatoes, collard greens, hot coffee and cider, and fresh baked bread. Edgar starts for a piece of chicken when Janine puts out her hand to stop him.

Dirk smiles and says, "Pastor, please honor us with the blessing."

"My pleasure," Roscoe says. "Martha and I like to hold hands when we pray." Roscoe says. They all hold hands and Roscoe prays, "Almighty Lawd Jesus, we ask your blessing on this food and to bless this food for our nourishment. We ask that you give us all strength and wisdom to carry out your will. We also pray that you watch over this family and keep them all safe from the evils of the world. We thank you Lawd Jesus. In your name we pray amen."

They all say, "Amen" then start to eat and enjoy each other's company and conversation.

Dirk asks, "Roscoe, how is it that came to be a pastor? How did you and Martha meet? Tell us about your lives, your families, your wants, and your desires."

"Well suh, I was fortunate to come from a plantation where the owner was a kind, gentle, and caring person such as yourself. I would take him and his wife to church every Sunday and tend to the horse and buggy while they attended the service. I would listen in from underneath the open window to the services most every time. I got to where I knew that Bible from one end to the other over the years by heart. Then one Sunday morning I got all fired up for the Lawd and the notion struck me, since I knew the Bible and the Holy Scriptures so well forward and backward, why not give a church service of my own to the Blacks that were a waiting outside for their Masters. Back home one day, I was down at the river a praying to the Lawd." Roscoe adds, "I says Lawd!" As I was standing with my back to the river and my hands raised up in the air. If you wants to be your servant to preach 'Your Word', to the multitudes, you really need to give me a sign or some sort of confirming approval." Roscoe then looks at everyone and says, "Do you know what happened next?"

Janine says, "I don't know about the rest of the table but I am mesmerized, please, do go on."

Dirk mumbles through a full mouth and just shakes his head.

Roscoe then says, "This here gigantic blast of wind lifts me right off of my feet and throws me in the river up over my head. I then came straightway out of the water and wade to the shore and says, 'Lawd, was that my Babtism? At that moment, a lightning bolt hits only a rock throw away from me with a loud clap of thunder, all of the trees quaked and leaves fell to the ground. Do you know what else?"

"No! What?" Edgar says with a wide open mouthful of food, mesmerized in amazement.

Janine says to Edgar, "Close your mouth when it is full of food."

Edgar closes his mouth still mesmerized by Roscoe's story.

Roscoe then continues, "There was only one little teeny tiny cloud in the sky at that time. I then smiles and says, 'Thank you Lawd.' This one Sunday morning at the service that I was giving, a young and most beautiful woman showed up for the first time."

Martha looks down in embarrassment. Dirk smiles and points to Martha.

"That is right. I could hardly get through my sermon for the want of looking at her all through the service. Six months later, we were husband and wife. That was twenty five years and two boys ago. We would like to have our own church building sometime."

Dirk says, "We would sure appreciate if you could come by at least one Saturday out of the month. We will even put out the invite to a couple of other plantation owners that we feel might be interested."

"That would be wonderful," Martha says.

"What about your two sons?" Janine asks.

"Elijah and Jonah, they are both up in the Ohio country free and doing well. We hear from them two maybe three times a year," Martha says.

"Yes," Roscoe says, "We brought them up in the Lawd and managed to get them to Ohio. They both have a daughter each and will be a raising them in the Lawd."

Dirk looks at his watch and says, "We have about ten minutes before we need to get to the pavilion for the church service."

Roscoe says, "I am really excited for your folks here."

"As we are also," Janine says. They get up from the table.

Martha says, "That was a most enjoyable meal and we do thank the both of you."

"The pleasure was all ours." Janine says.

By the time they get to the pavilion, there isn't any room left hardly to squeeze in sideways. Jefferson and Lucille are sitting close together holding hands. Harlan is there complete with bandaged up face. Georgie and Mammy Em, Jensen and Maybelle were already there. Everyone is there already with their own chairs, boxes, or whatever they could find to sit on.

"Roscoe," Dirk says. "It would appear that you are going to have to rival that 'thunder clap' in order for everyone to hear you today."

"I believe that you are right," Roscoe says. "I'll be a needin' to get up to the stage so I can begin my sermon."

As Roscoe starts up to the stage the crowd parts like 'The Red Sea' enabling him to get to the stage unhindered.

"Oh, now there's a miracle just getting through the masses." says Roscoe. "It is so good to see all of you that thirst after the Lawd. The good Lawd says, 'Come and drink of the waters of righteousness and ye shall be satisfied. Today being Saturday don't matter to Lawd one iota. The Lawd should be worshipped every single day, in private, in church such as now, or anytime and anywhere. Let us bow ours heads in prayer as we dedicate this service to the Lawd God Almighty."

Roscoe begins his prayer. "Lawd God, creator of all that is, was, and ever will be, we, your children, humble ourselves before thee giving you praise and worship. We beseech Thee almighty God in the 'Name of Jesus' that thee bless these people here this Saturday afternoon that thirst after thee. In your Holy Name we pray, amen and amen."

Amens can be heard from the people as well.

"Normally, we have an instrument or two to accompany the 'joyful noise unto the Lawd' when we sing."

Franklin immediately raises his hand and says, "I'll be right back with mah fiddle Suh."

Roscoe then says, "We didn't even have to ask and we are receiving. Thank you Lawd."

Franklin is back with his fiddle. "Ah knows most all the gospel songs Mr. Roscoe."

"Rock of Ages," asks Roscoe.

"Let's git started." Franklin says.

Franklin plays, Roscoe, Martha, and Kahanes do most of the singing. Everyone else hums along.

"Let's sing 'Amazing Grace'." Franklin starts and they join in the singing.

"Thank you Franklin for the blessings you have bestowed upon us with music. The Lawd has truly blessed you." says Roscoe. "Now, for the 'Meat and Potatoes' of the Lawd God's Word. Today's sermon will be from the book of Matthew, chapter five, as he holds his Bible up in the air, 'The Beatitudes'. These are the 'attitudes to be'. The Beatitudes are what Jesus wants us to be like in our everyday life. Jesus preached to the multitudes in his 'Sermon on the Mountain'. Here is where hundreds of people and his Disciples had gathered to hear him teach. The words of the Lawd Jesus to the multitudes, 'blessed are the poor in spirit: for theirs is the Kingdom of Heaven'."

Roscoe continues, "Your spirit is your immortality, your character of person, your emotions, your free will, your influences, and your thinking of your inward self. Your spirit is aware of yourself. Your soul, likened to your spirit is aware of God. We are always trying and striving to be more like God. That my friends, is why we are 'poor in spirit'. We are always trying but because we are born into sin, we are always missing the mark. We have all sorts of needs, we have bondages, slothfulness and laziness, and the things of life itself be a holding us back. I am no better, but I keep on striving for the goal."

"The next Beatitude goes like this: Blessed are they that mourn; for they shall be comforted. Mourning, not to be confused with when the sun comes up in the morning but, mourning as in grieving, sadness, and the expression of sorrow." Roscoe continues on with his sermon and every eye and ear is riveted to him. "Mourning or sadness can be caused by a lot of things, death, disobedience, desolation, or loneliness and misery, discouragement, disease and sickness. Now, the Lawd God in his infinite love and mercy can take each one of these human problems and turn them into gladness, joy, hope, and all of heavens glory."

Janine elbows Dirk and points to Jefferson and Lucille. Lucille has her head resting on Jefferson's shoulder. They both smile at each other.

Then Janine whispers in Dirk's ear, "I believe Roscoe will performing a marriage ceremony sometime soon."

Dirk smiles at Janine and shakes his head.

"The Lawd has a whole passel of these beatitudes. I am only going to do one more because we are a runnin' outta time." Roscoe says. "The last one for today is this: Blessed are the meek, for they shall inherit the earth. There are other words to describe meek. One of those words is patience or 'the ability to bear trials and tribulations without complaining'. I'm sure you already know about that without me having to go any further."

A lot of head shaking can be seen.

"I am going to take this one step further. In the ancient Greek translation, those of you who don't know about Greeks, they are a bunch of olive eaters way across this ocean out here." Roscoe continues, "In the original translation from the Latin to the Greek, meekness means, 'strength under control'. I see an example already." Roscoe points to one of the men in the crowd holding his baby. "You suh, please stand up."

The man with the baby stands up.

"You see, this man has lots of muscles and obvious strength to him. Yet, he is able to hold and love and embrace and control this delicate little life in his hands. Thank you very much," Roscoe says to him. "I once saw a man catch a butterfly in his hands. He held it, he looked at it and let it go. My friends that is 'controlled strength', meekness, however you want to interpret it. Let us pray. Lawd God, I pray in Your Holy Name that your word has blessed the fine people. I thank you Lawd for the opportunity to share your Word. I ask you to bless each and every one here and a special blessing on the Kahanes for opening and sharing without fear of their world. In your precious and beautiful Name amen and amen."

Amens are throughout the pavilion. The people stand up and cheer, many a 'thank you' can be heard. A throng of people surround Roscoe. Jefferson and Lucille go up hand in hand and introduce themselves to the pastor and to thank him personally for his sermon.

Jefferson says, "When will yuh be a comin' back Pastor?"

"In about four weeks. I'll be here once a month for everyone God willing."

"We'll be a lookin' fowad' to that Pastor," Jefferson says.

"Yes Pastor, thank yuh very much suh." Lucille says.

Dirk and Janine go to Pastor Roscoe and Martha. "Excellent service Roscoe, we and all those here really appreciate you coming here. You'll be staying up in the long house and Wanda will take care of your dinner this evening."

Janine adds, "Breakfast will be at seven AM and then we can all head into church together in the morning."

"That is great," says Martha, "I would like to take a nap."

"I am really tired too," Roscoe says.

Dirk says, "One more thing Roscoe, I have something for you."

Dirk reaches into his coat pocket and pulls out his billfold. Dirk gives Roscoe a ten dollar bill. Roscoe humbly accepts the money.

"Thank you very much, Mr. Kahane, we really appreciate this." Roscoe says.

"We'll see you in the morning then," says Dirk.

Janine looks at Timothy and says, "Timothy, if you want to go to church, show up for breakfast and then we'll all go together."

"Oh thank you Aunt Janine. I'll see you all in the morning," responds Timothy.

———

The next morning, Maybelle and Jensen deliver a feast fit for a king. Roscoe gives the blessing for the food. They all have a good meal. Ham, eggs, pancakes, potatoes, freshly churned butter, honey, coffee, apple juice, and fresh melon from the garden.

Dirk says, "Jensen and Maybelle, it looks as though we have a lot of food here, why don't you two join us."

"Oh Massa Dirk, we jus' cudn't," says Maybelle.

Janine then says with a smile, "Shall I get you two your plates or do you want to get them?"

"Thank you Massa Dirk an' Missa Janine."

Jensen and Maybelle join them for breakfast. With breakfast over, they all get into their buggies and head for church.

They travel down the same road where they had their encounter the Sunday before. They arrive at the location where Dirk had to fight for everyone's lives. That spot in the road is forever engrained in the deep recesses of their minds. Janine hugs Babs and Lulu as they pass the exact place. Dirk keeps on without saying a word. Timothy and Edgar don't say a thing but just sit there as though nothing had happened.

They all arrive at church in good order. Dirk puts the derringer under the seat without trying to be discreet as before. Roscoe and Martha make short talk with Dirk and Janine. Roscoe and Martha go to the tree for their service. The Kahanes and Timothy see Dr. Holden and Ruth.

"Good morning," says Dirk. "How are the Holdens this morning?"

"Real good. Janine," says Dr. Holden. "It looks as though you are progressing nicely."

"Oh I am feeling pretty good now that most of the morning sickness is behind me."

About that moment two other women and their husbands join in on the conversations.

One says, "Did you hear what happened last Sunday?"

Ruth Holden says, "No! What are you talking about?"

"Late in the afternoon there were these two horses that had two bodies strapped to them. One had his head almost cut off and the other had been shot in the head in the most gruesome way."

Timothy starts to say something. Dirk just looks at him sternly straight into the eyes without saying a word and Timothy clams up immediately.

"Come to find out," she continues, "According to the local constabulary they were wanted in Georgia for murder, robbery, rape, and numerous other things. The constable even said that there was a reward out for them dead or alive, preferably dead."

Dirk says, "It sounds as if someone has done the world a favor."

About that time Pastor Merle walks over and says, "Good morning everyone."

"Good morning pastor," they respond in unison. "We were just talking about the two highway men that were found last week."

"Yes, I heard about that," Pastor Merle responds. Pastor Merle then says, "It sounds to me that whoever took the lives of those two knew how to fight and knew exactly what to do in a combat situation." Pastor Merle gives Dirk a quick glance sideways.

Dirk then says, "Well, I think we'll go find us a seat."

Timothy sees Madeline, Alejandro, and Marguerite and goes over to be with them.

With the church service over, everyone files out. The Kahanes and the Holdens converse.

Dirk says, "Next Saturday don't forget, the barbeque and the music."

"If you need to spend the night, we have lots of room," Janine says, "I'll remind the Webster's also."

"I'll be right back." Dirk says, "I need to remind Timothy to be sure that the Simones are coming also."

About that time Timothy walks over and says that Alejandro, Marguerite, and Madeline are looking forward to next Saturday.

Janine returns and says, "We are all going to have a good time next week."

Dirk says, "I am going to say good bye to Roscoe and Martha and tell them that we will see them next month."

Dirk does so then everyone gets in the buggy and heads home. After they arrive at Spanish Oaks they grab a quick bite to eat, then Dirk and Janine spend the rest of the day in leisure.

The kids don't want to sit around relaxing, though.

"Daddy," says Edgar. "Can I go swimming at the waterfall?"

"Well sure, but under one condition," says Dirk.

"What?" asks Edgar.

"Take Babs and Lulu with you."

Edgar turns around and there are Babs and Lulu ready and waiting to go with their bathing costumes.

"We'll be back later," says Edgar.

"Bye." says Dirk.

The kids leave for the waterfall. Dirk winks at Janine and takes her hand and walks upstairs.

Janine says, "We have to be real careful."

"Okay." Dirk says, "Careful is my middle name."

"Yeh! Right!" says Janine.

Edgar, Babs, and Lulu are walking through the quarters with their swim clothes.

Little Willie sees them and asks, "Going swimming?"

"Yes, come on," says Edgar.

Soon Benjamin and Gabooti see them and ask, "Can we come too?"

"Sure come on," says Babs.

They get to the waterfall and swimming hole. Everyone finds his own private bush to put on his swimming suits. Edgar is the first to jump in the water. Soon they are all in the water except Lulu.

"What's wrong, Lulu?" asks Babs.

"Ah can't swim," responds Lulu.

"Well, now is as good a time as ever to learn."

Babs goes through the motions of swimming and shows her what Edgar, Willie, Benjamin, and Gabooti are doing.

"I'll hold you up and you practice the strokes like I showed you." Babs says.

"Ah is scared." Lulu says.

"I'll be standing right next to you and you can stand also, so there is nothing to be afraid of," reassures Babs.

Babs holds her up as Lulu goes through the motions.

"That's good, keep it up," Babs says.

The boys are all splashing each other and having a good time. The boys then get on each other's shoulders and try to knock the other off the other ones' shoulders. Lulu is making a lot of splashing when Babs lowers her slightly in the water slightly. Lulu starts to panic when the water gets to her face.

"Everything is okay," Babs says. "It is only water, just like when you wash your face at the big house."

The boys are still having their mock battles.

Babs says to Lulu, "Stand up and we'll try something else."

Lulu stands up.

"Watch me," Babs says. Babs walks out a little deeper then lunges towards the shoreline swimming. "Now you try it and if you get scared, then just stand up."

Lulu tries it and starts to sink then stands up.

"Ah jus' can't get this swimming thing, Babs." Lulu says.

The boys are taking a little respite from their battles. Edgar comes over to see what is going on.

"I'm trying to teach Lulu how to swim," Babs says.

"This is how I learned," Edgar says. "Hold your breath and go under the water like this." Edgar takes in air and just dunks his head under the water for a few seconds and stands back up. "Do that a few times Lulu so you can get used to holding your breath in the water."

Lulu does so.

"Do it a whole bunch of times till it doesn't bother you anymore." Edgar says.

Lulu holds her breath and goes under water and comes out several times.

"That is good," Babs says to Lulu.

Edgar then says, "This is how I learned to swim. I went to the deep part and pushed myself to the bottom and sprung back up with my legs. With air in my lungs and holding my breath I came back up real fast to the top and held on to the rocks."

"Will ah get to stand up?" asks Lulu.

"No, but Babs and I will be right next to you so you won't have anything to worry about."

"Ahs scared, Edgar." Lulu whimpers.

Babs gives Lulu a reassuring squeeze and says, "Everything will be alright."

Willie, Benjamin, and Gabooti are sunning themselves on the rocks. Edgar, Babs, and Lulu work their way to a deeper portion of the swimming hole by holding on to the big rocks.

"Okay Lulu, take a deep breath and hold it like we did in the shallow part," Edgar says. "Now push yourself down with me and I'll be holding on to you all the time."

Down they go to the bottom and they push themselves back up to the surface. Edgar still has a hold of Lulu when they get to the surface. Lulu takes a big breath of air when she gets to the top as does Edgar.

"Ah did it, ah did it!" Lulu says full of excitement.

Babs says, "That's good."

"Now," says Edgar, "comes the easy part."

"What's that, Edgar?" Lulu says.

Edgar says, "You swim on the surface to Babs, you already done it under water. I'll be swimming right alongside of you all the way."

Benjamin and Gabooti sit up and take notice.

"Are you ready?" Edgar says.

"Ah am scared Edgar," Lulu says.

"I am going to be right next to you and you will be able to see me all the time. I won't let anything happen to you." Edgar reassures Lulu. "Okay then, let's swim to Babs at the other end."

They start their swimming. Lulu starts to tread water and gains more confidence with every stroke with Edgar by her side all the way.

Babs says, "Lulu, you are swimming. Look at you go."

Babs starts to clap her hands and Edgar says, "You are doing so good, I just can't believe it."

Benjamin and Gabooti jump up and down and start to cheer for Lulu.

"You are swimming Lulu, you're swimming," Babs says.

Lulu gets to where Babs is standing and stands up herself. Babs and Edgar give her a big hug. Benjamin and Gabooti are cheering for her.

Edgar then says, "Take a rest then you will be ready for the next lesson."

"What is the next lesson Edgar?" Lulu asks.

"You will swim the whole length of the pond by yourself."

"No!" screams Lulu hysterically. "Ah am afraid to."

"You will be alright Lulu," Edgar says. "We all are going to walk alongside of you as you swim."

"You are going to do just fine," Babs says. "You already know how to swim."

"You just did it." Edgar says. "Benjamin, me, Gabooti, and Babs will all be here watching you."

"Ah am still scared." Lulu says.

"You'll be just fine." says Babs.

Lulu says, "Okay then, here ah goes." Lulu takes off swimming and doing very well for the novice that she is. They all cheer her on and give her words of encouragement as she swims.

"Lulu, you are doing good, now turn around and head back to the other end," says Edgar.

Lulu turns without saying a word and heads back to the shallow end. She swims to the shallow end and they all jump in and give her hugs and tell her how proud they are of her.

"Did Ah do ah right, Edgar?" asks Lulu.

"Yes, you did the best that I think anyone could do."

They hear the sounds of a horse and wagon pulling up. Turning around, they see Dirk and Janine walking towards them.

Dirk says, "We just wanted to see how everyone is doing."

"You all have been gone for a long time," Janine says.

Edgar says, "We have been busy teaching Lulu how to swim."

"What!" Janine says with a worried sound to her in her voice.

Dirk holds her arm and says, "I'm sure all is well. See, nobody is dead."

Lulu says, "Mommy, Daddy, watch."

Lulu starts to swim out to the deep end. Janine gasps and puts her hand over her mouth as Dirk holds her upper arm. Dirk does not seem to be worried at all.

Dirk says to Janine, "There are four of us here keeping a close eye on her."

Lulu turns and heads back to the shallow end.

"Oh Lulu, that is wonderful," Janine says.

"Who taught you how to swim?" Dirk asks.

"Babs and Edgar did. Benjamin and Gabooti were there if ah needed help."

"Well done guys!" Dirk says, as he and Janine clap their hands. "Come on, let's go."

They all jump in the wagon and head for home.

XVI

Monday morning finds Dirk at the pavilion talking with the workers. Lucille is at Jefferson's side. The two seem to be inseparable.

"Marcus and Nathan." says Dirk. "As soon as you are done nailing the boards together, start loading them up in the wagon and dropping them off where ever you see the logs starting at Timothy's place and working back to the waterfall. How much longer do you need till they are ready to go?"

Nathan says, "We should be done sometime in the next two days Suh."

"I still have to get more items before the project is finished," Dirk says. "Timothy, take the wagon into Charleston and I'll have a list for you when you stop by the big house. Jasper, do we have drill bits for drilling in wood?"

"Yes Massa Dirk, we has quite a few."

"One more thing, this is Monday. On Saturday, we have our barbeque and music. I invited a couple of other plantation owners and Dr. and Mrs. Holden here also for the festivities."

There is some mumbling from the crowd that Dirk overhears.

Dirk continues, "They are good people or I would not have extended the invite to them. Jefferson, they are all yours."

"It's go ta work time," Jefferson says.

Dirk looks at Timothy and says, "I'll see you at the house in a few minutes."

Timothy arrives at the big house and Dirk has a list for three hundred feet of one inch hose, ten sheets of tanned leather, twenty one inch water valves, pipe goop, a roll of canvas sheeting three feet in width, twenty one inch flange couplings for the water lines from the flume, a couple pounds of three-quarter inch brass screws for the flange pieces, and twenty pounds of salt for the brine solution.

"Here you go Timothy," Dirk says. "You might consider spending the night there this is a big order to fill. One more thing, don't forget the whiskey and cigars."

"Okay Uncle Dirk," and off Timothy goes for Charleston.

Dirk then returns to the working area. Dirk first stops by the barn to talk with Jasper.

"Jasper," Dirk says. "Show me the bits for drilling the wood."

"Raght heah suh." Jasper says. Jasper shows the vast array of wood bits and hand drills available.

"This is great," Dirk says. "Thank you Jasper."

Dirk then goes over to Marcus and Nathan. "Looks real good guys you are doing a fine job."

"Thank yuh suh," Marcus and Nathan say.

"The last thing that we are going to need for this project is to cut several squares from some of these boards," Dirk says. "The squares will be cut in half twice and nailed close to the flange openings for each line causing the water to pool up slightly, ensuring enough water to be available for each line. We should have plenty of boards. Good job guys."

Dirk then turns and leaves. Dirk goes over to Rufus.

"Good morning Rufus," says Dirk.

"Mornin' Massa Dirk," replies Rufus.

"Do we have plenty of meat for Saturday?"

"Oh yeh suh," says Rufus. "We has a whole hog ready for the roastin' spit an' whole mess of chickens. Lil' Ray's barbeque sauce is a ready for everything. We also has lots of corn on duh cob, watermelon, potatoes for baking, an' lots of fresh tomatoes."

"Well Rufus, I don't know about you, but myself, Janine, Timothy, and the kids are all looking forward to this Saturday."

"Dats all we been a talkin' bout roun' heah for awhile here also suh. We specialy wants ta hear dis music yuh been a promising us."

"Trust me, if you don't like it then you must be sick, dead, or not normal." says Dirk. "Who can cook and prepare the barbeque?"

"Dat would be me suh," Rufus says.

"Well then Rufus, the job is yours. Who do want to help you? Actually, I have an idea. Edgar needs to learn some skills. Barbecuing and preparing food is one he should learn."

"Dat would be fine suh. Ah can teach him real gud suh." says Rufus.

"Excellent," Dirk says. "Edgar doesn't know it yet, but he is going to be most happy to help you."

"Fine suh," Rufus says.

———

Timothy arrives in Charleston and goes into the hardware store to place his order. He gives his list to the clerk behind the counter.

The clerk says, "This is a mighty big order to fill and is going to take most of the day to fill it."

"That is fine," Timothy says. "I'll go and get a room and something to eat, so take your time. I'll probably head back tomorrow morning so I will leave the wagon here."

"That will be fine Sir," says the clerk.

Timothy grabs his overnight bag and takes the horses to the livery stable. Timothy goes to the hotel to check in. Returning from his room to the dining area he takes a seat.

A black waiter hands him a menu smiles and says "Good afta noon suh."

Timothy responds in like manner with a smile. As Timothy pores over the menu's selections, he can overhear a couple of well dressed persons with an English accent spewing seditious talk against the North to whosoever will listen. At one point one Englishman is heard to say the best thing for the South in recent times was the death of Daniel Webster. The other one then says not to forget the death of the traitor Henry Clay.

Timothy places his order and asks the waiter, "Who are those people?"

The waiter responds and says. "Ah doesn't know suh. He an' a couple of others that sounds like him have been roun' heah for almos' two weeks a talkin' like that bout' how bad the North is a treatin' the South."

"Thanks," Timothy says. "Why would the Brits care?"

"Ah doesn't know suh." responds the waiter. "Ah is a goin' ta git yuh order goin' suh."

"Thank you," replies Timothy.

Timothy listens to the two Englishman as a bigger crowd draws near to listen. The two Brits continue to bad-mouth the Northern States and talk about how the banks are making a lot of money at high interest rates off the Southern plantations when most of the money should be staying in the South.

At one point, one Englishman says, "The Southern ports, like this one here in Charleston should have a direct route for your cotton trade to the ports of England instead of going to Sandy Hook in New York harbor. The Northerners are making most of the money off your cotton, off the sweat and labor here in the South and not doing anything except reaping most of the benefits."

Timothy's dinner arrives. He enjoys his meal and leaves a little money on the table. He then goes to his room for a nap while the two British men continue to rant and rave. Timothy gets up in a couple of hours and heads down the stairs to a large crowd that has gathered outside the hotel. There are now three Englishmen expounding details on how the North is exploiting the South's money and labor. There is a lot of grumbling coming from the crowd. Timothy stops to listen. People from the crowd are asking a lot of questions.

One man from the crowd asks, "Just how much cotton is going to New York?"

The Englishman looks at him straight in the eyes and says, "Upwards of 800,000 tons and growing."

More grumbling and cussing can be heard.

Another from the crowd asks, "How much money is that?"

One of the Englishmen turns and says to everyone, "This amounts to millions and millions of dollars which should be staying here in the South."

More cussing and grumbling can be heard as the crowd grows angrier by the minute.

Timothy can't stand it any longer and says, "Hey Mr. Limey, what is in this for you? How come you care so much about what goes on here so far away from England?"

The crowd then turns to face Timothy.

"Well," one of them hums and haws, then clears his throat. "We know what it is like to be oppressed and taken advantage of. England loves the Southern U.S. Now run along before I have someone help you along."

"Would you still love us if we didn't have any cotton?"

The crowd then turns to face the Englishman. One of the Englishmen walks toward Timothy and hits him in the nose causing him to bleed profusely and knocks him down.

He looks at Timothy and says, "Now move on out of here boy!"

Timothy gets up slowly and goes back into the hotel and up to his room. Timothy stays in his room for the rest of the night. The next morning he goes the mercantile store to buy cigars then to the saloon to buy a bottle of whiskey. Timothy goes to the livery stable to get the horse and on to the hardware store. Timothy finishes the transaction and leaves for Spanish Oaks with a swollen, bruised, and very red nose.

He arrives at Spanish Oaks at noon time. He pulls up in front of the big house and brings in the cigars and whiskey for Dirk. Dirk and Janine look at him and rush outside.

"Oh my God, Timothy, what happened?" Janine asks.

Dirk says, "Let's go inside so you can tell us the story."

The kids look at him with their mouths agape.

"Jensen," Janine says.

"Yes Missa Janine," Jensen replies.

"Please bring Timothy some dinner."

"Right away Missa Janine," Jensen replies as he looks at Timothy's red and bulbous nose in awe and wonderment.

Timothy recounts the entire incidents from inside the hotel and outside with the gathering crowd and his queries that led to the bashing of his nose.

Janine says, "What are the British doing trying to create all this discontent?"

"In my travels to Liverpool and other English cities, I can only surmise that they are afraid of losing cheap cotton for their many textile factories." Dirk says. "I remember a lot of finished clothing coming back to this country from England as a result of all the cotton sent over there. It sounds to me that they are in 'quick sand' and grasping for straws."

Timothy says, "What would you have done Uncle Dirk?"

"I learned something along time ago," Dirk says. "That is, 'to keep my eyes and ears open and my mouth shut. That is good advice to all. Discretion is the better part of valor. One more thing, he who runs away lives to fight another day."

"I guess so," Timothy says. "But you fought the bandits and the runaway slave."

"They were a threat to me and to my family. Otherwise I would have left them alone."

Timothy then says, "Who was Daniel Webster?"

"Daniel Webster," says Dirk, "was a Senator from Massachusetts. His words carried more weight than the president's. Senator Webster was opposed to slavery and he always was in favor for a person's individual rights. His words were well known and famous in Europe as well as here in the U.S. Henry Clay, a Senator from Kentucky, along with Daniel

Webster bandied about new states entering the Union as 'free' states and not slave states. "

"That man, Henry Clay, was another name the Englishmen were bad mouthing." Timothy says.

"Webster then switched horses in the middle of the stream by supporting the capture and return of fugitive slaves," Dirk says. "I don't know who he was trying to appease. The next time we go into Charleston we'll just do a lot of listening and making of 'mental notes' to ourselves. Enough of all that. Hey every one, guess what Edgar gets to do on Saturday?"

They all look at Dirk.

Edgar says "What?"

"You get to help Rufus with the barbequing."

"I am, I do?" says Edgar.

"Yes." says Dirk. "I volunteered you, aren't you happy?"

Edgar just sits there with a mouthful of food saying nothing.

Dirk adds, "You need to learn some skills on cooking and preparing food. This will be a good opportunity for you. You just never know when you'll need to call upon these learning experiences. "

"You grasp things easy, have a good memory, and this is something all young people should be introduced to as early as possible." Janine says, as she looks at Edgar, "I love a good rack of ribs and a good piece of barbecued chicken Edgar. I am happy for you that Rufus is the one giving you his experience."

"Well, okay then," says Edgar.

"Timothy, let's get the wagon unloaded," Dirk says. "Then we'll have Mammy Em take a look at your red signal light."

Dirk and Timothy go to the barn and unload the wagon. With the wagon unloaded, they then go over to Georgie and Mammy Em's cabin and knock on the door. Franklin answers the door.

"Gud aftanoon, Massa Dirk and Massa Timothy," says Franklin.

Mammy Em comes to the door and takes one look at Timothy and says, "Gud Lawd, git in heah an' let me see what Ah can do for dat."

Georgie saunters over and says, "Massa Timothy, it seems that yuh didn't duck at all."

Dirk says, "Timothy hit some guy's fist with his nose. What can you do for him Mammy Em?"

Georgie says, "Well Massa Timothy, ah am sure his fist don' look near as bad as yuh nose suh."

Dirk and Franklin start to laugh.

Dirk says, "Mammy Em, please take care of him."

"Massa Timothy is a gon' ta be jus' fin suh," Mammy Em says.

"Thank you Mammy Em, thank you Georgie. I'll leave you in Mammy Em's capable hands." Dirk says to Timothy.

Dirk turns and leaves. Dirk heads for the pavilion and notices movement behind it. Dirk walks over and sees Jefferson and Lucille locked in a deep and passionate kissing embrace. Dirk returns to the front of the pavilion and mingles with everyone else. Lucille walks in fixing her hair and fluttering her eyes. Gabooti looks at her, elbows Benjamin in the side, and they both point and laugh. Lucille looks back at them, frowns and shakes her finger at them. They both just cover their mouths and giggle. Jefferson shows up smiling. Dirk looks at him, looks at Lucille and how they look at each other. Dirk can see the deep love that they have for each other and knows that there is going to be a wedding sometime in the near future.

"Jefferson," says Dirk.

No response at all from Jefferson other than a stare to some far away distant land. Dirk just smiles and goes over to Jefferson and waves his hands in front of Jefferson's face.

Jefferson just looks at Dirk and says, "Huh." Then Jefferson blinks his eyes several times as if he were wakening from a deep trance. "Oh yeh suh Massa Dirk!" as he comes to his senses.

"I'm headed for the barn, they're all yours." Dirk says.

Dirk turns and heads for the barn. Dirk looks at the leather that was brought in. He then lays one flat on a table takes a straight edge and lays it on the hide leaving a one half inch strip to cut with a knife.

Dirk takes out Sweet Thing and makes his cut down the length of the straight edge on the leather hide. Dirk holds up a strip of leather one half inch wide by two and half feet long. Dirk holds up the leather strip and thinks to himself, "Just right."

About that time Nathan, Marcus, and Jasper arrive at the barn.

"Hi guys," Dirk says to them. "We are going to need several hundred of these leather strips to lash the ends of the logs together. Jasper, please start cutting on the leather when you get the opportunity. Then we start soaking them in the brine solution. I'll get one of the guys to help you. Nathan and Marcus, I'll give you a hand with the flume boards and I'll also get Lil' Ray, Ambrose, and Harlan if he is up to it to help also." "Start loading up the wagon with the flume boards," Dirk says. "Jasper, please get the hand drill and the one inch wood bit."

"Yeh suh Massa Dirk," replies Jasper.

"I'll go get the others and I am going to have Harlan come down here to help with the cutting of the leather strips," says Dirk.

Dirk leaves. Nathan and Marcus continue to nail the flume boards together. Lil' Ray and Ambrose show up a few minutes later and start to load the wagon. Harlan and Dirk arrive back at the barn.

"Harlan, you stay here with Jasper and he'll show you what to do," Dirk says.

"Yeh suh Massa Dirk," replies Harlan.

Dirk says, "Well it looks like we have a good wagon load already. Let's start dropping these off at Timothy's house and work our way to the big house and on up through the cabins here. Take one of those cut off pieces to block off the end of the flume or else there is going to be a flood at Timothy's place. We'll cut a section of the flume to divert the excess water to a small ditch and create another small stream at Timothy's place. We'll just keep at this all day till quitting time."

They go to Timothy's house and start dropping off the flume boards and work their way towards the big house and on around to the worker's cabins. With the first wagon load dropped off, they start to load up the wagon again. Jasper and Harlan are cutting the leather strips and dropping them into the brine for soaking.

Dirk looks at them and says, "You two are coming right along with this project."

"Yeh suh Massa Dirk, we will be done real soon," Jasper says.

"Okay then, Harlan, in the morning I'll show you how to drill the holes for the water lines and to install the flanges with the brass screws and nail in the pieces for the water pooling for each flange unit. Go ahead and finish loading the wagon and cutting the strips of leather and then call it quits for the day."

"Thank yuh Massa Dirk." they say.

Dirk checks on Timothy to see how he is doing. He then heads over to the big house. Janine meets him at the door and asks how Timothy is doing.

"He'll be sporting a red signal light for a couple of days but he is going to be alright," Dirk responds.

Dirk gives Janine a big hug and kiss. Dirk sees Lulu sitting on the sofa looking at a book.

"Lulu," Dirk says. "What are you looking at?"

"Ah is a lookin' at Babs' book on baby animals agin."

Dirk winks at Janine and goes and sits next to Lulu. "Well let's just have a look-see at what interests you so much."

Dirk sits next to her and says, "Oh, it's the baby bunnies again."

Lulu sighs and says, "They are so cute."

Dirk adds, "Yes, but they grow up, they have to eat every day, their pen has to be cleaned, and if it going to be a pet you have to give it a lot of love and attention all of the time."

"That sounds okay to me," Lulu says.

Janine has her head cocked to one side smiling and admiring the conversation between the two and saying to herself, "How cute is that?"

Dirk then says, "Having a pet is a big responsibility for such a young little girl such as you."

"Ah don' think so," responds Lulu.

"We'll see what mommy has to say about that," says Dirk.

"Me!" Janine says with her mouth fully agape.

Dirk just smiles and shakes his head yes. Janine's mouth is still wide open.

"What are Babs and Edgar doing?" asks Dirk.

"They are upstairs doing whatever," Janine says.

Dirk hollers upstairs, "Kids what, are you doing?"

Babs answers back, "I am reading a book."

Edgar answers, "I am looking at the guns again."

Janine hears that and gasps, "Dirk!" she says worriedly.

"Don't worry I am going to teach him the right way soon." Dirk says with his hands up in the air then proceeds up the stairs.

Dirk sticks his head into Babs' room and says, "Hi sweetheart."

"Hi daddy!" she responds.

"Dinner should be ready real soon."

"Okay, thank you," she responds.

Dirk goes to Edgar and the gun collection. Dirk looks at Edgar and says, "Anything in particular catch your fancy?"

"They all do since I don't know a thing about any of these," Edgar says.

"Maybe next week we can get started on teaching you how to shoot and be safe. I did see a lot of deer tracks on the way to the forest. Maybe I'll teach you how to hunt and how to use cover and concealment once you become real good with the use of firearms."

"Oh daddy, I can hardly wait," says Edgar excitedly.

"We have a lot to choose from," Dirk says. "I'll start you out real small in the art of aiming, being accurate, and stretching your arm muscles to aid in that accuracy in controlling your shots. Most important, is SAFETY. I don't want you killing yourself or anyone by accident."

About that time Janine hollers that supper is ready.

"Let us eat." says Dirk. As Dirk and Edgar walk down the stairs, Dirk says, "Maybe Sunday afternoon when we get back from church we'll take out one of the firearms and give you your first lesson."

"Oh, I won't be able to sleep," Edgar says.

They all sit down to dinner. Maybelle has prepared another great feast, beef stew with biscuits, buttermilk, apple cider, and peach cobbler for dessert.

Janine says, "Just look at this food. We have never had it so good and we don't have to do anything but administrate all of this."

The kids just look at each other in bewilderment as to what the conversation is all about.

"You are right!" Dirk says. "Jensen and Maybelle, would you two please come here?"

Jensen and Maybelle arrive at the table with the most puzzled looks on their faces as do Janine and the kids.

Dirk then says, "You two have never made a bad meal or given bad service and have done everything asked of you. Each household is being paid twenty dollars a month. Your household is getting a one dollar a month raise for your excellent work."

"Thank yuh." says Jensen.

"Oh yes, thank yuh Massa Dirk and Missa Janine."

Dirk then says, "We'll be done here shortly and thank you again for the good jobs that you are doing."

Jensen and Maybelle give a slight bow and exit the room.

"Edgar," says Dirk. "Don't forget, you'll be working with Rufus barbecuing for Saturdays festivities."

"I remember," Edgar says.

They all finish their supper and relax for the rest of the day.

Friday morning at the pavilion finds everyone milling around in idle chitchat. Jefferson and Lucille are at each other's side.

Dirk looks at Harlan and says, "How are you feeling today?"

"Real good suh." responds Harlan.

Dirk then says, "Nathan, Ambrose, Marcus, Lil' Ray, and Jasper, what do we have left to do?"

Jasper responds, "All the leather is a cut inta the strips an' a; soakin' in the brine suh."

"Good, we'll start using them tomorrow. Jefferson," Dirk says.

Jefferson is in another one of his deep trance stares into Lucille's eyes and doesn't even hear his name.

"Timothy," says Dirk.

"Yes Uncle Dirk," Timothy responds.

"As soon as Jefferson and Lucille are done with their 'eye orgasms' tell him that they are all his."

Timothy smiles and says "Okay Uncle Dirk."

"Okay, the water flume crew, let's do it to it."

Dirk and the crew head to the barn.

"Harlan, you can get started with the drilling holes and screwing in the flanges for the waterlines." Dirk says. "I'll go with you for the first few to make sure all goes well. The rest of you continue on with the dropping off of the flume boards. After that we can start with the hose lines to each cabin, Timothy's place, and the big house. Also, don't forget the triangular pieces like I showed you how to cut earlier, one triangular piece for each of hose and flange units to be nailed on the lower side of the unit. Let's get started."

They all start doing their respective tasks. Harlan starts off with his drill, bits, brass screws, hammer and nails. The loaded wagon is hitched and off go Lil' Ray, Marcus, Ambrose, and Nathan. The work goes on all day, loading the wagon with flume boards and taking them out to be unloaded at the various locations and back again. Harlan is making good time with his project, drilling holes, installing the water flanges, and nailing the triangular pieces. Dirk checks on the crew to see how they are doing.

Dirk goes up to the guys and says. "You all are doing a fine job, let's quite early. We'll finish the rest of these tomorrow and Monday."

They all smile and start to head in. They get back to the living area and do as they well please.

Dirk hunts down Rufus. "Rufus, when do you want Edgar here?"

"We can start about mid mornin' wid duh fire so it can burn down to coals befo' we puts the hog on duh spit fo' a roastin'," Rufus says.

"Great, I'll have him here on time and give you a hand if need be," says Dirk.

Dirk heads for the big house. Janine gives him a big hug and kiss.

"In the morning, I'll get Edgar to the pavilion to help Rufus with the roasting of the hog and whatever else needs to be done for the evening. It has been a long hot day. I'm tired, hungry, and that's not all." Dirk says with a smile and a wink.

"Can you possibly wait till after supper and give us a chance to clean up?" Janine says.

"Well of course, dear." Dirk replies.

———

The next day, Dirk is at the pavilion early. The workers are already there.

"Mornin' Massa Dirk," some of them say.

"A good morning to all of you," responds Dirk.

They smile back at Dirk.

"We are going to a good time today with the eats and the music."

Rebecca comes up to Dirk and says, "Massa Dirk, this is all we bin' a talkin' bout' for duh las' two weeks. We all is jus' so cited' bout' today we all kin' hardly wait."

"I am too as well as Janine, we're all looking for this with great anticipation." Dirk says. "Jefferson, we are only going to work half the morning so we can get ready for this afternoon."

Jefferson replies with a big smile, "Yeh Suh Massa Dirk."

"They are all yours," says Dirk. Dirk heads for the barn. The crew is loading up the wagon again with the water flumes.

"Hi guys, looks like you have everything under control," Dirk says. "Lil' Ray, I am going to have you and Edgar give Rufus a hand with the barbequing. Since it is your homemade sauce it is only fitting that you are there to make sure that everything goes well with your recipe. Also, make sure that Edgar gets his hands in there and learns how to cook and barbeque. I want him to have some sort of skills even if it cooking over an open fire."

"We will learn him real gud suh," Lil' Ray says.

"Excellent, go ahead and drop these flumes off then knock off the rest of the day," Dirk says.

Smiles are everywhere.

"Thank yuh suh," they reply.

"I'll see you all at the party."

Dirk turns heads back to the big house to get himself and Edgar a bite to eat. Dirk goes upstairs to wake up Edgar.

"Hey big guy it's time to get up."

No movement from Edgar. Dirk stands at his feet and gives him a small tap on his foot.

"Edgar, it is time to get up."

Still no movement. Dirk grabs the sheet and pulls it off of him. Dirk stands there and finally Edgar shows some signs of life by going through the motions of trying to pull up the cover. Dirk still just stands there with his arms crossed over his chest. Edgar moans a little and turns over and barely opens his eyes then closes them again. Suddenly, Edgar screams himself awake. Edgar is fully awake now and slightly shaken at Dirk's presence standing close to him.

"Well," Dirk says, "it's not like I didn't try to wake you up already. I have something made to eat. It is time to go and help Rufus with the barbeque. I'll meet you down in the kitchen."

"Okay," Edgar says sleepily.

Edgar comes down to the kitchen in a few minutes, eats, and leaves with Dirk for the pavilion. They meet Rufus.

"Rufus," says Dirk, "He is all yours. Teach him well."

Dirk heads for the barn. Dirk gets there just as the flume crew gets back from dropping off the last load.

"Well done gentlemen. Take off the rest of the day and I'll see you later on."

"Thank yuh suh," they reply and off they go.

———

Rufus and Edgar gather hickory wood for the fire. They start with bringing in the big blocks for the main fire and stack them up next to the fire pit and then find the smaller pieces to build up before the big blocks are added.

Rufus says to Edgar, "We gots to make a small kindlin' fire to get the big wood to catch fire. Fust' thing is to get our wood ready. Afta' the kindling fire starts ta burn real good we then puts on bigger wood and then the big blocks to burn down into coals for a roastin' duh hog and later on duh chickens an' corn. Raht now we jus' sits an' waits fo' duh wood to render down inta coals. Pork meat has ta cook real gud so's none of us gets sick from eatin' red pork. Edgar, we need ta get duh hog ready for a roastin. Les' go to da barn an' git duh horse an' wagon an' to da smoke house an' git duh hog."

Edgar and Rufus muscle the hog onto the wagon and bring it to the roasting pit.

"The firs' thing we gots to do is put this heah hog on a roastin' spit."

"Spit!" says Edgar.

"Yeh, this heah rod is duh 'spit' used in a roastin' duh meat," Rufus explains.

They skewer the hog and fasten it to the roasting spit.

"Now" says Rufus, "We are a goin' ta lift the hog an' place it on duh suppots' so's we start ta roast this heah hog."

Rufus and Edgar muscle the two hundred pound hog from the wagon with the spit on each of their shoulders. Edgar strains under the weight but manages to do his part. They place the hog over the fire on the supports.

"Oh, dis is a gonna to be gud," Rufus says. "When duh fat drippins hit duh burnin' coals, it is agonna make sum' mo' flavor fo' duh smoke. Now ahm a gonna git duh sauce dat Lil' Ray made and you kin' give dis a turn every now an' den. Now we dusn' want to burn any of duh

meat so's yuh keep a gud eye on dis an' ah will be right back. Yuh goin'
ta be awraght?"

"Yeh, I think so," Edgar says.

"Ah will be right back," Rufus says.

Rufus returns in a few minutes with the barbeque sauce and some
garlic.

"Is everything goin' gud Edgar?" Rufus asks.

"Just fine Rufus." Edgar replies.

"We is agoin' to have us an extra special treat with dis heah garlic."
says Rufus. "Afta' we coats dis hog wid' duh sauce, we are a goin' ta put
pieces of dis garlic between the meat deep down inside. Go ahead an'
start coating duh hog wid' dis sauce while ah gives it a turn."

Rufus turns the spit as Edgar coats the hog with the barbeque
sauce.

"Now, ah am a goin' to the barn to get some different wood for duh
fire an ah be right back. You keep coatin' with the sauce an' turnin'
duh hog."

Edgar turns the spit and brushes on more barbeque sauce. Rufus
returns in a few minutes with an arm load of wood and lays it down
next to the other wood.

"Oh! yuh is a doin' gud Edgar," says Rufus. "That is real gud. Yo
mommy n' daddy is goin' ta be raght proud of you. You is a gonna ta be
a right proud cook. We almos' have duh perfec' bed of coals we need.
Nex' we takes dis heah knife an cut duh garlic pieces an' makes duh
cuts in duh meat for duh garlic an puts dem deep inside. When duh
hog heats an' cooks, duh garlic also heats and cooks inside an' sends it's
flava' all aroun' inside duh meat."

Rufus continues, "Nex' we takes dis fok an' jabs duh meats so's duh
sauce goes inside fo' mo' flava'. We is a gonna do dis all day long till duh
meats is ready an' duh chickens too later on when we cooks dem. We
has a gud bed of coals heah. Dis otha' wood ah jus' set down is sum'
cherry an' apple wood. We is a gonna' put some of dis wood for sum'
mo' better flava' long' wid duh hickry wood. Mos' of duh wuk is done

now. We jus' gots ta keep turnin' duh' spit, an keeps a puttin' on duh', an' jabbin' duh meat, an' make sho' dat duh meats don' burn. You is a doin' raght fine Edgar."

Rufus says, "Ah tell yah what Edgar, wha' don' yuh go git sumthin' ta eat and when yah dun' cum back an watch dis den' ah will go git sumtin' eat, okay?"

"Okay!" says Edgar.

Edgar leaves for the big house as Rufus coats the hog again and continues to turn the spit. Edgar returns within the hour to relieve Rufus so he can get a bite to eat. Edgar continues to turn the spit and coat the hog with the sauce. Rufus returns in a short time to check on things. Rufus picks up some of the apple and cherry wood and places a couple of pieces on the coals.

"Oh Edgar," says Rufus, "We is a gonna be a eatin' real gud."

They continue in idle chitchat as they turn the spit, jab the hog with the fork, and apply more of the sauce. Edgar and Rufus appear to be having more fun and laughing than anything else. As the hog turns and the sauce is applied, there is more laughing and giggling going on between the two. Dirk and Janine show up holding hands to check on things.

Dirk says, "What is so funny?"

"You two look as though you are having too much of a good time," Janine says.

"We are just telling jokes and swapping stories," Edgar says.

"Okay then, Edgar," says Dirk. "Tell me a joke."

Edgar then says, "Mommy, how far can you walk into a forest?"

Janine looks at Dirk as Dirk just shrugs his shoulders in return.

Janine then says, "As far as you want to I guess."

Rufus and Edgar smile just at each other.

Edgar then says, "Nope, you can only walk into until you reach the middle then you start walking out."

"See!" says Dirk to Janine.

"See what!" says Janine. "You weren't any help."

"You guys got us on that one," Dirk says.

"Okay Missa Janine," Rufus says. "If der' wuz a roosta' chicken a sittin' right smack dab on sah point of dat der barn roof an' da roosta' lays an egg up der, which side of dah roof wud duh egg fall on?"

Janine looks at Dirk puzzled as can be. Dirk just keeps a straight 'poker face' about him.

Janine says, "Well, I guess if the wind was blowing like it does most days here, the egg would fall on the left side since the breeze is coming from the right side."

Edgar and Rufus just smile.

Edgar says, "Mommy, roosters don't lay eggs."

Janine looks at Dirk with his wide grin and says, "Oh Dirky dear, your son is a 'wise ass'." Janine says, "Don't you guys have one for him?" Janine then points to Dirk. Rufus whispers something into Edgar's ear.

"Oh, yeah!" Edgar says. "Okay daddy, a train is going from South Carolina to North Carolina. Right on the border of the two states the train has a bad crash and some of the passengers are killed. In which state would the survivors be buried?"

"Oh, I guess South Carolina since it was coming from there."

Rufus and Edgar laugh out loud.

Rufus says, "Massa Dirk, people dusn' bury live suvivas'."

Janine smiles at Dirk, sticks her thumbs in her ears, wiggles her fingers, and gives him the 'raspberries' sound effects.

Dirk then says, "I know, I know, I just wanted to see if they knew."

Dirk closes one eye, raises the eyebrow of the other, and crinkles up his lips. Dirk just smiles and takes it all in stride. Everyone has a good laugh.

"Well, it looks as though everything is under control," Dirk says. "The hog looks real good guys and smells fine. The musicians should be arriving sometime this afternoon so we are going to go back and wait at the big house."

Dirk and Janine go hand in hand back to the big house.

"Afta' while we is agona git duh chickens an' start ta roastin' dem on dis utha' spit an' turn an' puts on duh sauce jus' likes dis hog." Rufus says. "Ah has some small coppa' pins dat ah is agoin' ta push down in dah hog meat an' dah chickens. Dis will make the cookin' fasta' deep down inside dah meat. The las' thing we duz is ta put duh con' an' sweet taters on."

"Edgar," says Rufus, "put on a couple mo' pieces of duh' apple an' cherry wood." Edgar does so. "All we has ta do now is jus' puts on duh' sauce an' turn duh spit fo' ah while."

Dirk and Janine are sitting on the verandah enjoying each other's company. Dirk is smoking a cigar and sipping whiskey while Janine is having a glass of sweet tea.

Dirk says, "You know all that wine we have upstairs?"

"Yes, " says Janine.

"Well, why don't we bring out some of those bottles for the festivities tonight? I bet they have never had a taste of wine in their lives."

"I don't see why not," replies Janine. "We have more wine than we know what to do with anyway. We'll bring down several bottles and lots of cups. They can have all day Sunday to recuperate if need be."

Babs and Lulu come outside.

"Hi guys," Dirk says.

"What have you two been up to today?" asks Janine.

Lulu says with a big sigh, "Ah jus' been a lookin' at the baby animal book agin, thas all."

Janine gives Dirk the 'eye'. Dirk notices.

Dirk looks at Babs and says, "What have you been doing?"

"Oh nothing much, just anxious for school to start that's all."

"School will be coming up in a few short weeks," Janine says.

Lulu looks up at something coming into Spanish Oaks from the main road.

"Ah wonder what that is?" Lulu says.

Dirk and Janine look up also.

"That must be the musicians," Dirk says.

Dirk, Janine, Babs, and Lulu all stand at the top of the steps when the musicians pull up in their two wagons. Dirk steps out to meet them.

"Gentlemen," Dirk says, "So glad to see you again." Dirk motions for the rest of the family to come down. "This is my wife Janine, our daughter Babs, and our other daughter Lulu. Our son Edgar is at the pavilion where you'll be playing helping and learning how to barbeque with one of our workers. I'll have Babs show to the pavilion to drop off your things and show you to the long house where you'll spend the night. I know I only talked with you a couple of weeks ago but I have forgotten your name already." Dirk says to the manager.

"Mah name is Maynard Charlebois and our music is called 'Le Zaricot'." Maynard continues in his French Creole accent. "Le Zaricot is better known in the English language as 'snap beans'."

Dirk turns to Janine and says, "I knew it was called something like that, I just couldn't remember the correct word for it."

Janine says, "Maynard and the rest of you, 'welcome'."

Dirk says, "We have quite an evening planned and we hope you all brought appetites with you. We will see you all later on. Go and get settled in for the evening."

"Okay Babs, show them the way."

Babs gets up in the first wagon and they head out to the pavilion with their gear.

Babs says, "Right over here Mr. Charlebois is the pavilion. Come on in with your things and put them up on the stage."

Rufus and Edgar are still tending the hog and just now placing the chickens on another spit for roasting.

Babs says to Maynard, "This is my brother Edgar and this is Rufus."

They exchange greetings and Edgar says 'hi'. The wagons are unloaded. Babs then takes the musicians to the long house and lets them in.

"I am going back to the big house now and we'll all see you later on." Babs says.

"Thank you Miss Babs." Maynard says as he tips his hat.

Babs arrives at the big house. The Simones have arrived. Dr. and Mrs. Holden are coming down the road.

"Good afternoon Miss Babs," Alejandro says.

"Hi Babs," Marguerite and Madeline say.

Dirk says, "Welcome."

Dirk and Alejandro shake hands. The Holdens pull in and are welcomed in similar manner. Janine and the ladies exchange pleasantries.

Janine says to Lulu, "Go over and let Timothy know that our guests have arrived."

"Okay mommy," Lulu responds.

She leaves for Timothy's. They hear another wagon pulling about that time.

Dirk says, "That must be the Websters."

The Websters arrive in short order.

"Good afternoon," Dirk says.

They all smile and shake hands.

"Let's go inside and I'll get a couple of the guys to come get the wagons and put the horses up for the evening."

"Let me show you to your rooms, then, we can relax for awhile." Janine says.

They all meet on the veranda after their bags are put up.

"Where is your son Edgar?" asks Dr. Holden.

"Edgar is in the pavilion with Rufus helping with barbequing the hog and chickens." Dirk says.

Janine says, "Let us show you around."

"Oh thank you," Christine Webster says.

Janine then says, "We are all going to have a lot of fun this evening. Good barbeque, corn on the cob, baked yams, cider, and we are even going to bring out several bottles of wine."

Dirk excuses himself to go get a couple of the guys to get the horses and wagons. Maybelle and Jensen arrive with a pitcher of sweet tea and several glasses for everyone.

"Thank you Maybelle, thank you Jensen." Janine says.

They sit at the table and sip their sweet tea and engage in conversation.

Dirk arrives back in short order with Cornelius, Andrew, and Marcus to put the horses and wagons up for the night.

"Thanks guys," Dirk says to them.

"Welcum' Massa Dirk," they say.

The guys leave for the barn with the horses and wagons. Dirk returns to the big house. Dirk has a glass of tea with everyone.

Dirk finishes his tea then says, "Who wants whiskey?"

Janine frowns at him. Alejandro smiles, Woodrow nods his head 'yes' with a big smile, and Doc Holden holds his index finger close to the thumb indicating just a small amount.

Dirk says, "I'll be right back."

He returns shortly with a bottle and four glasses.

"Gentlemen," Dirk says. "God loves us, hence 'whiskey'."

They go out to the veranda and sit down. Dirk pours each a shot.

Dirk holds his glass up and says, "To good friends and good whiskey,"

They all clink glasses in salute.

"While I have all of you here, I want to run something past you," Dirk says. "We have given all our workers their 'freedom papers, built them all new cabins, and are paying each household twenty dollars a month. Next week we are going to have running water for each cabin as well as this house and Timothy's place. They have all the food they want. Janine and treat them as family as opposed to slaves as much of the South is." Dirk continues, "Janine and I want to have Babs and Edgar to teach them how to read, write, and your basic arithmetic."

"Dirk," says Woodrow. "You can be fined and jailed for doing that."

Dr. Holden interjects, "That's right. I just heard of a plantation owner over in the next county that just had a hefty fine for that very same thing."

"Well," says Dirk, "I want to do what is right and upstanding. If we are to suffer for doing what is right then, so be it. We'll be able to get to sleep at night knowing that what we are doing is a righteous act. If any of you want to bring any of your workers over that will be fine with Janine and me in spite of the consequences. We'll let you know when we start school."

Timothy and Lulu arrive. Timothy shakes hands with everyone and goes over to Madeline and gives her a big smile, which does not go unnoticed by Alejandro, Marguerite, and Janine.

"Timothy, if you want a shot of whiskey go get yourself a glass."

"Thank you." Timothy says.

Edgar arrives and says, "Everything should be ready for eating in about thirty minutes."

Janine asks, "How does everything look?"

"Mommy, the hog and chickens smell so good I can hardly wait to eat. I am headed back now to give Rufus help in cutting up the hog and chickens. Rufus really knows how to cook and he says we should be over there real soon."

"Well then," Dirk says, "I am going to bring some of the wine my uncle had."

"He had quite the collection," Janine says,

"He was an avid connoisseur as his collection shows," Dirk says, "If you gentlemen would be so kind as to give me a hand with the wine."

They go to the wine cellar with a lantern and pick out several bottles.

"Who is a wine expert here?" asks Dirk.

Alejandro steps forward. "I know some about the wines and the characters of them."

"Please do the honors," says Dirk as he motions with his hands toward the wines.

Alejandro looks and says, "This Merlot is a good one. It has a full body, and has a 'plummy chocolaty flavor."

Dirk takes a couple of bottles.

As Alejandro scans the vast array of wines again, he then lets out an "Ah, look at all the Zinfandels. This Zinfandel has a 'robust' flavor and can stand up against any and all spiciness."

Dirk takes a couple of bottles and hands them off. Alejandro continues his mission.

Alejandro then says, "Mercy me, look at the bottles of Chianti complete in their 'fiascos'. The 'fiascos' are the straw baskets that they are packaged in." Alejandro states. "Chianti is a red Italian wine grown in the Tuscany region of Italy. Chianti is a dry wine that goes well with many different foods, like what we are having tonight,"

Alejandro scans again and finds to his excitement a 'pinot noir'.

"Pinot noir," Alejandro says with excitement. "This is a delicious, young wine with intensity."

Janine hollers from the top of the stairs, "Dirk, it's time to go."

"Be right there," responds Dirk.

Dirk takes two more bottles and up the stairs they go.

Janine says, "Looks like we better take a few glasses with us for all the wine."

They take as many glasses as they can.

As they head out the back door Janine says to Jensen and Maybelle, "We are headed over so whenever you two want come on over."

"We be along directly Missa Janine." Jensen says.

They all arrive at the pavilion and the air is filled with the fragrances of barbequed hog and chickens. Rufus and Edgar are pulling out the copper rods from the meat. The chickens are laid out on a big platter for cutting up into portions. Next, Rufus and Edgar muscle the hog, complete with an apple in its mouth, onto a canvas covered board on a nearby table. Rufus cuts into one of the hams and starts to cut the meat up into slices and stacks them on a plate. Rufus next cuts into the ribs. Then he takes a saw and cuts out the ribs sections on both sides and cuts them into manageable portions.

They then go to the chickens and start whittling them into drumsticks, thighs, breasts, and wings. The corn on the cob and the sweet potatoes are close to the coals to keep warm. There are melons of all types, tomatoes and cucumbers are being sliced up by a couple of the ladies. The apple cider is ready to go. The biscuits, butter, honey, and all the condiments are just begging for everyone to dig in. Dirk and company set the wine and glasses down on one of the tables. The pavilion fills up with hungry people.

The musicians arrive and start setting up for the evening. Georgie, Mammy Em, and Franklin walk in. They look around and see Dirk and Janine and go up and thank them for what is about to happen this evening. Franklin smiles and says thank you also. Franklin looks up at the stage where the musicians are setting up and his mouth drops open.

Mammy Em sees Franklin and asks, "What is it Franklin, yuh looks as if yuh had seed a ghost."

Franklin says, "Momma, ah thinks ah has. Ah knows everyone of those guys. Duh fiddle player teached me how ta play duh fiddle. Momma n' daddy com' an' lets talk to them."

Franklin, Georgie, and Mammy Em all approach the stage. Maynard looks over and sees Franklin. Maynard and Franklin booth have an ear to grin when they see each other. Maynard jumps down from the stage and they give each other a hug.

"Ah thought you wuz' gone fo'eva," Maynard says.

"Well, ah is, right heah," replies Franklin. "Maynard, dese is mah momma an' daddy. Dis is Maynard Charlebois and dese are the guys in duh band."

Franklin introduces each one to Georgie and Mammy Em.

Maynard says, "We is a gonna' bring dis here house down tonight an Franklin, you is a gonna' hep' do it."

From out of the crowd a loud booming voice yells, "Chow Time."

Janine looks at Dirk and says, "Dirk, do you have to call it chow?"

"Well, what do you want me to call it grits, grease, grub, gedunk, shit on a shingle, ptomaine? A hungry empty stomach doesn't care much what it is called. But," Dirk continues, "Since I love you better, you are the love of my life and my life's mission is to make you happy how is this?" Dirk clears his throat, and says in a loud voice, "Ladies and gentlemen, may I have your attention please, let us partake in this evening's nourishment and may you find it most pleasing to your palates."

Janine looks over at Christine, Marguerite, Ruth and says, "One extreme to the other and I had to say, 'I Do' to the preacher. I just hope he doesn't run out of whiskey."

Janine looks over at Dirk with her hands on her hips and yells, "And you don't love me better."

The ladies commence to laugh out loud. Every one of the workers, musicians, Jensen, Maybelle, and invited guests line up and fill their plates. Lucille is holding two plates while Jefferson is placing the food on their plates. They are inseparable as they have been for quite some time. A lot of the workers are a little apprehensive of some of the invited guests but are polite and congenial just the same. Everybody eats and has a good time.

Edgar goes over to Dirk and Janine, "Mommy, daddy, I am going to eat with Rufus and Wanda."

"Have fun," says Dirk.

Babs and Lulu are eating with little Willie and Lil' Ray. Franklin, Maynard, Georgie, Mammy Em, and the musicians are all together eating. There is a lot of talking going on amongst every one and all seem to be having a good time. Jefferson and Lucille are taking turns feeding each other bites of food. Janine elbows Dirk and motions toward Jefferson and Lucille. Dirk smiles and looks back at Janine. The Simones, Holdens, and the Websters are all enjoying their feast.

Woodrow looks up at Dirk and Janine then says, "You two have outdone yourselves."

"Yes indeed says." Christine adds.

Timothy and Madeline are off by themselves having polite conversation while they are eating. Alejandro nudges Marguerite and motions toward Timothy and Madeline. Marguerite just smiles at Alejandro as he smiles back.

Dirk leans backs and says, "I am so full I'm getting stretch marks."

Janine looks over at him and says, "It is nice to have company," as she pats her stomach.

They all spend some relaxing. Some are still eating their corn on the cob, ribs, ham, melons and anything else that isn't nailed down. The workers have never been so happy and content in all their lives, except for Georgie and Mammy Em's delight at Franklin's return. Wanda and a couple of the other ladies start to clean things up. Soon everyone is helping in the cleanup process.

Dirk says, "Any leftover food, divide it up and take it home with you."

The place is cleaned up in no time at all.

Dirk goes over to Maynard and says, "The rest of the evening belongs to you. Go ahead and take it away."

Maynard takes the stage and says, "Ah don' bout' y'all, but this child is full an' can hardly move. Ah don' member' the las' time ah et' that gud. Gud evnin' ta y'all."

Good evenings are returned.

"Ma' name is Maynard Charlebois an' we is the 'Snap Beans' from Southwest Louisiana close to Texas. Our LaLa music is called Le Zaricot. An' thas not all, we is a gonna' dance an' bring this heah house down ta night. But firs', we needs ta tell sum' of our musical instruments dat we plays. One of the main instruments that we use is the squeeze box accordion, we got that idea from some German folks a few years back. Our Acadian friends, better known as 'Cajuns' also use this."

Maynard looks at the accordion player and says, "Give 'em a taste."

The accordion player gives them a few bars of playing. Everyone gasps in awe.

Maynard continues, "We also use this heah drum. Our drummer borrowed this from a soldier boy quite some time ago when he wasn't looking."

Maynard looks at him and says, "Given 'em a taste."

The drummer gives out a rendition that has everyone smiling.

"This next piece we call the 'frottoir' or better known as the 'scrub board'. Give a smell."

He takes a couple of spoons and gives a quick rendition. The crowd is all smiles.

"Our Cajun brothers also use the fiddle" Maynard says. "Give 'em a hint."

The fiddle player shows them what he has.

"Later on, we are a gonna' have Franklin up heah playing also. Franklin wuz' learned how to play cuz he had a gud teacher, me." Maynard points to himself. "The las' two things that we an' our Cajun use are the guitar an' the 'la ti' fer' or the triangle. Give them sum honey in the ears."

The guitar player and the triangle player give them an earful.

"Now, we are agonna play sum 'lala Le Zaricot and' bring this house down."

The band starts to play. Everyone starts to dance in any which way they can. The band sings in their native Creole/ French. No one understands the words but they do understand good music and cannot keep still. The band plays song after song after song. There isn't one still body in the pavilion. Everyone dances and has a good time. Dirk, Janine, Timothy, Madeline, Edgar, and Lulu are all dancing with each other. Baba and little Willie are out there giving it their best. Dr. Holden and Ruth are swaying back and forth. Alejandro and Marguerite are dancing in the back. Georgie, Mammy Em, Jenson and Maybelle are out there keeping up with the best of them. Jefferson and Lucille never miss a song. Andrew, Cornelius, Lil' Ray, Ambrose, Nathan and Marcus are all out dancing. After about forty-five minutes of non-stop play the band stops.

Maynard says, "We be a needin' a short pause bout' raght now."

Everyone claps and gives out a their 'hoots and hollers' in appreciation.

Maynard says, "When we come back, we are a gonna' have Franklin come up a play a spell with us."

Franklin smiles at everyone. Everyone is sweating and huffing and puffing from the workout.

Dirk and Alejandro open up the wine bottles and pour a few glasses from each bottle. Wanda, Rebecca, Beulah, and Molly all show up for a taste of wine.

Dirk says, "Well ladies, are you having a good time to night?"

Wanda says, "Massa Dirk we have neva' had such a gud time as now."

"Thas raght Massa Dirk," say the rest of them.

Dirk and Alejandro smile.

Alejandro says, "Marguerite, Madeline, and I are also enjoying ourselves."

Dirk says, "Let Alejandro tell you some about this wine, then decide which one you want."

"This first wine is called, 'Merlot'. Merlot has a full body and a plumy chocolaty flavor."

"Ah'l have some of dat," Rebecca says.

Alejandro goes to the next bottle and says, "This is a Zinfandel. Zinfandel is robust and has a spicyness to it."

Beulah says, "Dat wun is fo' me."

"This next wine is called 'Chianti'. Chianti goes good with anything."

"Ah'l have dat wun," says Molly.

"This last one is a "Pinot Noir," Alejandro says. "Pinot Noir is deliciously young with an intense flavor."

Wanda says, "Ah'l be raght back."

Wanda leaves the pavilion and returns shortly with a cup of something. Wanda joins up with Rebecca, Beulah, and Molly. They are sitting conversing outside the pavilion in the night air.

Rebecca says, "Yah knows sumthin', mah Jasper is like dis heah Merlot wine, full body and chocolaty," as she smacks her lips.

"An' yah knows sumthin' else," says Beulah "Mah Caesar is lak dis heah Zinfandel wine, cuz he is so spicy and robust." Beulah takes her tongue and wipes her lips.

Molly then says, "Well' mah Zachary is lak dis Chianti wine cuz he goes gud wid' anything ah got," as a chill runs up her spine.

The three all look over at Wanda.

"Well!" says Rebecca. "What is Rufus lak?"

Wanda takes a sip from her cup and says, "Mah Rufus is lak dis heah 'Red Eye' cuz when he dun to dah wee hours of duh monin', his eye balls is all blood shot an' red."

Molly looks at Wanda and says, "You fool, don' yuh know dat 'Red Eye' is not wine, it is a hard lika."

Wanda's eyes roll back in her head as she leans back against the pavilion wall and says, "Dats raght, my Rufus is a hard lika," as she lets out a long sigh.

"Gud lawd girl!" Rebecca says.

Beulah says, "Dat Rufus been hangin' roun' too many whaht foks."

Molly chimes in and says, "Can ah borrow Rufus for a bit?"

Rebecca says, "Ah wants him afta her."

"Y'all jus' stay away frum mah Rufus," Wanda says.

The band is back on stage ready to play again.

Maynard says, "Awraght, how'd y'all like dat music?"

Cheers and whistling resounded through the night air.

"We ain't dun' yet, the night is still early. Franklin, cum' on up heah wid' yo' fiddle."

Franklin goes up on stage with fiddle in hand with the rest of the group. The band starts playing again with Franklin in the lead and the rest of the band following his lead. Dirk and Janine are dancing with each other as are Alejandro and Marguerite. Everyone is on the floor dancing. Woodrow and Christine are keeping up with the best of them. Georgie and Mammy Em are keeping in tune with the music and so proud of their son Franklin. Edgar is dancing with one of the worker's daughters. The accordion, scrub board, fiddles, triangle, and drum are all in sync. Jefferson and Lucille haven't missed a step since the music started. They appear to be as one person.

At the end of that song Maynard says, "All right y'all, we are going to change the pace just a bit. Our next song is going to be a slow waltz. Looks like y'all need a break from the lively ones."

The band strikes up a waltz. They all dance close and slow. Dr. Holden and Ruth are out on the floor dancing. Jensen and Maybelle are out the floor dancing. Everyone is having the time of their lives.

Janine says to Dirk, "Let's sit this one out and watch for awhile."

"Good idea," Dirk says in agreement. "I'll get you a cup of wine and something for myself."

"Gee, I wonder what you are going to have," Janine says sarcastically.

Dirk turns around and says, "The music is too loud, I can't hear you."

He returns with the wine and a shot of whiskey. As Dirk and Janine sip their drinks and observe, they notice Timothy and Madeline slow dancing. Another slow waltz is playing. Some are drinking cider, some are drinking wine, all in all, everyone is having a good time. Dirk and Janine hold each other close and just smile at each other with a sense of accomplishment and pride at what they have done in the lives they have affected. Timothy and Madeline walk by hand in hand. Timothy just smiles as they walk by. They do not go unnoticed by Alejandro and Marguerite.

Marguerite looks and smiles up at Alejandro then gives him a hug and says, "Our baby girl is growing up."

"We better get used to it," Alejandro says.

"We better get used to changes also," adds Marguerite.

"I'm afraid so," replies Alejandro.

Dirk and Janine are listening to the variety of songs and music. Jefferson and Lucille come up to them.

"Are you two having a good time?" Dirk asks.

"Oh yeh suh Massa Dirk and Missa Janine," Lucille replies.

Jefferson clears his throat and says, "Ah wants ta marry Lucille and be her husband."

Lucille looks stunned and just stands there with hand covering her partially open mouth and her eyes start to tear up. Janine looks at Dirk and Dirk looks back at Janine.

Dirk then says to Jefferson, "Does Lucille know that?"

Janine says, "I think she does now."

"Do you really want to marry her and be her husband?" asks Dirk.

"Yeh suh Massa Dirk, ah duz'" Jefferson says.

"Okay then, after the next song, you can get up on stage and ask her so everyone can enjoy your happiness along with you."

"That is different." says Janine.

"Come on!" Dirk says. "Let's get up there."

Dirk and Jefferson go up to the stage. Dirk motions to Maynard that he has to say something. The music stops and everyone turns toward the stage to see what is going on. Jefferson goes up on the stage as everyone looks in bewilderment. Jefferson takes center stage and again clears his throat.

Jefferson looks at Lucille and says "Lucille, Ah loves you and have for quite some time. Ah wants ta be your husband an' ah wants yuh ta be mah wife. Lucille, will you marry me?"

Lucille covers her face in uncontrollable crying and blubbering as the tears roll down her face.

Janine goes over to Lucille and puts her arm around her and says, "If you want to marry him now is the time to let him know."

Lucille looks up at Jefferson still crying like a baby and says, "Yeh Jefferson, as many stars as there is in duh night sky 'yeh'. Ah wants ta be yuh wife."

Maynard says, "The entire band congratulates the newly engaged couple and this is a real gud time to take another break."

Jefferson hops down from the stage to be with Lucille who is still crying. Jefferson goes over to her and kisses her tears as they roll down her face. Then they give each other a deep embrace. Dirk and Janine give Lucille a hug and Dirk shakes Jefferson's hand. The women all gather around Lucille.

Wanda says to Lucille, "We be a needin' ta talk real soon."

The men folk all pat Jefferson on the back. Timothy and Madeline are all smiles.

Dirk says to Janine, "Let's get some wine for them and we'll make a toast to them."

"Good idea," Janine says.

They both get some wine and bring back to Jefferson and Lucille.

Dirk then says to everyone, "Folks, a toast to the bride and groom to be."

Lucille starts in on her crying again. Those that have cups raise them in their honor and drink. Lucille takes a drink and doesn't know what to think of the new taste as her facial expression indicates. Everyone is mulling around and Jefferson and Lucille are still being honored in their upcoming union. Dirk and Janine go over to Woodrow and Christine.

"Well, are you two having a good time?" Janine asks.

"Dirk, Janine, we don't know when we had this much fun," Christine says, "We can't thank you enough."

Dirk says, "You two having a good time is thanks enough."

"The food is the best and our compliments to your son and Rufus. They really know how to barbeque," Woodrow says.

"The music," Christine adds, "Where did you come up these musicians, they are wonderful. We love it."

"I ran across this type of music when I was in one of my port o' calls in New Orleans a few years back when I was in the Marine Corps. We had several days to kill so a few of us took a stage west not knowing where we'd end up. We stopped somewhere just east of Texas." Dirk continues, "I think the name of the place was 'Charles Town', named after some French landowners there. We went into a saloon and a group of these musicians were playing. We were the only white people in the saloon, but they didn't seem to care much and paid us no never mind. We really liked the music and did our best not to look too obvious that we wanted to dance. We all had a few drinks and a bite to eat. The band took a break and the lead musician came over to talk with me. I could hardly understand him with his Creole/French accent. He said not too many white folks come in here. I replied, they don't know what they are missing and this kind of food is excellent."

Dirk continues, "I asked him what is this here stew-looking soup called that we are eating. Gumbo, he said. He said it had shrimp, crawfish, chicken, rice, okra, and I don't for sure what else. We ate and listened to some more music. We pooled our pocket change together and managed to scrape up a couple of dollars, which we laid up on the stage at their feet. The leader smiled from ear to ear as we tipped our hats to the band."

"That is quite a story," Woodrow says.

"Yes indeed, most interesting," Christine adds. "Well it looks like they are ready to start playing again."

"I think this will probably be it for the night, so enjoy your selves."

"Oh we are," they say.

Dirk goes on to see Timothy and Madeline.

"You two haven't missed a step yet," Dirk says.

"Uncle Dirk, I don't ever remember having this much fun and good eats to boot."

"Yes Mr. Kahane," says Madeline. "I would really like to thank you for this evening."

"Madeline, please call me Dirk. I'm happy that you are having a good time. I believe they are going to wind things up pretty quick, so get in as much dancing as you can."

Dirk tips his hat to them and departs.

"Georgie and Mammy Em, how are you enjoying this evening?" Dirk asks.

"Massa Dirk, we is ahavin' duh bes' tam'. We really enjoy duh music."

Janine shows up at Dirks side.

"Missa Janine, how is you an' yuh new life inside a doin'?"

"I've been feeling real good," Janine responds.

Mammy Em lays her hand on Janine's stomach. Janine smiles as she is being touched. Janine does not see the tear in Mammy Em's eyes. Mammy Em kisses Janine's stomach.

"Take cares of yuh sef Missa Janine," Mammy Em says.

"Oh, I am doing just fine. Thank you, Mammy Em."

Dirk and Janine get in a quick dance. Jefferson and Lucille are at peace with the world. Dirk and Janine go up to the kids. They are all standing together by the apple cider.

"You guys doing alright?" asks Dirk.

"Oh! Hi daddy," Babs says.

"Well it looks as though you all are having a good time."

"Lulu, are you having a good time?" Janine asks.

"Yeh ah is mommy," Lulu says.

Benjamin and Gabooti come up for a drink of apple cider.

Janine asks, "How are you two doing?"

"We is a doin' jus' fan' Missa Janine."

"Have you both had enough food to eat and cider to drink?"

Benjamin says, "Yeh Missa Janine," as he smiles from ear to ear.

Just then, the music stops. Maynard announces, "This does it for y'all tonight. We had us a good time, good eats, and good drinks. We all heah wants ta thank each an' every one of yuh y'all for havin' us heah this evening. Congratulations agin ta Jefferson and Lucille."

Lucille lays her head on Jefferson's shoulder as she smiles.

"Y'all have a good evenin'."

Dirk and Janine gather up the kids, find their overnight guests and head for the big house. They get to the big house all tired from the evening's festivities. Timothy is with Madeline, Alejandro, and Marguerite.

"Tomorrow is church. We'll have us a nice breakfast and be on our way." Dirk says. "See you all in the morning."

———

The morning arrives and they all straggle down with their bags to the breakfast table. They all have coffee.

"Edgar," Dirk says, "Would you please go and get a couple of the guys to bring the wagons up here?"

Edgar leaves for the workers' area. Jensen and Maybelle deliver a big breakfast. They are all talking about the events of the previous evening and the good time they all had. Edgar, Ambrose, Cornelius, and Nathan show up with the wagons and horses in short order. Dirk excuses himself and goes outside and thanks the guys for bringing the horses and wagons. Edgar comes in and has a bite to eat. Soon they all pack up the wagons and 'wagon train' it on in to church.

Timothy rides with the Simones. They arrive at church in about thirty minutes. Dirk removes the Derringer from his coat pocket and puts under the seat. They all head towards the church. Dirk and Janine say hello to the 'gossip' lady. Janine points out to Dirk that there is Roscoe and Martha.

Dirk turns to Edgar and says, "Go in and save Mommy and me a couple of seats and we'll be right in."

"Okay Daddy," Edgar responds.

"Good mornin', Mr. and Mrs. Kahane," Roscoe says as they approach them.

"How are the Bells this morning?" Dirk asks.

Janine gives Martha a hug.

"We are a doin' jus' fan suh," Roscoe says.

Janine says, "Next time you come to our place, we have a couple that want to be married."

"Oh! how wonderful," Martha says as she clasps her hands to her breasts and smiles.

"Who is the couple?" asks Roscoe.

"Jefferson, our foreman and Lucille," says Dirk.

"They were the young couple that were sitting together on your last trip," Janine says.

"I do recall a very attractive and beautiful young thing in the congregation when we were there."

Martha puts her hands on her hips and looks sternly into Roscoe's eyes as her foot taps on the ground and says, "Well, did you manage to recall anything else Pastor?"

"An attractive and beautiful young thing in the 'Eyes of the Lawd'," Roscoe says with a wide 'ear to ear' grin as he looks at Martha and blinks his eyes rapidly several times.

Martha looks at him and says, "Well, you'll be a sleepin' with the Lawd' tonight." As she snaps her shoulders away and looks in the other direction.

Roscoe says, "I'll have a counseling session with the couple nex' time we are out there." Roscoe whispers in Dirk's ear, "everything will be jus' fan' with Martha an' me."

"Okay then, we'll talk with again when you come to our place," Janine says.

"We'll see you in a couple of weeks," Dirk says.

They head on into church. Dirk and Janine snicker at Roscoe's predicament. They sit down next to the kids as Pastor Merle and wife Joyce are making their rounds greeting everyone in the congregation.

Pastor Merle says to Dirk, "One of these days we'll have to talk about our exploits in Mexico."

Dirk responds, "I'm sure that we both have some interesting tales from that place. Some I would just as soon forget."

"I understand fully," Pastor Merle responds. "Well, we need to get the service started."

They shake hands and the pastor goes to the pulpit. Joyce takes a seat in one of the pews. They sing some hymns and listen to the sermon. The 'gossip ladies' are whispering to themselves. Lulu is fast asleep in Janine's lap. Dirk is finding it hard to stay awake. Janine elbows him to keep him from snoring. Finally the service is over. Everyone exits the church and mulls around outside for awhile prior to heading home.

Timothy and the Simones arrive. They all bid each other farewell. Dr. Holden and Ruth say goodbye and thank them again for Saturday night. Woodrow and Christine say their goodbyes. The gossip ladies are never in need of a subject.

Dirk and Janine wave goodbye to Roscoe and Martha who are just finishing up with their service under the tree. They all head home.

Dirk and Janine want to spend the rest of the day relaxing. They all have a quick bite to eat.

Edgar asks, "Can we go swimming?"

Janine looks at Dirk and Dirk looks at Edgar and says, "Have fun and watch after your sisters."

"Okay Daddy," responds Edgar.

He looks at Babs and Lulu and says, "Let's go."

They race upstairs to get their swimming clothes on. The kids race back downstairs and are out the door.

Janine says to Dirk, "Let's take a nap."

Dirk smiles back and says, "In due time," again with a big smile.

Janine says back, "I am getting bigger each day now and there is a lot of activity going on inside me."

"I promise not to hurt anyone," responds Dirk.

Dirk takes hold of Janine's hand and leads her upstairs.

———

The kids are walking through the workers cabin area. They pass by all the flume boards and cedar logs. They get to the swimming hole a few minutes later. Cornelius, Andrew, and little Willie are already there swimming and having a good time.

"Lulu" says Babs, "Do you remember everything we taught you and how to swim from last time?"

Lulu just looks at Babs and jumps in the water without any hesitation.

Andrew looks at Cornelius and says, "Did you see that?"

Edgar says, "We have enough for two teams to knock each other off in the water."

Willy gets up on Edgar's back and Cornelius on Andrew's.

"Let the games begin," Edgar says.

They push and shove each other. Cornelius throws Edgar off Willie's shoulders into the water. Cornelius pounds his chest in victory.

"Okay Willie, you get on my shoulders," Edgar says. "Just because Cornelius is bigger don't mean nothing other than he is going to make a bigger splash."

"Okay, les' git 'em," Willie says.

They go at it laughing all the way. Willie grabs Cornelius's foot and throws him off Andrew's shoulders.

"I didn't know we could do that," says Edgar.

"We can do anything we want," Willie says.

Babs and Lulu enjoy watching the boys play and laugh at them. Lulu swims like she was a fish. Soon, they all get out of the water and rest on the side of the swimming hole. They rest a little longer and jump back in the water. They all play, splashing and flailing the water at each other. It starts to get late, so they all head back.

When they are about halfway back, they see Dirk and Janine hand in hand, out for a walk.

"How is everyone doing?" Janine asks.

"Real gud suh," Andrew says. "We had a good time playing horse and rider."

"We all got thrown in duh' wata' Massa Dirk," Cornelius says. "Yeh', an' Willie cheats."

Willie looks at him and says, "Duh' rules are dat der' are no rules."

Dirk and Janine laugh. As they are walking Dirk notices how good the cotton crop is coming along and knows that the harvest will be real soon and no time for rest. They walk into the living quarters of the workers and say their hellos. Franklin is on the porch of his cabin playing the fiddle. Dirk and Janine nod and wave. Franklin smiles back as he plays. Edgar sees Rufus tending to the livestock.

"Daddy," says Edgar. "Can I have Rufus teach me how to ride a horse?"

Dirk looks at Edgar and says, "You need to learn sometime and now is as good a time as any."

Janine says, "Edgar, please be careful!"

"I will mommy."

Janine looks at Dirk and says, "Oh, I do worry about him so much and the things that he wants to do."

"He'll be just fine. He should have learned a long time ago how to ride properly. I was never in the mounted cavalry so I wouldn't be as good a teacher as Rufus who is with the horses every day. But, I can teach him how to shoot, how to protect himself, how to survive, and several other skills I have learned over the years that would be most beneficial to him and those around him."

Janine says, "I've seen some of those skills first hand I believe."

They all get back to the big house and fix something to eat and save a plate for Edgar.

XVII

≈

$\mathbf{D}$irk is at the pavilion as the hands are mulling about readying for the day's work.

Dirk calls Jefferson over and says, "Janine and I spoke with Pastor Roscoe yesterday at church. He is going to want to a have a talk with you and Lucille concerning your wanting to get married."

Jefferson smiles and says with a wide grin, "Oh thank yuh Massa Dirk, I'll tell Lucille."

Jefferson goes off to find Lucille.

"Caesar," Dirk says. "I'll be wanting you with the water flume crew from now till it gets done. Go ahead and get the guys and we'll meet in the barn."

A high pitched squeal echoes through the pavilion. Everyone looks in that direction. It is Lucille hugging Jefferson as she jumps up and down with excitement. All are smiling. Jefferson returns to Dirk all smiles. Dirk is also smiling when Jefferson returns.

Dirk says, "I am taking Jasper and the water flume crew today and till the project is finished."

Timothy shows up wiping the sleep out of his eyes.

"Go with Jefferson," Dirk says. "Jefferson, take over."

Dirk, Jasper, and the water flume crew head for the barn.

"Caesar, take Nathan, the triangular wooden pooling pieces, the hand drill, flanges, pipe adapters, leather for the flange gaskets, and load them in the wagon. Marcus and Ambrose, load up the leather strips that are in the barrel into the wagon. Lil' Ray and Marcus, get the ladders, gloves, and pliers and let's get going."

They load up and off they go.

Dirk says, "Jasper, you and Nathan nail in the pooling units, finish the drilling and mount the flanges with gaskets at each cabin spot and about five evenly spaced locations between here and the waterfall. We are going to the waterfall and will work ourselves backwards with the log tripods and the laying of the flume boards. We'll see you guys at supper time."

Dirk and the guys arrive at the waterfall.

Dirk says, "Lay the three logs side by side."

With the logs laying side by side, Dirk takes one of the leather strips and makes two wraps around the logs and between each log a couple of turns tying the logs together. Then the logs are set upright and made into a 'tripod'.

"Lil' Ray, Marcus, take the first flume board up and lay one end down about this far from the water."

As they take the flume boards up, Dirk and Nathan set the ladder up and position the tripod logs. Lil' Ray and Marcus set the first flume boards down and Nathan holds the end up as Dirk puts the tripod under the end.

"Come on down," Dirk says to Lil' Ray and Marcus. "Let's do the next one now."

They move the other ladder into position. The logs are tied together with the brine soaked leather strips and moved into their position. The flume boards are moved so that the first flume will flow into the second flume board. The second tripod supports the second flume board. They then move into the third set of flume boards and tripod and set it up. Things move rapidly just like clockwork. By the time suppertime arrives, they are about one fourth of the way towards the cabins. Caesar and Nathan are making good time also with the nailing of the pooling units, flanges and gaskets. By the time supper arrives they are making faster progress than Dirk had ever expected.

Dirk and crew head back to get something to eat. They meet Jasper and Nathan in the cabin area. They too are making great progress on their project.

Dirk says to everyone, "See after supper."

As Dirk heads for the Big House he sees Edgar riding the stallion Beau, with Rufus pointing and talking to Edgar.

Rufus says to Dirk, "Massa Dirk, Edgar heah is a boan rider. Jus' look at him go an' he jus' got on his firs' horse yestaday'."

Edgar is riding like a natural horseman as if he were born in the saddle. Edgar stops, starts, and makes the horse do quick turns and maneuvers.

"Please watch over him real good," Dirk says.

"Ah will Massa Dirk," Rufus replies.

Edgar sees Dirk and gallops over to him.

Edgar smiles and says, "Did you see me riding?"

"I sure did and you look like you were made to ride," Dirk smiles. "Rufus says that you are doing real good. You pay close attention to Rufus now. I'm going to go eat now and you be real careful."

"I will daddy." responds Edgar. "Watch this!"

Edgar dismounts and walks away from Beau to the other side of the corral. He turns and makes a whistling sound that a cricket would make. Beau runs over to Edgar and nuzzles his head into Edgar's chest. Edgar gives him a hug around his neck.

"Very impressive," Dirk says as he claps his hands in approval. "I'll see you at the big house."

Dirk gets to the big house and tells Janine all about Edgar and his activities. Janine just wrings her hands together in fear for her child and danger. Lulu comes in again with Babs' book on baby animals and sits at the table with Dirk and Janine. Lulu looks at the book and then looks up at Dirk and Janine and just gives out a big sigh.

Janine looks at Dirk and says, "Hint taken."

"We are making record time with the water flume project," Dirk says to Janine. "By the end of the week we should all have running water here."

They enjoy lunch and Dirk is off to the water flume project again. Dirk passes by the corral where Edgar is still riding. Rufus is there eating his noon meal as he watches Edgar. Edgar waves at Dirk as he passes by and Dirk waves back.

Everyone is ready to go to their assigned tasks. Timothy and Jefferson are ready for the fields. Dirk and crew set off for their project. Caesar and Nathan are back at theirs. Dirk and crew secure the logs together and set them up into a tripod. The ladder is set up and the water flume boards are set in place. They move on to the next and repeat the procedure again. They continue the process throughout the rest of the afternoon.

"Let's call it a day," Dirk says to everyone.

When they get back to the living quarters they see Caesar and Nathan hard at it. They are just about all through the cabins and just have Georgie and Mammy Em's place left to do.

"Very impressive work you two are doing!" Dirk says to Caesar. "We are just about at the halfway point. A few water stations between here and the falls and then we'll be ready for the water. See you all tomorrow. Ambrose, how about you and Marcus take the wagon and horse back to the barn?"

Dirk walks back to the big house and sees Edgar still on the horse.

"Did you eat anything today?" Dirk asks.

"No, I was too busy with Beau here. Watch this," Edgar says.

Edgar gets to one end of the corral and takes the reins and slaps the horse on the rump. Beau takes off running at full speed to the other end of the corral. Dirk grimaces as Edgar and Beau near the end of the corral. About twenty feet from the end, Edgar pulls back on the reins and Beau digs his rear legs into the dirt as the horse's rear end almost scrapes the dirt stopping. Dirk grabs his chest in relief that he is stopped in time.

Rufus comes over to Dirk and shakes his head and says, "Edgar is a learnin' so fas', ah can barely keeps up wid' him."

"That kid is going to make me age before I'm supposed to," Dirk says.

Rufus adds, "Edgar is a doin' so good, ah think dat he could start ta teach me a few things. Dat horse Beaudandy has choosed Edgar, Edgar didn' chose him."

Dirk just smiles. "Have him take care of the horse for the night and send him to the big house so we can take the rest of the day off."

Dirk gets to the big house where Janine greets him with a big hug and kiss. They all sit at the table for dinner. Jensen brings them their dinner.

"Thank you Jensen," Janine says.

Edgar shows up in a few minutes.

Edgar says, "Mommy, you should see me riding Beau. I'm really doing good aren't I daddy?"

"That you are," Dirk says.

Edgar continues excitedly, "Mommy, Daddy, I really love that horse."

Janine looks at him and says, "Having a horse is a big responsibility."

Dirk adds, "You have to make sure that he is fed properly, combed and brushed. Also from what I have noticed, he is going to require a lot of love and affection from you."

"I already am doing that," Edgar says.

Dirk looks at Edgar and says, "Okay then, Beaudandy now belongs to you."

Edgar's mouth drops wide open and tears well up in his eyes and roll down his face.

"Just like mommy said, you have a big responsibility and I want you to learn as much as you can from Rufus, he is still your teacher. Bring Beau a treat every day to eat. Something like a carrot, an apple, or a honey ball rolled in oats."

Edgar's mouth is still open and he just nods his head 'yes'.

Babs says, "When can I ride him?"

"Me too," Lulu says.

"You'll all get a chance, I'm sure." Dirk says.

Janine looks at Babs and says, "School will starting in a couple of weeks and you two will be riding him to school every day."

Jensen asks, "Will there be anything else this evening?"

"We're fine, thank you Jensen."

Jensen gives Edgar a pat on the head and smiles at him. .

———

The next day finds everyone at their assigned tasks. Dirk and the water flume crew start in where they left off the previous day. They tie the cedar logs together, set them up, and position the flume boards in place. They move on to the next ones and do the same. This continues on throughout the morning and on into to the afternoon after they eat. They meet Caesar and Nathan who are making good time with the flanges and adapters.

"We are going to be done in another day I believe." Dirk says.

———

The next day they set up in the living quarters and install the lines on the flange adapters. They make their way past the barn to the big house and on to Timothy's house. Dirk has them take the small tree ends and make smaller tripods to support the lines coming off the flume with the lines lashed to a horizontal piece for elevated support. The end of the lines are brought to the front of each cabin, the barn, the pavilion, and fastened to the outside wall; then a valve is installed. This is done on the big house and Timothy's also.

"You all have done a great job," Dirk says to everyone. "Tomorrow is Saturday and we are all going to sit in the pavilion making canvas and cotton jackets to wrap each one of the lines coming off the flume. If we don't, all we'll have is hot water in the summer and icy cold water, if not frozen, in the winter. Lil' Ray, Ambrose, Marcus, and Nathan, you guys bring the glue and all the other things that are needed. Caesar, you and Harlan make sure that we have some sharpened knives and straight edges for cutting. Pastor Roscoe and Martha will be here tomorrow so we don't want to make too big a mess that will take a long time to clean up. See you in the morning."

Dirk arrives at the big house. He sees Janine at the table with payroll book.

"Is it payday already?"

"I just about have everything ready to go for the morning." Janine responds.

XVIII

～

Saturday morning in the pavilion finds everyone there for the morning's work.

"Jefferson," Dirk says, "short workday, Pastor Roscoe and Martha will be here."

Lucille smiles with a toothy grin and looks lovingly at Jefferson.

"Today is payday for all of you, so we need to get in early."

"Yeh suh, Massa Dirk, we'll all be in early."

Caesar and the crew are busy bringing in the materials for the waterline coverings. Timothy, Jefferson, and crew head for the fields.

"Okay," Dirk says, "I need to think on this before we get started. We have one inch waterlines and we'll need at least one inch of cotton surrounding each line. With the outside diameter of each line and the surrounding cotton that is going to make each line roughly ten inches around. We'll need an overlap to glue the canvas closed. So, we are going to cut the canvas in fourteen inch widths. Caesar, roll out the canvas on one of the benches."

With the canvas rolled out, Dirk measures a fourteen inch wide mark several times down the length of the material. He then takes the straight edge and makes a line to each mark. The piece of canvas is cut off at a twelve foot length. Dirk then measures four inches in from edge and makes marks down the twelve foot length.

"Harlan and Ambrose, you two start spreading the glue on the entire piece but don't go over this line. Marcus and Lil' Ray, you two start laying down the cotton about this thick on the wet glue."

Dirk says to Caesar, "You and Nathan start cutting the canvas just like I did."

They are all hard at it. Dirk sits back and observes their work.

"I am going out into the fields and I'll be back to check on you before I go to the big house to help with the payroll."

Dirk sets off for the fields. He notices Lucille, Benjamin, and Gabooti setting things up for breaks. Dirk meets up with Timothy and Jefferson.

"It seems as though it has been a long time since I've been out here with all the projects going on."

"Massa Dirk," Jefferson says, "Duh cotton harvus' is a comin' on fast and we has a lot of cotton to pick an' bale."

"When it comes, you get to run the harvest," Dirk says. "Timothy and I know nothing about that. Just let us know what you need. I'll see you guys later on at the pavilion."

Dirk heads on over to where Lucille, Benjamin, and Gabooti are.

"Good morning, how is everything today?" Dirk says.

"Mornin' Massa Dirk," Lucille says.

"How are you two guys doing today?"

"We all is a doin' fin suh."

"Benjamin, let me fix your hat," says Dirk.

Dirk takes Benjamin's hat and pulls it over his eyes.

"Ah can' see nuthin' now." Benjamin says as he rights his hat with a big smile.

Lucille and Gabooti laugh as they point their fingers at Benjamin. The first group of workers comes in from the field for a bite to eat and drink.

"How are we all doing this morning?" Dirk asks.

"Jus' fin' suh," one of them replies.

"Well, we have a short day today. We have to get all of you paid and Pastor Roscoe and Martha will be here later on."

Dirk goes back to the pavilion to check on the flume crew. He gets about halfway there and up rides Edgar on Beau.

"Hi, what's up?" asks Dirk as he pets and strokes Beau. "Did you give Beau a treat this morning?"

"I sure did, I gave him a big red apple." Edgar answers back. "He sure did like it."

"Yes, horses love apples." Dirk says as he continues to pat Beau on the neck. "You take good care of him and he'll take care of you. I need to go get mommy so that we can get everyone paid today."

Dirk gives Beau one more pat and leaves. Edgar continues his ride. Dirk arrives at the big house as Janine is just finishing up the final preparations for the payroll disbursements.

"I am ready anytime you are," Janine says.

"Okay, I'm going upstairs and I'll be right down."

Janine readies the books and gathers things up as Dirk returns from upstairs.

Dirk and Janine arrive at the pavilion. Most of the crews are now returning from the fields. Janine sets up her books with all the names in order. Timothy, Jefferson, Lucille along with Benjamin and Gabooti are bringing in the food and drinks from the fields. The workers file into the pavilion. With all the money close by, Dirk keeps his attention and eyes diligently surveying the surroundings for any possible trouble, not that he is expecting any. They all file in front of Janine. They make their mark as Janine then 'co-signs' and witnesses their mark.

Dirk calls over Benjamin and Gabooti and says, "You two are a great big help to Lucille. Once again, you two don't have to be told what to do, you just do it . I am still really proud of you two."

Dirk reaches into his pocket and produces two shiny silver dollars and hands each one of them a coin. Benjamin and Gabooti take them in their hands and just stare at them with 'ear to ear' grins. Dirk stands between them both and gives them both a strong handshake. Edgar rides up on Beau and ties him up.

"Have a good ride?" Dirk asks.

"I sure did." Edgar replies. "Here's Pastor Roscoe and Martha."

Dirk looks up and goes over to greet them. Dirk shakes Roscoe's hand and tips his hat to Martha.

"We are just about to finish up with the payroll here."

Roscoe says, "Where are Jefferson and Lucille?"

"I don't know, they were here just a while ago. I'll have Edgar go find them"

Dirk goes to Edgar with his request. Dirk goes back to Roscoe and Martha. Janine joins them and gives them both a big smile warm smile. They are talking for a short while when Jefferson and Lucille show up.

Roscoe says, "Martha honey, who do they remind you of?"

Martha looks at them and says, "You two remind us of us."

Lucille smiles and rests her head on Jefferson's shoulders.

"Jefferson and Lucille," Pastor Roscoe says, "Before the service begins today, I wants you two to be here early so's Martha and I can talk wid yuhs."

"Yes Pastor, we will be here," Jefferson says.

Lucille squeals with delight. Dirk, Janine, Roscoe, and Martha head for the big house.

Dirk says to Ambrose, "Ambrose, please put the horse and buggy up and bring their bags to the big house."

"Yeh suh Massa Dirk, right away."

They get to the big house and sit at the table. Jensen and Maybelle bring in supper for everyone. Babs and Lulu join them. Lulu has a small chalk board and is drawing pictures of baby bunnies. Lulu goes to Janine and shows her the pictures.

"Oh! That is a very nice picture of a baby bunny rabbit," Janine says.

She holds the picture for everyone to see.

"Very pretty," says Dirk.

Edgar rides up on Beau and ties him up out front and comes on in the big house. Lulu goes outside and starts drawing a picture of Beau.

"Hi Beau," Lulu says.

Back in the big house all enjoy a fine meal and fine conversation. Lulu returns from outside and goes to Janine.

"Look mommy, I drew a picture of Beau," and she hands the chalk board to her.

Janine smiles and takes the chalk board. Janine examines it for a few seconds and breaks out in hysterical laughter as the tears roll down her face. Janine hands the board to Dirk.

"What's wrong?" Lulu asks.

"Nothing dear, you only drew what you saw," Janine says.

Everyone at the table is curious as to what is going on. Dirk breaks out in laughter. Lulu is baffled. Edgar gets up and goes over to see.

Edgar looks at it and says, "Beau doesn't have five legs!"

Edgar then opens his mouth with a loud gasp and covers his mouth. By this time Pastor Roscoe and Martha are laughing also.

Janine brings Lulu to her side and gives her a hug and says, "Everything is just fine sweetheart," then gives her a kiss on top of her head. Babs is sitting there taking everything in with a smile.

With the meal almost over Pastor Roscoe says that he and Martha must go meet with Jefferson and Lucille.

"Edgar," says Janine, "Go and find Jefferson and Lucille and have them go to the pavilion so Pastor and Martha can speak with them."

"Okay mommy," Edgar responds.

Edgar gets up on Beau and rides off. In a few minutes Pastor Roscoe and Martha excuse themselves to go meet with Jefferson and Lucille.

"We'll be over in a bit." Dirk says.

Jefferson and Lucille are already waiting for Pastor Roscoe and Martha by the time they get there. They are all smiles as Pastor Roscoe and Martha sit down with them.

"Jefferson an' Lucille, so yuh two wants ta get married."

"Oh yes Pastor," Lucille says.

"Thas' a mos' honorable institution blessed by God."

Martha adds, "This is not to be taken lightly."

"Oh yeh'," Pastor Roscoe says. "This is a permanent bond centered and based on love, trust and obedience to each other. Marriage is like the Lawd Jesus' union wid' his church." Roscoe adds as Martha nods her head in the affirmative.

As they are talking the workers and families are starting to arrive. Pastor Roscoe and Martha are still talking. Soon, Dirk, Janine, and the kids arrive. Pastor Roscoe and Martha finish up their counseling with Jefferson and Lucille. They stand and give each other a big hug. As everyone is taking whatever seat of some kind, Pastor Roscoe takes to the stage.

"Good to see all of yuh' here today," Pastor Roscoe says, "Martha and I jus' had a nice long talk wid' Jefferson an' Lucille. They is a gon' ta git married the nex' time we come out heah. Give them both a big hand clappin'. Yuh two has one month to think sum moah 'bout this blessed union."

Every one claps and smiles at Jefferson and Lucille. Janine smiles and puts her head on Dirks shoulder.

Pastor Roscoe clears his throat and says, "Franklin, are yuh heah taday?"

From in the back of the pavilion can be heard the sounds of a fiddle.

"Praise the Lawd," Pastor Roscoe says. "What ah wants ta preach taday is all about the 'Blood of Jesus'. Ya see, in our flesh and blood bodies that we live in right now, the blood cleanses the body of impurities. The blood rebuilds our bodies. The blood has the power to control the development of any part of our bodies. The blood in our bodies has the power to reach into the future. The 'Blood of the Lawd Jesus' is POWER to cleanse us our sin and transgressions. The 'Blood of the Lawd Jesus" is the power of love. Befo' we goes on any further Martha an' ah are a gonna' sing a hymn bout' the "Blood of Jesus'. Franklin, you are a gonna' have to join in as you see fit."

Martha says, "This song is about a fountain, a different kind of fountain, a fountain filled with blood."

Franklin says, "Ah knows dat song, ah played it alla' time when ah wuz in Loosiana."

Martha and Pastor Roscoe sing:

Drawn from Emanuel's veins,
And sinners plunged beneath that flood
Lose all their guilty stains, lose all their guilty stains,
Lose all their guilty stains, lose all their guilty stains,
And sinners plunged beneath that flood
lose all their guilty stains.
There is a fountain filled with blood.

They finish the hymn. Pastor Roscoe raises his hands high the air in praise and says, "Dear dying lamb, thy precious blood shall never lose its power that your flowing wounds supply."

"Hallelujah! Hallelujah! Praises to duh Lawd God Almighty."

Both Pastor Roscoe and Martha have tears rolling down their faces when they finish.

"Praise duh Lawd for there is 'Power in His Blood'." Pastor Roscoe yells at the crowd. "Without the shedding of the Lawd Jesus' Blood, there is no remission of sin, there is no forgiveness of sin. We are born into it plain an' simple. Yuh see, the Israelites of old thought they could sacrifice some of their animals as a 'blood sacrifice' to God. But you see, they sinned so much, their herds was getting thinned out to just small flocks. So God did the only thing he could, send His only begotten Son to die once and for all for every one for all times. The Lawd Jesus was the 'Blood Sacrifice' the essence of life. Let us pray."

After the prayer everyone just sits there. Some had tears rolling down their faces.

"Next time Martha and I are here and afta' duh wedding ceremony, we'll have an altar call and anyone that wishes to be saved, we'll all go to duh river for a Baptism. Franklin, play us something."

Franklin plays, 'Just As I Am'. Several come up to Pastor Roscoe and Martha giving them thanks and gratitude for the service. Dirk and Janine come up to Pastor Roscoe and Martha.

Dirk says, "Well done. We are going to the big house, we'll see you there."

Janine says, "I still have my wedding dress. I'm going to dig it out for her."

Dirk says, "Timothy should have his wedding suit or something appropriate also."

Pastor Roscoe and Martha arrive shortly thereafter.

"Excellent service today," Dirk says.

Pastor Roscoe replies, "Thank you."

Janine says, "We've put your belongings up in the guest room."

"Before I forget, here." Dirk hands him ten dollars.

Pastor Roscoe and Martha smile and thank them for the money.

"I don't know about you folks, but this child is tired and going to take a nap before dinner." Dirk says.

"Good idea," Pastor Roscoe says.

Janine and Martha both nod their heads.

"We'll see you in a couple of hours," Janine says.

They show them their room and everyone takes a nap for a couple of hours.

When dinner is served, they all sit down for the evening meal.

Dirk brings up a controversial subject in the conversation," In another week or so the families and all will be taught to read, write, and do basic arithmetic. Babs and Edgar will get to do that."

Janine adds, "We have also thrown that out to a couple other plantations owners, suggesting that they can bring anyone of their workers over."

Martha says, "We have heard reports of the white folks gettin' inta trouble for doing that."

Dirk looks at Pastor Roscoe and says, "Do you know what I say to that?"

He looks at Dirk and says, "Ah is almost 'fraid ta ask."

Dirk says, "Well, I'll tell you."

Janine gives him a worried look that he is going say something embarrassing.

Dirk says, "They can just go and 'breed' themselves if they don't like it."

Janine has the 'thousand yard stare in a ten foot room look on her face' as she gives off a sigh of disgust.

Dirk looks at her and says, "I could have said worse."

"Oh how well I know," Janine responds. Pastor Roscoe can be seen smiling.

"After they learn some basic arithmetic and money values, I want to take some small groups to town so they can spend some of their money with us present during the transactions," Janine says.

They have an enjoyable remainder of the day socializing and drinking sweet tea on the veranda. They while away the hours talking and laughing. Soon they all get ready to turn in for the night.

"See you at breakfast they we can leave for church together in the morning."

XIX

===

Monday morning finds everyone at the pavilion again as usual.
"Jefferson and Timothy," Dirk says, "We should have things up and running with water flowing before supper time."

Dirk turns to the water flume crew and says, "Get a couple of shovels and some buckets and pick me up here."

Dirk talks with Jefferson and Timothy. "Janine has her wedding dress still and she says that it would probably fit Lucille. Timothy, you and Jefferson are about the same size, do you have something he could use for a wedding suit?"

Timothy responds, "I sure do. I have a dark suit that I'm sure would fit you perfectly and just made for a wedding."

"Oh! Thank yuh both. Lucille an' me wuz' both worried."

"Everything is all taken care of," Dirk says.

The wagon and the flume crew show up and Dirk jumps in the wagon. Off they go to the waterfall. Upon arrival at the waterfall they all get out. Dirk examines the surroundings.

"Lil' Ray and Nathan, take the shovels and go up to the waterfall and I'll be up in a minute. The rest of you, take the buckets and fill them up with as many small rocks as you can carry, about this size here." Dirk picks up a rock about one inch round. "We need to make a rock bed for the water to keep the flume board out of the mud. We are also going to need six good size boulders to stabilize and keep the flume board from moving under the water pressure going down the trough. Okay, let's do it!"

Dirk goes up to the waterfall and takes a shovel.

"You two lift the flume board up while I dig," says Dirk.

Dirk start to dig a 'VEE' trench up to just shy of the water flow. Up come the first buckets of small rocks. Dirk then puts the rocks in the trench and smooths them out into a nice bed. Caesar and Ambrose are muscling up a big boulder.

"Put it down right here," as Dirk points to a spot. "We are going to need five more. Let's all go and get some boulders."

The flume board is laid down as they all get boulders. With the boulders all set in place and the flume board picked up, Dirk takes the shovel and opens up the last shovel's load of dirt to allow a small amount of water to flow. Dirk gradually takes more shovel loads of dirt allowing a larger amount of water to flow.

Dirk says, "It is about time to eat. We'll have running water right after supper. Let's go."

With the meal over and done with, they meet up at the pavilion.

Dirk says, "Lil' Ray, you and I are going to stay here. Caesar, you and the rest go back to the waterfall and take one of the short boards with you. Put the short board down to block the flow of water into the flume. Put the flume into the rock bed and place the boulders next to it one each side then slowly allow a small amount of water in. I don't want a big water surge all at once. Slowly at first then increase it till the board is completely allowing all the water in."

Caesar and the crew go to the waterfall. Dirk and Lil' Ray go to Jasper and Rebecca's cabin. They are both out front ready to go to the fields.

"Why don't you two hang back for a spell," Dirk says. "You should be having some running water real soon."

"Yeh suh Massa Dirk," Jasper says.

Dirk and Lil' Ray head for another cabin. Caesar and crew are at the water with the board in place with the boulders firmly securing the flume. Caesar lifts the board slowly and a small amount water begins to flow down the flume. The flume can be heard to creak under the weight of the water. A short time later, Caesar lifts the board a little more. Again the creaks and groans can be heard under the weight of more water.

Dirk and Lil' Ray are at the cabins when the first signs of water show up. The creaks and pooping of flume boards under stress can be heard. More sounds of stress can be heard as more water weight is increased. Some of the flanges and gaskets are showing signs of water dripping. Water can be heard running down the flume.

Caesar pulls up the board the rest of the way. The water is really rushing down the flume now. A pretty good torrent is flowing in the flume.

Caesar says, "Okay, let's head back and see what is going on."

The water is really rushing through the living areas. More rushing water can be heard. Dirk and Lil' Ray head for Timothy's place. The excess water is spilling over into a man-made creek bed and onto the river.

"Excellent," Dirk says.

Jasper and Rebecca are at their cabin. With the water flowing and dripping at the flanges Jasper says, "Ah thinks we is ready now to try dis."

Jasper opens the valve. All that comes out is hot air.

Jasper looks at Rebecca and says, "Ah thinks Massa Dirk got dis one wrong, nuthin' 'cept hot air comin' outta dis."

Jasper holds the open valve and looks at it. As Jasper is talking to Rebecca all of the sudden a big blast of water hits Jasper in the face and all that can be heard is Jasper's gargling and gurgling as the water fills his mouth. The flume crew shows up as Dirk and Lil' Ray get back to the cabins.

Dirk says, "Okay, next we go to the valves and purge the air out of the lines till the water is running freely. Ambrose, you go to the long house and Marcus, you take the barn."

The water is running freely at all locations. The wood swells up from the water and closes off most of the drips and leaks. They all meet again in the cabin area.

"Tomorrow, we'll take the cotton jackets, glue, leather strips, and wrap the lines," Dirk says. "Then this project is history. Let's go home for the rest of the day. You all have done an excellent job."

———

The next morning the crew starts the wrapping of all the lines. The workers are all in the fields doing their various tasks. Everything is going well. Dirk notices how well Edgar is progressing in his horsemanship and maneuvers on Beau. Janine is showing more and more of her pregnancy as each day goes by. Franklin is out in the fields everyday with his fiddle playing his music. The cotton harvest will be coming on real soon. The other crops are being harvested for consumption and canning for the winter. Dirk is very happy and content as are all the inhabitants of Spanish Oaks. Babs and Edgar will be starting school in another week and teaching the residents of the plantation reading, writing, and arithmetic. Life is good.

The next three weeks go by quickly. Jefferson and Lucille's wedding date is fast approaching. Janine digs out her wedding dress from a big trunk and holds it up over her protruding stomach.

"Lucille will look so good in this," Janine says to herself. Janine brings the dress out and downstairs to the parlor.

Dirk comes into the room smiles and says, "It has been a long time since I've seen that dress."

They both smile at each other and just look at the dress as they both reminisce about their wedding years ago, Janine in her flowing white gown and Dirk in his 'Dress Blues' uniform. They hug and kiss.

Dirk looks into Janine's blue eyes and says, "I love you more now than ever before and my love for you grows and grows more as each day goes by."

Janine looks up at him as tears roll down her cheeks. "I love you more each day also," Janine says as she wraps her arms around him and they give each other loving embraces.

Janine says, "You better have Timothy dig out his suit so that Jefferson can see if it fits okay. We need to get Lucille up here to try this on also. Let's keep this dress as a surprise for Jefferson."

Dirk says, "Benjamin and Gabooti can handle the food and drinks for awhile without Lucille. I'll have her come up here right after I get back and I'll have Timothy and Jefferson go to his place for the suit. I'll go out into the fields while Timothy and Jefferson are gone. Now let's eat."

They have a quick bite then Dirk heads out to the Pavilion. Dirk is conversing with Jefferson and Timothy and tells them to go to Timothy's for the wedding suit. They then head for Timothy's house. Lucille is just entering the pavilion. Dirk goes to her and has her go to the big house to see Janine.

"Benjamin and Gabooti, you two can handle the drinks and food till Lucille gets back. I'll be out in the fields till Jefferson and Timothy return. Okay, let's do it to it."

Everyone smiles at Dirk and off they go to do their particular jobs. The wrapping crew goes off to continue their project.

Janine and Lucile are in the parlor. Janine has Lucille hold the dress up against herself.

"Look at yourself in the mirror," Janine says.

Lucille turns and gazes at herself in the mirror. Lucille starts to cry.

"Missa Janine, dis is da mos' buteful thing ah has ever see'd."

Janine gives Lucille a big hug and says, "This is your wedding dress and it appears that it is going to fit okay. Step into this room and try it on."

Lucille goes into the room and returns in a few minutes. Janine takes one look at her and gasps as she puts her hands up to her mouth.

"Lucille, you are beautiful," Janine says with excitement. "Here is the bridal veil."

Lucille puts on the veil.

"Go look at yourself in the mirror," Janine says.

Lucille sees herself in the mirror. Her mouth opens wide and she starts to cry. Babs and Lulu walk in and see Lucille and just stare with mouths agape. Babs and Lulu turn and look at each other with their mouths still wide open and turn again to look at Lucille.

Janine smiles and says to them, "Well, what do you two think?"

Babs says, "Lucille, you are so beautiful."

"Pretty too," Lulu says.

"Babs," says Janine, "Go get Maybelle."

Babs turns to go get Maybelle. Maybelle and Babs return shortly.

Maybelle looks at Lucille in the wedding dress and says, "Good Lawd Almighty, yuh is duh mos' buteful thang ah has ever laid eyes on."

Lucille is so excited 'goose bumps' can be seen rising on her skin.

"I also have the perfect pair of shoes to go with this," adds Janine. "Maybelle, can you bake a big cake for the wedding?"

"Yuh bet ah can," Maybelle responds.

"I'll put the dress up in the closet till the wedding," Janine says. "One more thing," Janine reaches into her dress pocket and pulls out a gold wedding band. Here is the ring that you can give to Jefferson."

"Missa Janine, dis is so buteful'," Lucille says.

"This belonged to my father and I know that he would want it to go to good use."

Lucille looks at the ring again with tears in her eyes.

"You have earned this." Janine says.

Timothy has Jefferson trying on several suit pants. All are too short, but, passable for the occasion. The suit coat and white shirt fit okay. The wedding clothes are ready for both bride and groom as best as they can be. Timothy goes over to a drawer and produces a diamond wedding ring.

"Here might as well put this to good use."

———

The week passes by fast. The wrapping crew is done with their project. Jefferson and Lucille are anxiously awaiting for Saturday to arrive for their big day. Before they know it, it is Saturday morning. The workday has been cut short for the wedding.

The preparations are all made. The pavilion is decorated with flowers and white table cloths are over the all the tables. Maybelle has made a very large cake. There is cider and lemonade. Pastor Roscoe and Martha are at the big house where Lucille is already dressed in her wedding attire. Jefferson is at Timothy's house with his wedding suit on. The families are all gathered in the pavilion. Franklin is playing music for young lovers. Dirk, Edgar, Babs, and Lulu are already there. Georgie and Mammy Em are seated. Timothy and Jefferson walk in.

A couple of the people notice that Jefferson's 'high-water' trousers don't quite reach the full length that they should and smile ever so slightly. Pastor Roscoe walks in and goes up onto the stage and takes his place facing the crowd. Janine, Lucille and Martha make their entrance.

Oh, ahs', and gasps are heard throughout the entire pavilion as Lucille walks in. All are awe struck at Lucille's overpowering and radiant beauty. Janine and Martha have done a praiseworthy job on Lucille. Jefferson starts to cry audibly when he gazes upon the love of his life soon to be wife. Dirk goes up and comforts Jefferson along with Timothy. Mammy Em is looking at Lucille in a different and peculiar manner different than anyone else in the pavilion. Mammy Em then looks up and closes her eyes and whispers something to herself ever so slightly. Franklin still plays his fiddle softly.

Pastor Roscoe smiles, clears his throat, and says, " Befo' we gits started I need to clarify somethin'. Martha an' me has bin' to a lot of weddins performed by white preachers for the black foks'. Duh' white preachers don' marry duh' black foks' in way duh' Lawd God says ta. When duh' white preacher is all dun, dey sez, 'you is married'. Well, 'whoop tee do an' la de dah!" is all ah has ta say bout' dat. We heah is a gonna' obey duh' Lawd Creator God Almighty."

Pastor Roscoe nods at Franklin. Franklin starts playing very new song that no one has heard before. It is "Here Comes the Bride."

Franklin had learned it from Maynard who heard it on one of his trips to New York.

Everyone stands. Pastor Roscoe motions for Lucille and Dirk to come forward. Dirk then takes Lucille under her right forearm and walks her to Pastor Roscoe and Jefferson.

Pastor Roscoe then asks, "Who gives Lucille away in marriage?"

Dirk says, "Janine and I do."

Dirk then departs from their presence and goes to sit with the kids. Pastor Roscoe looks at Franklin, smiles and nods. Franklin then stops playing.

"Befo' ah gits started, der' is sum' things that must be said. Last month when we wuz' heah, we had us a nice long talk bout' dis heah marriage. Now, ah jus' say ah sumthin' mo'. Yuh' see, marriage is instituted by duh' Lawd God. Marriage is not to be taken lightly. Marriage is duh' honorable, permanent, intimate bond between Duh Lawd God, a man, an' a woman. Marriage is worthy of duh' Lawd Jesus' presence. Marriage is duh' means of having children and duh' marriage can only be dissolved by death. One last thing," Pastor Roscoe says in a loud voice with his arms raised in the air, "What Duh Lawd God has brought together, let NO man tear asunder!"

Pastor Roscoe turns his attention to Jefferson and says, "Now repeat after me, 'I Jefferson," He does so.' "Take you Lucille" He does so. "To be my lawfully wedded wife." Jefferson does so. "To have and to hold from this day forward." Jefferson repeats. "For better or for worse, for richer, for poorer." Jefferson repeats. "In sickness and in health." Jefferson repeats. "To love and to cherish from this day fo'wad until death do us part." Jefferson does so.

Pastor Roscoe then looks at Lucille and has her say the same vows. Lucille does so flawlessly.

"Jefferson, you may place the ring on Lucille's finger."

Jefferson does so.

"Lucille," Pastor Roscoe says, "You may place the ring on Jefferson's finger."

Janine hands her the ring and she places it on Jefferson's finger.

Pastor Roscoe then says, "By the powers of God, the powers vested in me, and the State of South Carolina, I now pronounce you 'Husband and Wife'. You may now kiss the bride."

Jefferson lifts Lucille's veil, cups her cheeks in his hands, and gives her a warm passionate kiss. Lucille's right leg bends slightly at the knee.

"Face the people," Pastor Roscoe says, "I give you Jefferson and Lucille."

At the moment, Janine feels the baby move inside her and she puts her hands on her stomach. Mammy Em looks over at Janine with reverence and love in her countenance. Pastor Roscoe nods at Franklin and Franklin starts playing again.

Everyone is congratulating Jefferson and Lucille. Janine and the kids start to put the cake on the plates. Mammy Em makes her way to Lucille.

Mammy Em smiles, takes Lucille's hand in hers, and looks deeply into Lucille's eyes, the 'windows to her soul' and says, "We need to talk real soon."

Lucille looks at Mammy Em without expression.

FINI

ACKNOWLEDEMENTS

I take immense pleasure in this opportunity to acknowledge those of whom assisted, aided, and helped promote this book making it possible.

I want to acknowledge the 'un-known' proofreader that ameliorated and remedied numerous passages throughout this book. The 'un-known' proofreader's knowledge and expertise is beyond compare. Without the proofreader's arduous work, I would still be trying to navigate through the 'swamps and quicksand' with a broken compass on a dark and moonless night.

I want to acknowledge Annette Amerman and Owen Conner of the UNITED STATES MARINE CORPS MUSEUM in Quantico, VA for their historical information and knowledge whenever called upon. My cover, (hat) is off to them.

I take pleasure in acknowledging Stephen Yafa, author of 'COTTON' for our conversations on the subject and of the historical recorded history. The recorded historical information will also be used in subsequent writings.

I want to thank those within The Dept. Of Homeland Security whom I work with for their uplifting and stimulating encouragement that kept me writing when I didn't feel like writing.

I want to acknowledge my wife wife Janice, my daughter Barbara, and my son Edward for their support and patience with me.

I acknowledge, Images: Salvatore Vuono/Andy Newson/FreeDigital Photo.net

AND

I acknowledge the, Cover Design: Jay Holmes/jayholmes.b3an.com

DEDICATION

I dedicate this book to those of humanity whom perform to achieve what is right and justified. I dedicate this book to those that are weathering the 'stormy seas of adversity and condemnation'. I dedicate this book to those that have succeeded into the sailing of the 'smooth and calm seas' of the Creator's approval.

Last, I dedicate this book to ME, 'The Great Procrastinator', for my 'singleness of purpose' in finishing this first task filled journey of, 'labor and love'.

LaVergne, TN USA
07 October 2010
199847LV00004B/3/P